The
INN
at
TANSY
FALLS

CATE WOODS

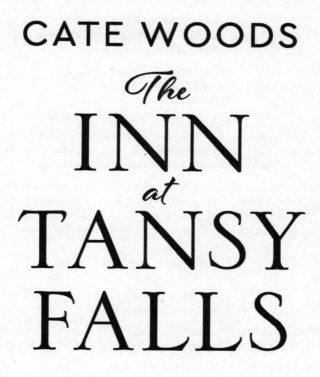

The
INN
at
TANSY
FALLS

FOREVER

NEW YORK BOSTON

Copyright © 2021 by Cate Woods
Reading group guide copyright © 2022 by Cate Woods and
Hachette Book Group, Inc.

Cover design by Eileen Carey
Cover image by Aleksandar Novoselski/Stocksy
Additional imagery by Shutterstock
Cover copyright © 2022 by Hachette Book Group, Inc.

Forever
Hachette Book Group
1290 Avenue of the Americas, New York, NY 10104
read-forever.com
twitter.com/readforeverpub

Originally published in paperback in 2021 by Bookouture, an imprint of Storyfire Ltd., Carmelite House, 50 Victoria Embankment, London EC4 0DZ

First Forever Trade Paperback Edition: October 2022

Forever is an imprint of Grand Central Publishing. The Forever name and logo are trademarks of Hachette Book Group, Inc.

The publisher is not responsible for websites (or their content) that are not owned by the publisher.

The Hachette Speakers Bureau provides a wide range of authors for speaking events. To find out more, go to www.hachettespeakersbureau.com or call (866) 376-6591.

Library of Congress Control Number: 2022937263

ISBNs: 9781538724880 (trade paperback)

Printed in Canada

FRI

10 9 8 7 6 5 4 3 2 1

The
INN
at
TANSY
FALLS

Chapter One

Nell gazed up at the flight departure screens with a swooping sensation close to vertigo. ROME. LAGOS. LOS ANGELES. BANGKOK. It was dizzying, the thought that from this spot you could travel across the globe to wherever you wished in a matter of hours. Anywhere in the world—except right now the only place Nell wanted to be was back home in her not-quite-right apartment, preferably in bed, with the curtains closed. It wasn't as if her bed was even that comfortable: the mattress still sagged down on one side from the memory of the man who had last slept on it a year ago. Every time she turned over at night, she was reminded of him.

Scanning the list of destinations, Nell finally found it: NEW YORK, departing at 8:20 a.m. and, in bold green capitals alongside, ON TIME. Her stomach lurched, and she reached a hand for the pop-up handle of her borrowed suitcase. If the events of the past months hadn't already disproved the idea that you could "manifest" your heart's desire simply by "asking the universe," then this settled matters once and for all, because how many times over the past few days had Nell begged the universe to cancel this flight? Yet here it was, waiting for her on the asphalt outside. It didn't even have the decency to be delayed. Could you get airsick while still on the ground, wondered Nell, swallowing down her rising panic.

It wasn't yet 6 a.m., but the woman at the check-in desk looked ready for a night out drinking martinis. Nell's hand shot up to her own reddish-blondish bob; she had tumbled out of bed at 4:30 a.m. and fallen straight into a taxi, without a single thought about her appearance, but under the surgically bright lights of the airport terminal she was regretting not taking a brush to her hair at the very least. She was no supermodel—she was about a foot too short for one thing—but with her fine features, apple cheeks and rosebud lips, she was often described as elfin, which secretly pleased Nell as it made her think of Liv Tyler in *Lord of the Rings*—who, to be fair, she looked nothing like. This morning, however, she was decidedly more orc than elf.

"How many bags will you be checking in today?" asked the clerk.

"Just the one, thank you."

"And are you carrying any of these objects inside your bag?" The clerk held up a laminated list of restricted items and tapped at it with a long red nail. As Nell scanned the list she felt her face grow hot; she grinned at the clerk, aiming for breezy innocence but ending up looking more suspected shoplifter. Honestly, she might as well have had a neon sign on her head reading: SMUGGLERS R US. Thankfully, however, the precious cargo she had hidden in her suitcase, wrapped up in a favorite sweater, didn't appear on the restricted list. Still, she couldn't help worrying what would happen to her if it was discovered.

In all her thirty-seven years, Nell's experience of air travel had been limited to the occasional hop from her home in England across to Europe. It wasn't that Nell didn't like the idea of travel—quite the contrary, she dreamed of going on safari in Africa or hiking in the Himalayas—but like so many of the dreams she'd had over the years she'd never quite managed to make it a reality, and now it was too late. Rather than Malibu or Milan, her life had calcified around a few square miles of unexciting outer London suburb, and with each passing year she felt her existence was shrinking ever smaller, until one day she supposed she would simply just...disappear.

"Aisle or window seat?" asked the check-in clerk.

"Whichever is closer to the emergency exit." Nell had been aiming for a jokey tone, but even to her own ears she sounded somewhere between timid and panicked.

The clerk rearranged her foundation and false lashes into a look of sympathy. "Nervous flyer, are we?"

"Oh, I'm fine, just a little out of practice."

"Nothing to worry about at all. Relax, have a breakfast G&T, watch a movie. It'll be fun! Right, here's your boarding pass. You'll be boarding at gate twenty-two at 7:30 a.m. Enjoy the flight, Miss Swift."

Nell picked her way along the aisle of the plane, ducking past passengers deadlifting their bags into the overhead lockers, until she found her seat right at the back next to the toilets. It was in the middle of a row of five seats, so neither by an aisle or window, and was about as far from the emergency exit as possible. The check-in clerk had evidently decided that Nell needed the physical reassurance of two people squished on either side of her rather than easy access to the inflatable emergency slide.

As she settled into her seat, a woman with a tangle of bags and children stopped at the end of the row.

"Hold up, guys, I think this is us. I said HOLD UP!" She grabbed a toddler who was making a run for it then fixed Nell with an apologetic grimace. "I'm sorry, I think you've drawn the short straw: we're sitting next to you."

"Oh, that's fine, please don't worry." Nell liked kids; besides, right now she welcomed any distraction from obsessing over how this lump of metal was going to stay up in the air for the eight hours it would take them to get to New York.

The woman smiled with relief. "Right, Tyler, Zoe, you sit on the other side of the lady." The two older kids started to clamber over Nell. "Tyler, watch your elbows! Really, I'm sorry."

"Honestly, it's not a problem," said Nell, helping the little girl into her seat. "But would you prefer to all sit together?"

"That's kind, but they'll behave better if they're split up."

After a frenetic few minutes organizing toys, drinks and snacks, and securing the toddler, the woman sank into the seat next to Nell. The older kids immediately got out their tablets, clamped on headphones and became as still and silent as waxworks.

As the plane started to taxi toward the runway, Nell swallowed down the lump that had appeared in her throat and got out the novel she'd bought at the airport. Trying to ignore the flutters of fear in her belly, she turned to the first page and attempted to read, though it may as well have been written in Lithuanian for all she actually took in. A moment later the fasten-seatbelt sign flashed again with a soft *boing* and the plane began picking up speed. Nell glanced around in alarm—couldn't anyone else hear that clanking noise?—and as the plane left the ground she gave up all pretense of reading and clamped hold of the armrests, her feet rammed against the floor as if slamming on the brakes.

"You okay, honey?" It was her neighbor. Nell's eyes were squeezed shut, but she could only imagine how *not* okay she was looking.

"I'm fine, thank you," muttered Nell, feeling her knuckles turn white and her insides plunge as the plane soared upward. "Just a little nervous."

"Would you like to talk? It might keep your mind off the flight, and I am *dying* for some adult conversation."

Nell managed a tiny nod.

"Great! Well, my name's Sara, and you are?"

"Nell," she mumbled, her entire being focused on keeping the plane aloft through willpower alone. "Lovely to meet you."

"You too, Nell. The kids and I are on our way home to Connecticut after going to visit my aunt, who lives in Windsor. You know, where the queen has a castle?"

"Mm-hmm."

"My husband, Eric, had to stay home unfortunately. Work." Sara sighed. "His boss is *brutal*. Eric's in finance, his office is in New York. Have you been there before?"

"No, I haven't." The engines had stopped thundering quite so alarmingly now, and Nell risked opening her eyes. "This is actually my first time visiting the States."

"Really? So what's bringing you to New York?"

"I'm just connecting to my next flight. My final destination is Vermont—a little town in the north called Tansy Falls."

"Oh, well, you're in for a treat! Vermont is so pretty, you'll love it."

"It does sound beautiful, but..." How to explain to a stranger how terrifying she was finding this: jetting to the other side of the world, all alone, to a town where she didn't know a soul? "I've never flown by myself before. And it's a long way from home," Nell managed.

"Sure, but isn't life all about getting out of your comfort zone and trying new things? What's that saying? 'Feel the fear and do it anyway!' Out of your comfort zone is where the magic happens!"

Nell smiled and nodded in a polite fashion, but honestly, this nice lady was seriously mistaken. Nell had never understood why it was considered such a positive thing to get out of your comfort zone. Come on, folks, the clue is in the name! *Comfort* zone? As for embracing your fears, surely the fight-or-flight reflex had evolved over millennia for good reason, and Nell chose flight every single time. Just not this particular one.

The seatbelt sign went off and the flight attendants got up and started preparing for the drinks service. Nell's grip loosened a little on the armrests, and she looked at Sara gratefully.

"You're doing great, Nell," said Sara, giving her arm a pat. "So, do you live in London?"

"Just outside. I have an apartment near a park. It's great for dog walks—I've got a Maltese Terrier called Moomin." Nell dug in her pocket and pulled out her phone, showing the photo she had as her screensaver. Just seeing Moomin's fluffy little face soothed her; she really should have brought him along as an emotional support dog.

"Oh, he's very cute. Who's looking after him while you're away? Your husband?"

Nell flinched. "No, he's staying with my parents. I'm not married."

"Lucky you," laughed Sara, rolling her eyes; if she'd noticed Nell's discomfort at the mention of husbands, she was kindly pretending she hadn't. "What are you going to be doing on your vacation?"

"Well, I'm not really on vacation, strictly speaking. I'm going to Tansy Falls on a sort of... mission, for my best friend."

"Oh? Does she live out there?"

"No, she..." Nell paused. The shape of the words she was about to say still felt so unnatural to her it felt like she was reciting a line from a movie. "She died. A month ago. She had cancer. Her name was Megan."

Sara looked horrified. "Oh, I'm so sorry, what a terrible thing to happen. And so young!"

"Yes, it really is." Nell stared at her hands, grief threatening to swallow her whole again. She had spent so much of the past few months in tears that they came easily when she was alone—sometimes without even a warning sob, just dripping from her eyes like a faulty faucet—but the idea of crying in public, in front of this kind stranger, horrified her. "You see, the reason I'm going to Vermont is because Megan asked me to scatter her ashes on a mountain that was special to her when she was growing up."

But really, what Megan was asking of her over the next two weeks was so much more than just that.

Chapter Two

"Good afternoon, and welcome to Burlington, Vermont, where the local time is 4:20 p.m. The weather on the ground is a chilly nineteen degrees Fahrenheit and snow flurries are forecast later tonight, so wrap up warm, folks! Safe travels, and thanks again for flying with us."

Nell peered out of the plane window, giddy with relief at finally being back on solid ground. The world outside wasn't putting on the most spectacular of welcomes: the sky was heavy with clouds, and the only snow she could see was piled up in dirty, well-tramped heaps edging the runway. In the distance she could just about make out the smudge of dark hills on the horizon. It wasn't quite the winter wonderland she had envisaged.

After the craziness of New York's JFK airport, however, the low-key coziness of Burlington was a relief, and within minutes she had made it through security and baggage claim, jumped into a taxi and was speeding through the grid of fast-food joints and outlet stores surrounding the airport. The driver wasn't in a talkative mood, which suited Nell, and within minutes the motion of the car lulled her to sleep.

When she opened her eyes again, nudged awake by the engine cutting out, it was dark. It took her a moment to remember where she was. Judging by the drool on her cheek she had been fast asleep, but then it must be well past midnight back in London.

"Miss? We're here," said the driver, meeting her eyes in the rearview mirror. "Welcome to Tansy Falls."

Nell peered dozily out of her window. From what she could see, they had pulled up on the town's main street: she could make out a few blocks of shops, marked by spotlit signs and flagpoles, and a little farther on, the slender spire of a church that reached several stories high like a gleaming white beacon, though without the ambient city light she was used to in London it was impossible to see more.

"Great, thank you," said Nell, rubbing her eyes. "I'm staying at the..." Her mind suddenly blank, she fumbled in her bag for Megan's letter to check the details. "The Covered Bridge Inn?"

The driver gestured out of his side window. "You're right here."

"Oh okay, thank you," she said, still groggy with sleep—she was thousands of miles from home and right now felt every single one of them—but then she looked where the driver had pointed and her heart floated up like a helium balloon as she got her first glimpse of the Covered Bridge Inn.

To Nell, it looked like a Hollywood movie set from one of those romcoms she loved to watch on Sunday afternoons where the heroine is adorably clumsy (yet always gets her man), cherry pie is a menu staple and kissing in the rain is the most romantic thing ever, rather than cold and squelchy. Stretching the length of the block, the inn's brick walls were painted dark red and a row of sash windows dressed with spruce-green shutters ran along each of its two stories. There was a grand front porch, supported by white columns and topped with a presidential-looking balcony, but it was the homey touches that enchanted Nell: the planters overflowing with foliage and dotted with fairy lights, the rocking chairs lined up along the deck, painted the same green as the shutters and a pair of dormer windows peeping like amused eyebrows above the roof. A white picket fence wrapped around the whole building like a ribbon trimming a gift, which was entirely appropriate because right now Nell felt as if Megan had given her the most wonderful present.

She stepped out of the taxi, relishing the sudden smack of cold, and wheeled her bag up to the entrance, over which hung a sign written in curly gold script: WELCOME TO THE COVERED BRIDGE INN, and underneath, in smaller letters, SHARING WHITE CHRISTMASES SINCE 1878. Nell broke into a delighted grin; she'd never had a white Christmas before and the idea that these seemed to be guaranteed in Tansy Falls made her like this place even more.

Once inside the lobby, Nell felt like she had wandered into somebody's den: there was a log fire, a floor-to-ceiling wall of bookshelves and an eclectic mix of ornaments that looked like they'd been lovingly collected over the years from vacations and antique stores rather than "curated" by an interior designer. It was a room that couldn't care less about being cool; its sole purpose was to give you a welcoming hug.

"Hi there, may I help you?" A woman had appeared from a doorway to the rear. She was dressed down in jeans and a checked shirt, her light brown hair in a messy bun skewered with a pen.

"I'd like to check in, please. My name is Penelope Swift."

"Sure thing." The woman opened a leather-bound book on the rustic wooden table that clearly served as the reception desk. "Ah yes, there you are. Welcome, Miss Swift. My name's Connie Austen and I'm the manager here at the Covered Bridge. How was your journey?"

"Oh, about 35,000 feet too high up in the air for my liking."

Connie smiled; Nell warmed to her instantly. "Well, why don't you take a seat by the fire while I go and print out the paperwork?

Just leave your bag here and I'll get it taken up to your room. I won't be a moment."

As she disappeared out back again, Nell sank into the cushions of the nearest couch. She couldn't quite believe that she'd done it: traveled thousands of miles across the world, on her own, without any disasters, tears or major dramas. For now, she gave herself permission to take her foot off the gas and relax; whatever challenges the next two weeks had in store could certainly wait until morning. The flickering and crackling of the flames worked like hypnosis, and Nell's eyelids had started to get heavy when one of the furry throws on the opposite couch suddenly shook itself, jumped on the floor and plodded over to greet her.

"Well hello there," said Nell, offering the elderly Labrador her hand to sniff, but he bypassed the formalities and immediately slumped at her feet, legs stuck up in the air, in the international language for "tummy rub, please."

"I see Boomer has already introduced himself," said Connie, who had just reappeared. "You okay with that? He doesn't have much respect for personal space."

"Oh, don't worry, I love dogs. Is he yours?"

"He's officially the owners' but really Boomer belongs to all of us at the inn, the guests too. Don't you, boy?" She gave him a scratch behind the ear. "Here, this is for you," she went on, holding out a steaming mug that smelled like Christmas. "Hot spiced cider."

Nell wasn't crazy about cider, but took a sip, just to be polite. *Wow.* Her eyes grew wide. This was like nothing at all like the vinegary fizzy stuff they served in pubs back home.

"That is seriously delicious," she said. "Like drinking liquid apple pie."

"It's from the Cedar Creek cider mill, just down the road," said Connie. "Well worth a visit if you have time. Do you have any plans while you're here? Will you be skiing?"

"No, I..." As much as Nell liked Connie, she couldn't face explaining the purpose for her trip right now. "I thought it might be too late in the season to ski?"

"Not at all, there's still plenty of snow up on Mount Maverick."

Nell had a vision of wading through thigh-high drifts and having to dig a hole in the snow to bury Megan's ashes; not quite the send-off she was hoping to give her friend. "I guess you must have pretty long winters up here?" she asked.

"Oh yes. As the saying goes, in Vermont we have nine months of winter and three months of darned poor sledding—though strictly speaking we're into mud season now. That's the time between winter and spring when the ground frost melts. Things can get pretty boggy around here."

Mud season? Judging by Connie's amused look, Nell's attempt to hide a grimace had failed. "Don't you worry," Connie went on, "you'll be fine as long as you've got a good pair of boots. You just need to take care if you're driving on any dirt roads: cars have a nasty habit of getting themselves stuck upcountry." She slid the check-in register in front of Nell. "If you could just sign here... Great. Breakfast is served from 7 a.m. until 10 a.m. in our restaurant, which is just through there. Can I get you anything to eat sent up to your room now?"

"I'm good, thanks. In fact, I'm pretty tired. I think I'll probably call it a night."

"Okay, let's get you settled in."

Nell gave Boomer a goodbye pat, then followed Connie up a wooden staircase and along a carpeted corridor. Her feet were leaden, and even the thought of changing into her pajamas felt like too much effort, yet Nell couldn't help but be entranced by the surroundings of the inn. The walls were dotted with framed black-and-white photos of stern-looking couples in starchy period dress standing next to very large cows, while each door they passed bore a hand-painted plaque portraying a different bird.

"We have 20 rooms here at the Covered Bridge, each one named after a different native bird." Connie stopped outside a door at the end of the corridor and put the key in the lock. "And this one, Snow Goose, is my favorite."

Nell crossed the threshold, and her eyes lit up with delight. In her experience hotels were anonymous, impersonal sorts of places, but this room felt like it had been waiting especially for her. There was a four-poster bed covered with a patchwork quilt, the colors of which perfectly picked out the sage-and-white striped wallpaper, plus a Nell-sized armchair and antique writing desk with a wooden rocking chair.

"Pretty, isn't it?" said Connie. "This is the bedroom where we put our brides the night before they get married, but you're in luck, we don't have any weddings for the next two weeks."

About the closest I'm going to get to a wedding night, thought Nell, unwanted memories rushing in on her—but Connie was already moving on.

"I'll be around tomorrow if I can help with anything at all, but I'll leave you to settle in now. Good night, Miss Swift."

"Oh please, call me Nell."

Connie nodded, smiling. "Sleep well, Nell."

Once she'd left, Nell sat on the edge of the bed and gave the mattress an experimental bounce: not too hard, not too soft. There was a little box sitting on the pillow, together with a handwritten card. Inside were two chocolates; Nell popped one in her mouth and read the note.

Dear Miss Swift,

Welcome to the Covered Bridge Inn. We hope you enjoy your stay with us here in Tansy Falls.

Warmest wishes,
Piper and Spencer Gridley

Nell wondered if this couple, Piper and Spencer, had known Megan, and whether she would meet them while she was here. She couldn't begin to imagine breaking the news to people that Megan had died, as even telling Sara on the flight had nearly floored her, but it was a responsibility she would have to face up to. Megan hadn't been to Tansy Falls for years, so none of the people she had loved in this town would know she had passed away: it would be her duty to tell them.

Nell was too tired to unpack, but she unzipped her case and got out the casket of Megan's ashes, propping it next to her against the mass of pillows. She sat and stared at it for a while, trying to process the unthinkable fact that this was all that remained of her best friend.

"Well, we've made it, Meg," she said. "Was the flight okay? I know you're usually a business-class kind of girl, but at least you didn't have to sit next to me freaking out at every tiny bump. Honestly, I was pathetic. You'd have found it hilarious."

Nell grinned at the idea, but in the answering silence her smile quickly faded.

"So tomorrow I guess I'll have to get on with this crazy mission of yours. And yes, I promise I'll follow all your instructions to the letter. But then I'm quite sure you'll be looking down and keeping tabs on me, won't you?"

Nell knew it was ridiculous, but she was half expecting Megan to reply—and perhaps she did, because at that very moment she looked up and saw that it had started to snow, the blowsy flakes catching the light from her window as they drifted past. It was all so ridiculously perfect—this beautiful room, the falling snow, the sweetness of the chocolate on her tongue—yet the familiar weight of unhappiness was settling back on Nell's shoulders like an overstuffed backpack. She tried to recapture the rush of joy she'd felt when she first arrived at the inn, but could now only fumble for the memory of it, as it melted away like a snowflake on skin. Perhaps things would seem brighter tomorrow; right now, though, she needed to sleep.

Chapter Three

One Month Ago

Nell sat next to the bed where Megan was propped against a mass of pillows, the ridges of her ribs visible beneath her faded old college T-shirt and her once-golden skin now sickly pale. Since Megan had been admitted to the hospice a week ago there had been times when Nell had felt as if she had been plunged into a real-life horror movie and she'd had to run outside the building and force herself to take deep breaths to stop herself from screaming at what was happening to her best friend. Could it really have been only a couple of months ago that they had been sitting together enjoying spaghetti *cacio e pepe* at their favorite Italian restaurant? The cancer had been greedy, and fast: it had been diagnosed just six months ago and was now close to overwhelming her.

The hospice nurse had just been, 'round to give Megan some medication and Nell had marveled at how this woman could look death squarely in the eye every single day, yet still be so cheery and upbeat—because for Nell, rather than making her cherish every precious moment, Megan's illness had covered the world in a shroud of bleakness. All the little things that used to bring her joy—a blue sky, the first coffee of the day, a bunch of frilly candy-pink peonies—now felt as if they were taunting her, because if this was what life could do to a woman like Megan, then life was clearly no longer to be trusted.

Nell had been with Megan all morning, reading to her from celebrity magazines, but whereas once they would have giggled or gasped over the stories, Megan had barely managed a word. That was okay though, because everything they needed to say to each other had already been said a hundred times over: how much they loved each other, how Nell would always be there for Megan's husband, Ben, and their three daughters, how she would do everything she could to keep Megan's memory burning just as brightly as she had done when she was alive.

"How about we have a go at this crossword?" asked Nell, flicking through the pages. "Meg?"

She didn't answer, and when Nell glanced over Megan's eyes were closed. Taking care not to disturb her, Nell got up to cover her with the duvet before leaving her to rest, but as she brushed the cloud of dark curls off her face Megan stirred.

"Hey, hon." Her voice was barely a murmur.

"I thought you were asleep." Nell reached for her hand.

"Awake, asleep, it's all kind of the same thing now." Megan shifted her position, wincing a little, which put yet another dent in Nell's heart. "I keep forgetting, Nellie, I've got something I need to give you. Take a look in there."

Following Megan's gaze, Nell opened the drawer of the bedside cabinet and had a rummage inside. "Ooh, compression socks! And in my favorite shade of surgical beige, too. Just what I've always wanted. Thank you, my love."

Megan managed a weak smile. "No, silly. It's got your name on it."

Looking again, Nell spotted the envelope. She took it out of the drawer: it felt heavy, as if there were a number of sheets of paper folded together inside. She looked quizzically at Megan. "What's this?"

"A gift. Well, more of a favor, I suppose. But I think it will be a good thing—for both of us."

Curious, Nell went to open the envelope, but Megan put out a hand to stop her.

"Not now. Better to wait." Her eyes drifted shut again. "Then you can't say no."

She didn't need to add when, exactly, Nell should wait until.

A week later, Nell woke suddenly in the early hours. It was one of those zero-to-sixty wake-ups, when you go from comatose to fully alert in an instant. She lay still, trying to figure out what had disturbed her, but there was just the usual 4 a.m. silence broken only by Moomin snoring in his basket. Sleep had been elusive these past few weeks, so after a few minutes of half-hearted breathing exercises Nell decided she might as well get up. She was halfway through a second cup of tea when her phone started to ring, and at that moment she knew with sickening certainty what it was that had woken her.

She looked at the screen: it was Megan's husband, just as, deep down, she knew it would be.

"Ben?"

"She's gone, Nell," he said, his voice racked with pain. "An hour ago."

Once they had finished talking, Nell slumped on the floor staring at the wall. So this was it, the moment she'd been dreading all these months. She had been expecting a torrent of tears, but it was as if all the extremes of emotion crashing around inside her had canceled each other out, leaving only emptiness. She couldn't feel anything; it was as if she had been turned to stone.

The sun had come up and the outside world was busy with the sounds of rush hour when Nell suddenly remembered the letter Megan had given her in the hospice. It felt like a lifeline, a final chance for contact with her friend. She scrambled to her feet, grabbed it from the mantelpiece and tore open the envelope. At the sight of the familiar looped handwriting tears started to flow; she reached for a box of tissues, wiped her face and started to read.

Darling Nell,

I know we've already said everything we wanted to say to each other, and I'm so grateful we had that chance, but there is one more vitally important thing I need to tell you. Are you listening, Penelope Swift? Because this is very important.

It is this: life is wonderful. Yes, it truly is! I know this is a dark time, and I will allow you to mope (just for a bit), but the one thing I want you to do for me is to get out there and LIVE—for both of us. Things have been really tough for you lately, I know that, and you've had some unlucky knocks, but from now on I need you to grab each opportunity and squeeze every single ounce of joy out of life that you can because, honestly, Nellie, life can be glorious.

To that end, I have a proposition for you. I can imagine your horrified expression when you find out what it is, but don't you dare refuse. As your dead best friend, I INSIST you do this for me!

Nell broke off reading for a moment, sobbing and clutching the pages to her chest. It was as if Megan was in the room talking to her, and she was terrified at the prospect of reaching the end of the letter because then she would fall silent forever, yet at the same time, greedy for contact, she couldn't stop herself from reading on.

As I've told you before, when I was growing up in Boston we spent our vacations in Vermont, at my aunt and uncle's house in a little town up in the north of the state called Tansy Falls. It was idyllic—long lazy summers and gorgeous snowy winters—and it's one of my only regrets that I never managed to take the kids to visit, although I didn't count on dying at thirty-eight! Anyway, the reason I'm mentioning this now is that I can't think of anywhere I'd rather have my ashes scattered than on Mount Maverick, the mountain next to Tansy Falls, which was where I learned to ski, where I camped with friends in the summer, where I had my first kiss with the town's high school quarterback Brody Knott (did I ever tell you about him? Man, he was trouble...)—where I enjoyed so many happy times. And I can't think of anyone I'd rather have scatter them there than YOU. Besides, Ben is going to have his hands too full with the kids to even think about transatlantic travel for the next few years.

But that's not all. You see, what I want more than anything is for you to experience the magic of Tansy Falls for yourself, and the only way you're going to be able to do that is to immerse yourself in the place completely rather than just fly in, chuck me off the top of the mountain and then jet out again. I want you to experience Tansy Falls through MY eyes, the way I remember it. My aunt and uncle moved to Canada when I was twenty-two, so I haven't been back to Tansy Falls for about sixteen years, but it's the sort of place that won't have changed that much since then.

So, with all that in mind, I've put together an itinerary for you. It's a two-week schedule (yes, Nell, you CAN take a two-week vacation, your clients will cope without you) and every day you'll be visiting a different place in Tansy Falls and meeting a few of the 4,000-or-so locals who make the town so special. I guarantee it will be an adventure and there'll be surprises along the way, but if at any point you feel like giving up, you've got to trust me when I say that it will all be worth it in the end. In fact, you might just find that the end turns out to be a beginning. (Ooh, the mystery!) Anyway, you must promise to stick with it and follow this itinerary TO THE LETTER, because if you don't, then I will haunt you to the end of your days, okay?

Despite herself, Nell smiled at this: it was just so typically Megan. She glanced at the first sheet of the itinerary. It was dense with detail, from where she should stay to what she should eat; the first day alone covered a whole sheet. Right now, she couldn't begin to imagine the idea of going all the way to Vermont—she wouldn't even have been able to place it on a map—but then again, she couldn't imagine never seeing Megan again, either.

I better sign off now, honey. Know that I love you, dearest Nell, and that you have enriched my life in more ways than you can possibly imagine. Look after Ben and the kids, and don't let him marry anyone prettier than me! And I hope that Tansy Falls captures your heart in the way it did mine. You truly deserve each other.

Meg

Chapter Four

Nell opened her eyes a crack and instantly snapped them shut again. Her room was dazzling with sunlight; she'd obviously forgotten to close the drapes before she crashed last night. She stretched like a cat, reveling in the softness of the bed. Wasn't jet lag meant to mess up your sleep? Because she felt as well-rested as Sleeping Beauty after her one-hundred-year sleep-in—and also, she imagined, about as hungry. Prompted by her grumbling stomach, Nell got out of bed and padded over to the window to get her first real look at Tansy Falls.

Even after last night's glimpse in the darkness, nothing prepared her for the world laid out in front of her. From her apartment window back home she could see only a few hundred feet to the next high-rise block, but here the view stretched miles and miles to the horizon. And the sky! After the gray of London, Nell was transfixed by the endless expanse of blue.

Her room was at the front of the inn and looked out over the row of well-kept shops and businesses on the opposite side of the street, their rooftops dusted with snow, then beyond were great swaths of fields and woodland-clad hills. At the moment the trees were largely bare, apart from some splashes of dark-green conifers, but she could imagine how incredible it must look in the fall when the whole countryside would be ablaze with color. And towering over it all was a mountain: Mount Maverick, Nell presumed. Its jagged peak was covered with snow, while below the treeline a network of ski trails cut white slashes into the wooded slopes. It was beautiful, but also, Nell felt, rather menacing: the way it brooded over the chocolate-box countryside like a hunched ogre. Megan had asked for her ashes to be scattered at the top, but how on earth would Nell get up there? She had never been on skis, and the sturdiest footwear she'd brought with her was a pair of pink galoshes: fine for London puddles, not so great for hiking up snowy mountains. Not for the first time since starting this journey, Nell felt certain she would let Megan down. Well, no time for wallowing in self-pity now; she needed food.

Downstairs, the restaurant was already half full with families and couples. Nell sat at a table in the window that had been laid for one, glancing around with a stuck-on smile and a prickle of self-consciousness, and a few moments later a waitress came over with a menu, a pot of coffee and a jug of fresh juice. Nell ordered the cornmeal buttermilk pancakes with a side of bacon, just as Megan had suggested in the itinerary, and forced herself to turn her attention to her morning's plans.

Your first mission, should you choose to accept it (scrap that, you have no choice—ha!) is to visit Fiske's General Store, which is where I worked every summer when I was a teenager. In my day it was run by Darlene Fiske, the great-granddaughter of the original owner, who seemed to me about 100 years old yet was a total badass. I adored her, in fact I'd say she was like my surrogate grandma, except with combat boots and a shotgun instead of slippers and knitting. I can't imagine she's still there—although with Darlene anything's possible—but the store is still well worth a visit. It's a Tansy Falls institution: the heart of the town and the place to go for local gossip, Darlene's famously strong coffee and everything from fishing tackle to socks. Good luck!

Nell chewed her lip, worrying at a bit of chapped skin. Darlene had clearly been special to Megan, and Nell supposed a normal person would be hoping the old lady was still alive so they could share memories of Megan together. Not Nell, though. She couldn't quite put her finger on when meeting new people had gone from generally enjoyable to an ordeal that needed to be avoided at all costs, but nowadays anything beyond a quick exchange of pleasantries made her twitchy with nerves. It had been a gradual process, this closing in on herself, like an armadillo rolling into a protective ball. It had started a few years back when she lost her accountancy job at a big London bank and, determined to see it as a lemons-into-lemonade opportunity (rather than the knockout blow it felt like), Nell reinvented herself as a self-employed bookkeeper. She hustled round the clock and managed to build up a list of local clients, but once she was working from home her existence suddenly got a whole lot smaller and she could go for days without speaking to anyone else in person. And then, last year, the one person who Nell did see every day, and who made the long hours and isolation bearable, suddenly upped and left, taking the last shreds of her self-esteem along with him, and encounters that once would have been a breeze became fraught with anxiety. What if she said something stupid? What would people think of her? In the end, it just seemed easier to avoid them in the first place.

The pancakes arrived and, despite her jitters over the morning's task, Nell fell on them like a woman who hadn't had a meal since the matchbox-sized lasagna she'd picked at on the flight over from London.

"How was the food?" asked the waitress when she swooped by with more coffee.

"Absolutely amazing," sighed Nell, resting her hands contentedly on her belly. "I could happily eat that for every meal for the rest of my life."

"Just wait until you try the strawberry mascarpone brioche French toast," said the waitress, clearing the plate. "I've been known to have thirds."

Nell thought for a moment. "No time like the present. I think jet lag must have given me an appetite."

The waitress smiled. "Excellent. I'll be right back."

After another cup of coffee and the French toast, which was just as delicious as the waitress had suggested, Nell was strongly tempted to crawl back into bed for a nap, but she knew it would just have been a delaying tactic.

"Could you point me in the direction of Fiske's General Store?" she asked the waitress, when she returned with the check.

"Sure, it's just down the street to the right. You can't miss it."

Despite the sunshine it was bitterly cold, and Nell plunged her bare hands into her pockets as she set off down the street, making a mental note to dig out her gloves from the bottom of her suitcase. Tansy Falls had the relaxed air of a well-loved place: the sidewalks had already been cleared of the night's snowfall and early risers were going about their business, bundled up in coats and hats against the chill. Here and there in the gaps between the buildings, Nell caught glimpses of a river, iced over in the shallows, that meandered between thickets of trees as if playing a game of hide-and-seek.

Fiske's General Store stood a little way back from the street—though, as the waitress had said, it was impossible to miss. With its weathered wood exterior, railed porch and faded gold-lettered sign, it had the look of a Wild West saloon, albeit one where the cowboys had lovingly swept the boards of the deck and planted hanging baskets with spriggy yellow flowers. On one side of the front door there was a noticeboard papered with local ads and posters, while on the other a pile of winter squash was stacked up against the wall. The place looked like it hadn't changed in years, except for one clearly modern addition: the SALE PENDING sign that was stuck to the porch railings.

A bell jangled as Nell pushed open the front door to be greeted by a welcoming wave of warmth. After the brightness of the morning outside it was like walking into a cave, and once her eyes had adjusted to the dim light they grew saucer-like with astonishment. The place was a minimalist's nightmare: every inch of surface space was piled high with stuff. There were shelves lining all the walls, mismatched tables and old dressers stacked with goods and teetering columns of cardboard boxes dotted around the floor creating makeshift aisles that wandered off into darkness. Where there was a glimpse of bare wall between the shelving, random bric-a-brac had been mounted to fill the space: a rusty scythe with a wickedly curved blade, a vintage ad for cigarettes featuring a picture of a heavily pregnant woman looking thrilled to be smoking—"the smooth taste expectant mothers crave!"—and an antique wall clock hanging above the old-fashioned till, its ticking the only sound disturbing the dusty stillness. Here and there someone had made an attempt at a more conventional shop display—a pyramid of cookie boxes, or a fan of knitted alpaca socks ("from Tansy Falls' very own herd of alpacas!")—but generally it looked as if things had just been crammed into the available space without any thought.

Nell wandered around, marveling at the dazzling array of goods on sale. Run out of shotgun shells? *There they are, just along from the jigsaws, right next to the bottles of organic bubble bath.* Looking for a gift? *How about a box of candy (you'll find them to the left of the garden rakes) or perhaps this brooch fashioned from maple bark?* Need something to read? *Check out this shelf of very well-thumbed secondhand novels, alongside a whole stack of out-of-date issues of* Cheese Market Quarterly *magazine . . .*

"You need any help there, miss?"

With a start, Nell turned to find a woman scrutinizing her from behind the counter in the far corner of the store. She had ice-white hair gathered into a long braid and was wearing a man's black overcoat over a pair of denim overalls. There was a tangle of beaded necklaces at her throat, and her hands were dotted with silver rings and bangles, giving her the look of a wise old mystic. Could this be Darlene? She certainly didn't look one hundred and twenty years old; early seventies at a push, though she had the bearing of a much younger woman.

"Hi! Yes, um . . ." Nell picked her way across the store toward her, trying not to knock anything over. "I was wondering if Darlene Fiske still owns this place?"

"She does, though not for much longer. Who wants to know?"

"My name is Nell Swift and I—"

"That an Australian accent?"

"What? Oh no, I'm English."

"Hmmm." The woman pursed her lips, looking so stern Nell wondered if she should have stuck with Australian. "What's your business with Darlene?"

"Well, a friend of mine used to work here in the summer when she was younger—"

"If it's a job you're after, then I'm afraid you're out of luck." She folded her arms.

"Oh no, no, I'm not looking for work." Behind her, Nell heard the front door open, but she plowed on. "You see, this friend of mine, Megan Shaw, told me that I should stop by and—"

"Megan Shaw?" The woman's face lit up as if a switch had been flipped. "Well, what a wonderful surprise! What did you say your name was?"

"Nell Swift."

"Nell! Welcome, I'm Darlene, and it's a real joy to meet a friend of Megan's." Darlene reached across the counter, squeezing Nell's hands with the grip of a woman in the very prime of her life. "I must have a quick word with Chief Watkins over there about his order, the poor man's been waiting on his new fly rod for weeks, but I would love to hear all Megan's news. I think about her often, that girl was so very dear to me. Would you like a coffee? Take a seat, I won't be a minute. Such a wonderful surprise...!"

As Darlene went over to speak to the police officer, Nell perched on a stool by the counter and, with a sinking heart, wondered how she was going to break the news about Megan. Darlene had been so delighted just at the mention of Megan's name, she could only imagine how devastated she would be to find out she had died. Nell tried to visualize herself saying the words, but her chest instantly tensed up, as if her lungs were refusing to play any part in this terrible plan. It was such a horribly intimate conversation to have with a stranger. Yet as Nell watched Darlene laughing with the officer, the seed of an idea took root. Perhaps she could just *not* tell her that Megan had died? It wasn't like she was going to hear it from anyone else—and she would never see her again—so why cause this woman unnecessary grief? Yes, in a way, it would be far kinder simply to keep it to herself.

The front door jangled shut and soon after Darlene returned carrying two cups of black coffee from the machine in the corner.

"Right. Now, I'm all yours." Darlene pulled up a stool next to Nell and patted her knee, her eyes sparkling like a child at Christmas. "So, how's my sweet Megan? You know, that girl was just about the best help I'd ever had in the store. It must be—hmmm, let's see—well over ten years since her aunt and uncle left Tansy Falls, though it feels like she was stacking shelves here only last week! But then time does go funny on you when you reach my age. Tell me, did she end up becoming a lawyer? I've never known a young person to be so focused."

"Yes, a criminal barrister."

"Wonderful! And has she got herself a husband? A family of her own?"

"She..." Nell faltered; boy, this was tough going. "She married a lovely man named Ben, another lawyer, and they have three children."

"Three?" Darlene shook her head, chuckling with obvious pleasure. "Well, that girl never did things by halves. Boys? Girls? Both?"

"Three gorgeous girls." Nell felt a lump forming in her throat.

On seeing the delight in Darlene's eyes, Nell finally admitted defeat. There was no way she could lie about this. It felt deeply wrong, and it wasn't fair, to Darlene or to Megan. Nell took a breath, preparing herself for what was coming next, the wound she was about to inflict on the old woman.

"Darlene, I'm so sorry to have to tell you this, but Megan died a month ago."

It was like she'd thrown a bucket of ice water at her. Darlene gasped with shock and pain.

"She had cancer," Nell pressed on, rushing out the details like she was ripping off a Band-Aid. "It was very quick, she didn't suffer. She was so loved. We did everything we could."

"No... That can't be." Darlene's eyes were wide, her fingers quivering at her mouth. "Not Megan, surely?"

Nell was desperate to offer comfort, but there was nothing to say that would make this any less horrendous. "I'm just so sorry," was all she could manage.

The pair of them sat in silence for a moment, Darlene retreating into herself, processing the shock, while Nell relived the loss of Megan all over again through the woman's horror. When Darlene finally looked at Nell again, her eyes were glittering with tears. "You two were close?"

"About as close as friends could be."

Darlene shook her head. "That poor sweet girl. I just can't believe it."

Nell only now became aware that they were no longer alone in the store, and she glanced round to see a family dressed in expensive skiwear browsing the aisles. Judging by the dazed looks on their faces as they gazed around, this was their first time in here.

"Just a minute," muttered Darlene, swiping the tears from her face. "Sorry, folks, store's closed!" she barked, herding them toward the door. "We'll be open again in an hour." Shutting the door behind them, she flipped the CLOSED sign and shut the bolt. "Right, now we won't be disturbed. So Nell, please, tell me everything."

They talked until the coffee pot was empty, swapping stories and poring over the photos on Nell's phone. It was the first chance Nell had really had to talk about Megan since she had died. She'd been so careful not impose her grief on anyone else that she'd kept it all packed away, twisting and scrunching at her insides, and as the words poured out of her she could feel the tension drain away. Darlene was such a wonderful listener, easing the details out of her and matching her step-for-step with memories of her own, and Nell couldn't believe she'd ever considered keeping Megan's death from her, as if she were some enfeebled senior who wouldn't be able to cope with the shock. She was as sharp as someone a quarter of her age.

"But tell me, why have you come to Tansy Falls?" asked Darlene. "I'm guessing Megan suggested it, but why now?"

"Well, the main reason is that Megan wanted her ashes scattered on Mount Maverick."

Darlene gave a sad smile. "That figures. Any chance she got, that girl would be up on Maverick, running wild with the local kids."

"But she's also given me this itinerary for my visit: a list of places that meant something to her, things I should do, people she wanted me to meet. I suppose, well, I've had a few personal problems recently, and she seemed to think Tansy Falls would do me some good."

Darlene narrowed her eyes. "Like a vacation?"

"Yeah, but I get the feeling it was meant to be more than just that. I don't know, like I could learn some kind of lesson from Tansy Falls."

"Now what could that be, I wonder?"

"I have no idea—I wish I could ask her. And there was something else too. Meg said in her letter that I should stick with the itinerary, even if it got tough, because it would"—here Nell made air quotes with her fingers—"'all be worth it in the end,' and then something about endings being beginnings. Like there was going to be some sort of...*goal*, which would be revealed at the very end of the trip."

"Huh." Darlene wrinkled her forehead. "And my store was on this mysterious itinerary of hers?"

"It was the first place she wanted me to go. She described it as the heart of Tansy Falls. And she called *you* a badass."

"Ha! Not so badass nowadays, I'm afraid." Darlene smiled, fiddling with the beads around her neck.

Nell paused. "If you don't mind me asking, Darlene, how old are you?"

"Oh, I have no idea, sweetie! Stopped keeping count years ago. I do know I'm the exact same age as Jane Fonda, though, so look it up on Wikipedia if you're interested." She gave a shrug that suggested she absolutely wasn't. "How long are you in town?"

"Two weeks. I've got a lot of ground to cover."

"Will you come back and have dinner with me tomorrow night?"

Nell didn't hesitate. "I would love to, thank you."

"Wonderful," said Darlene, her eyes crinkling. "Now, where is Megan sending you next on this wild goose chase?"

"Tomorrow morning I've got to visit her aunt and uncle's old house. I don't suppose you know who lives there now?"

"In the old Philpott place? I most certainly do." The look on Darlene's face strongly suggested there was a story there, but she didn't elaborate further.

Nell prompted her. "Can you tell me anything about them?"

"Oh, I don't think Megan would want me giving you any clues now, would she?" Yes, that was definitely a glint of mischief in her eyes. "But let's just say I'm looking forward to hearing all about your visit there when you come over tomorrow night..."

Chapter Five

The next stop on your tour is the house where my Aunt Nancy and Uncle Bill Shaw lived throughout my childhood. Everyone in town refers to it as "the old Philpott house," although nobody can remember who the Philpotts actually were or when they lived there. The house is on a road called Birdsong Hill, which is a half-hour walk outside town. It sits on several acres of woods with a perfect sledding hill, a wildflower meadow and a creek with a pebble-bottomed swimming hole. Knowing Tansy Falls folk, I'm sure whoever lives there now would be happy for you to have a look around. Promise me you'll have a go on the tire swing—jumping off it into the creek is weather dependent, of course!

It may well have taken half an hour to get there outside of mud season, but Nell had been walking for a good deal longer than that and there was still no sign of the turning to Birdsong Hill. In fact, she was pretty sure she was lost.

The directions, according to Darlene, were simple: head straight out of town on the mountain road, after about a mile you'll pass a red barn on your left, then Birdsong Hill is the third turning on your right. Easy. When Nell had said she was planning to walk, Darlene had been adamant she should borrow her car, but Nell had insisted the fresh air would help with the jet lag. Ha! Right now, jet lag was the very least of her problems.

The mountain road ran along the valley bottom, cutting across farmland before heading up into the foothills of Mount Maverick. There was no sidewalk, so Nell was forced to take her chances either on the surprisingly busy road or in the boggy ditch that ran alongside. Numerous times she had picked up her foot while her boot had remained stubbornly stuck in the mud. Her hands were now caked in dirt from pulling out her boots, her jeans were filthy from wiping her hands, and her pink galoshes had long ago forgotten what color they were actually meant to be. She was fast becoming more mud than woman.

To make matters worse, the scattering of puffy clouds that had accompanied her when she set off had mutated, Incredible Hulk–style, into a furious mass that was now pelting her with icy sleet. Nell's coat wasn't remotely up to the task, so all she had to keep her dry was an umbrella, which was as good as useless as the sleet seemed to be coming at her sideways. She felt ridiculous, picking her way across the open countryside like a bedraggled Mary Poppins.

Nell had passed the red barn Darlene mentioned a while back and had since gone by multiple turnings, but as most had been little more than dirt tracks and, as nobody around here seemed to bother with street signs, Nell had no clue if any of them were Birdsong Hill.

An enormous truck rumbled up behind her, forcing her to scramble into the ditch again. As well as being drenched she was now very cold, her galoshes were leaking and the phrase "dying from exposure" was nibbling away at her weakening resolve. Perhaps she should head back to the Covered Bridge Inn? She glanced ahead: in a couple of hundred yards there was another turning, yet this one led to a road that looked considerably more substantial than the others she had passed. And was that...? Yes, there was definitely a signpost! Nell trudged onward, straining to read what it said, and gave a whoop of triumph when she got to close enough to see the wonderful words BIRDSONG HILL.

Not that this was the end of her problems, though, by any stretch.

"The old Philpott house is the first on the left," Darlene had told her, but unless Megan's aunt and uncle had lived in a tumble-down cowshed on the edge of a birch copse, ten minutes later Nell still hadn't found it. There was hardly any traffic on Birdsong Hill, so she could at least stick to the asphalt here, but the road climbed steeply from the valley floor and she was soon panting, her spirits dropping as her pulse rose. And then, just as she was considering desperate measures (*perhaps they have Uber in Tansy Falls?*) Nell rounded a bend and saw, alongside a turning into the woods, a red mailbox. The name QUAID was printed on the side, but she was sure this was the place. It must be, as it was apparently the only house in the vicinity.

As a rule, the prospect of turning up at a stranger's house unannounced would have made Nell break out in a cold sweat (she always felt so sorry for doorstep sales reps that she sometimes ended up buying whatever they were selling purely out of sympathy) but right now she was just relieved at the prospect of getting warm and ticking off the next stop on Megan's itinerary. The dirt driveway was built up on a raised bank that snaked through a forest of spruce, the trees packed in so tightly that the ground underneath them was untouched by snow. The sleet had eased off now, but the world was heavy with water: dripping off branches, trickling in rivulets down the muddy drive and gathering in pools of snowmelt on its mossy banks. Towering trees soared high above the evergreens, their bare branches clawing at the sky like witches' fingers. There was an otherworldly stillness to the place that made Nell feel as if she were walking into a fairy tale.

She passed an outbuilding, the doors of which were ajar, revealing a truck and what looked like farm machinery, and as she rounded a bend she caught a glimpse of a pretty gray house tucked in a dell a little farther below.

Then all of a sudden, the peace was shattered as a dog bounded out of the trees and squared up to her, barking furiously. She took a step back. It was the biggest dog she had ever seen, about the size of a small pony, but Nell knew dogs—in fact, she found them easier to read than people—and she was pretty sure this guy was all bark and no bite. She slowly got down into a crouch. "Easy now," she murmured, holding out her hand.

The dog woofed a few more times, then gave himself a shake and trotted over, tail at full wag. He was clearly well loved: his black-and-russet coat was glossy and well groomed and he was wearing a leather collar with identity tags.

"Simba!" Nell looked up to find a man striding up the driveway toward them. "Simba, here boy!"

At once, the dog bounded over to his master, dancing around his legs while gazing up at him adoringly. The man, who she presumed was the Mr. Quaid from the side of the mailbox, must have been tall—well over six feet, with a rugged build and broad shoulders—because Simba seemed almost normal-sized next to him. The man fondly ruffled the dog's coat, then turned his attention rather less fondly to Nell.

"Can I help you?" he asked, with a look that, if not outright hostile, wasn't exactly welcoming.

Nell's cheeks turned hot under his gaze, partly because it was obvious that the man didn't want her to be there, but also because her insides were being flooded with whatever hormone is released when you find someone instantly attractive. It wasn't just that the man was good-looking, although with his thick chestnut hair and a face that had the elegant angles and symmetry of a marble statue, Nell could see that he certainly was. He was, in fact, the living embodiment of "tall, dark and handsome," with an extra helping of handsome on top—though a dusting of freckles across his nose and cheekbones at least took the edge off the perfection. No, this was about whatever strange magic occurs when you meet someone and have a feeling that this person is somehow meant to be a part of your life. That was how Nell felt as she stood on this stranger's driveway, on the other side of the world from home: like the pair of them had been destined to meet. Even before the rational part of her brain had had a chance to inform her that this was a ridiculous idea (and, by the way, that this man was way out of her league) she had instinctively stood up a little straighter and scraped off a clump of hair from where it clung damply to her cheek.

"Hello! I'm sorry to bother you, but my name is Nell Swift and a friend of mine's aunt and uncle, the Shaws, used to live here." *Unless—perhaps this wasn't even the right place?* "This is the old Philpott house, isn't it?"

He folded his arms. "That's what people round here call it."

"Cool!" said Nell, grinning manically, and before she could stop herself, she did an actual thumbs-up.

The man just stared at her, while Nell wished fervently for a freak avalanche to cover her in snow so she couldn't embarrass herself any further.

"So, anyway," she forced herself to plow on, "this friend of mine had so many happy memories of her time staying here that she suggested I should stop by and ask to take a look if I was passing by."

"And you were...passing by?"

He looked dubious—understandably so. This place wasn't exactly *on* the beaten track.

"Yes! Well, sort of—I'm staying in town, but...Look, I know this must sound weird, but to cut a long story short it would mean a lot if I could just have a quick look round your backyard. My friend told me all about the meadow, and the creek with the swimming hole, and she told me I had to have a go on the tire swing!"

A smile flickered in his eyes, but it vanished before it could take hold. "Not really the weather for tire swinging," he said, with a glance up at the sky.

"No! Ha! No, of course, but it was more just to, you know, have a *virtual* swing on it. Just take a look, really. If it's not a bad time, of course."

The man ran a hand over his jaw; he was clearly finding this as awkward as she was. "The thing is, I'm afraid that it *is* a bad time."

Nell hadn't been expecting that. "It would only take a few minutes, if that. I wouldn't even need to see the swing up close. If you tell me which way it is, I could maybe just...wave in its general direction? Just so I can say that I've seen it."

She shot him a hopeful smile, which the man again noticeably failed to return.

"I'm sorry," he said. "I'm just heading out."

Judging by his jacket and boots this did appear to be true; still, Nell was at least expecting him to suggest she come back another time, and when he didn't she felt her insides curl up with embarrassment. What must he think of her, turning up on his doorstep, caked in mud, and demanding to go on his swing?

"Of course, I completely understand," she muttered, already turning to leave. "So sorry to have bothered you."

As she walked back up the drive, her pulse pounding, Nell felt a sudden flare of anger at Megan. Why on earth was she making her follow this stupid itinerary? Forcing her to run around town, chasing after ghosts. What was the point? Because if Megan had imagined Nell would fall in love with Tansy Falls after two weeks of excruciating encounters like this one, and then somehow, magically, become as spirited and adventurous and as, well, all-around *happy* as Megan had been, then she had been sorely mistaken.

She stumbled on a rock, pain stabbing at her toe, and she pressed her fist to her mouth to stop the tears that were threatening to explode messily out of her. It wasn't as if she *had* to follow Megan's itinerary, though, was it? Nobody was going to be checking up on her. Nell gritted her teeth. So, she wouldn't follow it. She would stay in her room at the inn, perhaps see Darlene a couple of times, but would ditch the rest of this dumb, pointless—

"Hey there! Nell, is it? Do you need a ride into town?"

To her horror, she heard footsteps approaching behind her.

"No, no, it's fine, thank you," she called over her shoulder, picking up her pace. "I'll enjoy the walk."

"Come on, you're soaked, and I'm headed that way. It's no trouble."

In the end her throbbing feet made the decision for her, slowing to a halt before she'd had the chance to persuade them otherwise. As much as she wasn't relishing the prospect of an awkward car journey with this man, on balance it was preferable to another hour spent battling the elements.

"Thank you, that would be great," she said, turning to face him. "I think I'd be in danger of going full Swamp Thing if I had to face that walk again."

And then, finally, he relaxed into a smile, and his face was transformed. Gone was the aloof ice man of before: he had a wide mouth and slightly crooked grin, which made him look a little less intimidatingly handsome, a bit goofy even. Nell decided she liked this new version far better.

She glanced down at her filthy clothes and grimaced. "I hope you've got something I can sit on."

"Don't worry, the truck's seen far worse." He nodded toward the outhouse. "It's just up here."

They set off together, walking side by side, but although it was only a couple of hundred yards Nell quickly became conscious of the silence looming between them, so she asked: "How long have you lived in Tansy Falls?"

"About four years."

"Are you from around here originally?"

"Oh no, I'm a flatlander."

Nell looked at him quizzically.

"It's what Vermonters call anyone from out of state. Which is kind of ironic, seeing as I'm from California and my hometown is probably at twice the elevation of Maverick."

He punctuated this with another warm smile, and as they reached the outhouse Nell felt glad she'd accepted his offer of a lift—and not just because she'd get the chance to defrost her extremities.

Nell had been expecting some kind of work vehicle, but this was more like the sort of thing a city dweller would refer to as a "truck": there was an open cargo bed at the back, but inside the cab it was like a family car, complete with a scattering of toys in the back seat. As the man settled into the driving seat, Nell took a peek at his left hand:

no wedding ring, although that didn't mean anything. *He's bound to be married*, she thought. *All the signs are there.*

"Where are you staying?" he asked, as they set off.

"The Covered Bridge Inn."

He nodded, turning the truck onto Birdsong Hill, and that appeared to be the end of their conversation, but after a little while he said: "You're English, right?"

"Yup, I live in London. I'm here on vacation."

He paused, thinking. "Interesting time of the year to choose to visit. Most tourists prefer to come here in the winter, or in summer or fall."

"Basically anytime of the year other than now, is that what you're saying?"

The corners of his mouth twitched upward. "Pretty much."

"What can I tell you? I like mud."

They briefly met each other's eyes, smiling.

"So what have you got planned while you're here?"

"Do you know, I'm really not sure," said Nell, with a flat chuckle.

The man furrowed his brow, looking at her for an explanation.

"I'm following an itinerary that my friend put together. Like a magical mystery tour of Tansy Falls."

"Sounds intriguing," he said, as they turned onto the mountain road. "And will this friend of yours be joining you?"

Nell hesitated, wondering whether she should explain about Megan—but decided against it. It was too personal for this polite, brief exchange with a stranger.

"No, I'm on my own for this adventure," she said, and left it at that.

Just then a giant dump truck thundered past them heading toward the mountain; Nell watched it disappear in the side mirror, wondering what it might be doing up there. Then out of the corner of her eye, she noticed the man glance at her.

"How long are you going to be in town?" he asked.

Nell's heart gave a little skip; perhaps he was going to invite her back to see the swing after all? The prospect made her strangely happy.

"Two weeks," she replied, smiling in anticipation of his reply.

"Well, you might want to think about getting yourself a better pair of boots."

What? Nell almost laughed. "I'll do that," she muttered, then swiveled to stare out of the side window, her back hunched and chin cradled in her hand. *See? Never a good idea to leave your comfort zone. Terrible, in fact.*

Thankfully, within just a few minutes they were pulling up outside the Covered Bridge Inn.

"Thank you for the ride," said Nell, her hand reaching for the door handle before they'd even stopped. "It was very kind of you."

"Sure, you're welcome."

As Nell shut the door behind her, their eyes met. She caught a glimpse of something in his gaze—uncertainty, perhaps, or more likely bemusement—then he raised his hand in farewell, spun the truck in a circle and headed back in the direction they'd come. It only then occurred to her that she hadn't even found out his name.

Chapter Six

"His name is Jackson Quaid."

Nell was having a drink with Darlene in her apartment above the store. Her living room was crammed with nearly nine decades' worth of photos, antiques and trinkets and lit by an array of old lamps—some with fringed shades, others ornately beaded—that cast puppet-like shadows on the wallpaper. They were drinking bottles of very good local beer and eating spiced nuts, while cooking scents from the kitchen mingled with the smoke from the fire.

"He's our local forester," Darlene went on. "Anyone with any trees on their property in Tansy Falls knows Jackson Quaid, which means that just about everybody does."

"Forester? Is that like a lumberjack?"

"No, Jackson doesn't cut down trees, he manages them. He's like a kind of woodland architect." She nodded, pleased at the analogy.

"Sounds interesting."

"If you like trees." Darlene shrugged, reaching for another handful of nuts. "Jackson moved here with his wife and baby son a few years back. He's from the west coast, but Cindy, that's his wife, grew up in Tansy Falls."

Well, that explains the toy cars in the back of the truck, thought Nell.

"So what did *you* think of him?" Darlene asked her.

She was scrutinizing her with such intensity that Nell had a sudden crazy notion that perhaps Darlene could read minds. With her mass of white hair and all those beads, she did have a hint of the ancient sage about her, after all.

"Oh, I reckon I must have got him on a bad day," replied Nell, before she thought anything incriminating. "It was clear he didn't want me poking about the place."

"Did you tell him about Megan?"

"I didn't. To be honest, I don't think I handled any of it very well. He clearly thought I was a bit of a loony."

"Oh, don't take it personally. Jackson's had a bad time of it lately."

"How so?"

Darlene twisted her beads and gazed up at the ceiling, perhaps wondering if she should say more. "Well, I'm not one to gossip," she said, after a surprisingly short pause, "but Cindy left him last year. Apparently she'd been having an affair for months, although from what I've heard Jackson didn't suspect a thing right up until the day she walked out. Cindy moved to Chicago to live with the rich guy she'd been cheating with, leaving Jackson to raise their son on his own. Joe's six—he's a terrific kid, but it must be tough."

"Gosh, that's terrible," said Nell.

"Folks can never know for sure what goes on inside a marriage, but I've never had cause to say a bad word about Jackson Quaid. That Cindy, though..." Darlene scowled, and Nell made a mental note never to get on the wrong side of her. "Now *she's* a piece of work. Nice to look at, sure, but doesn't she know it? Reckon she damn near broke Jackson's heart."

Neither spoke for a while, each wrapped up in her own thoughts. For her part, Nell was replaying when Jackson had smiled at her, and how it had made her light up inside—swiftly followed by that awkward moment in the car, which had brought her crashing back down to earth. Anyway, it was pointless spending any time thinking about Jackson Quaid, Nell reminded herself, because she'd be going back to London in a few days' time. More to the point, she was terrible at relationships, a fact that had been proved beyond all doubt a year ago. Just as she was certain that she was not a whiskey person or a Zumba person, Nell knew for sure she was not a love person.

"You know," mused Darlene, "if you told Jackson about Megan, and why you're here in Tansy Falls, I'm sure he'd be accommodating. I could phone him now if you'd like?"

"No!" Nell almost shouted. "No, that's extremely kind of you, Darlene, thank you, but I really don't want to bother him. Sounds like he's got enough on his plate."

"Well, if you change your mind…" Darlene glanced at the mantelpiece, where there must have been a clock hidden among all the clutter. "Time to eat! I hope you've brought your appetite, Miss Nell."

Over braised ham with greens, mustard and maple roast beets (Darlene was the sort of cook who made enough for thirds and also put a whole loaf of bread on the table, "just in case") Nell told the story of how she and Megan had met.

"It was my first week at college in London and I was at the Fresher's Fair, which is where you sign up to the college clubs and societies. I was feeling completely lost. I didn't know a soul, I couldn't act or play an instrument and I was rubbish at sports, so most of the clubs wouldn't have me. I was about to go back to my dorm and give up on ever having a social life when I noticed this stall a little way apart from the others that was being ignored by all the other students. I went to take a closer look and discovered that it was the Carnivorous Plants Society."

Darlene put her palms on the table and leaned forward. "The what society?"

"Carnivorous Plants," repeated Nell, tickled by the look on Darlene's face. "Venus flytraps, pitcher plants, that sort of thing."

"Well, that is most certainly niche."

"Right? Anyway, I felt so sorry for the guy who was manning the stall that I went over, planning to take a leaflet, maybe ask a few polite questions and make my excuses, but then this girl came bounding over and said in this incredibly cool American accent, 'Wow, this is so awesome! Tell me more about your bloodthirsty plants!'"

"And that was Megan?"

Nell nodded. She could picture the moment so clearly: the cool high-top Nike sneakers Megan had been wearing, her gap-tooth smile, her explosion of curls swept up in a red spotty scarf. Nell had wanted to be her friend even before they'd spoken.

"She'd just arrived from Boston and was so sweet and funny and enthusiastic about everything. Even carnivorous plants." Nell smiled, remembering how she'd been swept up by Megan's zest for life that day. "Anyway, long story short, she talked me into joining up with her. That first year, Megan, me and Clive—that was the PhD student who ran the society—were its only members."

"What in the world did you do in this society of yours?"

"Well, Clive had a lot of carnivorous plants, so basically we'd go to his room and feed them mealworms with tweezers. I think he was lonely, really. But that was another thing I loved about Megan: she could have been friends with anyone, been captain of all the sports teams, but she didn't care at all about being cool or popular. She just had the biggest heart." For the millionth time, Nell wondered why it'd had to be Megan, the very best of them, who'd been taken. "I've got a lot to thank Clive for," she plowed on, as brightly as she could. "Not only did he teach me the difference between a purple pitcher and a Cape sundew, it was because of him that I met Megan. We were pretty much inseparable after that."

"You two must have made quite the pair," said Darlene with a smile. "Megan so dark, with all that gorgeous hair, and you—"

"So pale?" Nell already had a sprinkling of freckles from the few minutes of sunshine she'd had on her walk that morning.

Darlene chuckled. "I was going to say a beautiful English rose, but I guess pale will do. Now, are you ready for some apple fritters?"

As Darlene busied herself serving dessert, Nell decided to ask a question that had been niggling at her since yesterday.

"Darlene, I couldn't help notice the SALE PENDING sign outside the store."

The older woman paused with her serving spoon in midair, then set it down with a sigh.

Nell had clearly touched on a sensitive subject. "I'm so sorry, Darlene, I shouldn't have mentioned it. Forget about it."

"Don't worry, dear, I'm fine. It's just the store's been in the Fiske family for generations, and it makes me a little sad to think about selling." She lifted her shoulders as if to say "What can you do?" then went back to dishing up the fritters. "I've kept the store going as long as I can, but even with extra help it's getting too much for me now. I've no kids of my own to pass it on to, and my niece Tati works in the movie industry in LA and has no interest in running some dusty old country store."

"So who's buying it?"

"The developers of Maverick Lodge."

Nell looked at her blankly.

"You've not heard about it? It's just about the biggest thing to happen to Tansy Falls in years. Ice cream?" Darlene held up a tub and Nell nodded. "They're building a fancy five-star hotel up at the mountain with glass-walled elevators and hot tubs and a different restaurant for every day of the week. They've even got a 'wellness center,' whatever the heck that is." Nell remembered noticing the trucks heading up toward the mountain that morning; it now made perfect sense. "The developers made me an offer for the store and it's not as if anyone else was biting my hand off, so I said yes."

She thrust a bowl at Nell; it was so heaped with fritters and ice cream that rivulets of melted vanilla were already trickling down the side.

"Thank you, Darlene. So what are these developers planning to do with Fiske's?"

"Well, I only agreed to sell it to them if they promised to keep it as the general store."

"And will that be written into the contract?" asked Nell.

"No, but I explained that it was a deal-breaker for me and they gave me their word. I've been dealing with the boss, Liza DiSouza her name is, and she's been ever so sweet. The company's run by her father and is based in Manhattan—very successful apparently—but Liza's renting a condo here in Tansy Falls while she oversees the project. I'm sure you'll meet her at some point."

Nell felt a prickle of concern. Back when she was in banking she'd worked in the mergers and acquisitions department, so she had a good deal of experience buying and selling companies, and it would have been unthinkable to have relied on another party's word during negotiations.

"Um...I don't mean to be nosy, Darlene, but have you signed the contract?"

"Not yet, but I'll be getting the valuation report any day, then we'll be good to go." Darlene frowned at Nell. "Now you don't have to worry about me getting hoodwinked, I'm getting my attorney to check the paperwork. I may be old, but I'm not foolish."

"Oh, believe me, I can see that," said Nell, laughing. "But if you did want a second opinion, I'd be very happy to take a look. I'm an accountant, and I used to deal with these sorts of transactions all the time."

"You're very kind, dear, thank you, but no need. Ted Libby has been my attorney for fifty-odd years and he knows his onions, and his carrots and taters too!" She patted Nell's hand, as if to settle her worries. "Now tell me, what's on Megan's itinerary for tomorrow?"

The itinerary. Nell's overly full stomach rolled unpleasantly: the prospect of tomorrow's task was like the thought of school on a Sunday evening. Yet despite being so sure she would abandon Megan's mission after the encounter with Jackson, that now felt inconceivable. Of course she would continue; she had to, for Megan's sake. She would grit her teeth and get on with it to honor her best friend's memory. Only another twelve days to go, then she could get back to her nice, safe, *predictable* life in London.

"Actually, Darlene, you might be able to help me. I've got to track down one of Megan's old friends tomorrow. Mallory something?"

"Ah, that'll be Mallory Hoffman, or Smith as she was before she got married. They were as thick as thieves whenever Megan came to stay. She's married to the second youngest of the Hoffman sons. They live over at the family farm."

Darlene's usually sunny demeanor had been clouding over while she'd been speaking and she now looked like there were a nasty smell beneath her nose.

"Um...if there's something I should know about this woman," said Nell, "I'd appreciate some warning."

"Oh no, Mallory's a sweet girl. It's her mother-in-law that's the problem. Deb Hoffman." Darlene spat out the name as if it were gristle.

"And what's the problem with her?"

"Oh, I would not know where to begin." Darlene's mouth formed a thin line.

Terrific, another tricky customer, thought Nell.

"Can I walk there?" she asked. "To the Hoffman farm?"

"What is this darn obsession you have with walking everywhere? You'll borrow my car. It's just sitting there, I barely use it. I'll go get the keys."

By now, Nell knew that it was pointless to argue. "Thank you, Darlene."

"You're welcome, sweetie," said Darlene, beaming angelically, but as she headed for the kitchen Nell heard her mutter, "You just better hope old Ma Hoffman's not home when you go visiting tomorrow."

Chapter Seven

As Nell headed back to her room after a very early breakfast the next morning, she saw Connie in the lobby talking to a pretty blond woman. Judging by her white apron and the tray of muffins she was carrying, she worked in the inn's kitchen—although with her chunky tortoiseshell glasses and coral lipstick she looked more like an Instagram influencer than a hotel cook. She was young, no more than mid-twenties, and her long hair was piled on her head in the sort of perfectly messy style that Nell could never hope to emulate.

"Morning, Nell," called Connie as she approached. "How are you today? Everything okay with your room?"

"Absolutely, you have such a gorgeous place here." Nell stopped to pet Boomer, who was stretched out right in the middle of the floor. "In fact, I'm thinking about moving in permanently. It would be worth it for the breakfasts alone."

Connie smiled, but it was the woman standing with her who answered. "I'm so pleased to hear that," she said, putting down her tray and offering Nell her hand. "I'm Piper Gridley. My husband, Spencer, and I run the Covered Bridge."

Nell just about managed to hide her surprise, but inside she was doing the math: this woman must be at least ten years younger than she was, yet she was the boss of a successful hotel, married *and* had mastered the art of the perfect casual updo. *Perhaps I should start wearing lipstick*, thought Nell, as she eyed Piper's flawless makeup; then she realized she was staring and that it would probably be polite to say something.

"Hi! It's a pleasure to meet you, Piper. Have you, um, been at the Inn long?"

"Well, I moved here from New York about eighteen months ago, but the Covered Bridge has been in my husband's family for years. Spencer's grandparents are officially still in charge, but they're now living in Florida, which is where Spencer is right now, trying to persuade them to agree with some changes we'd like to make to the inn. They still have very strong ideas about how things should be done round here!" Piper waggled a finger, mock-stern, and Connie smiled, but Nell got the impression that this arrangement wasn't as easy as Piper's jokey manner suggested. "For one thing," Piper continued, "I'm not sure Grandma Gridley would approve of the chia and cardamom I added to her banana muffin recipe." She offered the tray to Nell. "Would you like to try one?"

Nell took a bite. *Dammit, the girl can cook too.* "Delicious! Thank you."

Piper beamed. "So, what brings you to Tansy Falls?"

After yesterday's encounters with Darlene and Jackson, Nell had decided it would be far better to be upfront about her reason for visiting the town. And, as it turned out, neither Connie nor Piper had lived in Tansy Falls when Megan used to visit, which made Nell's task a little easier, and their sympathy and offers of help were clearly genuine. Still, as always, her heart ached as she put Megan's death into words. The problem was that she still couldn't accept that it was true. It seemed bizarre that someone as brilliant, beautiful and gloriously alive as Megan was now gone. Apparently, denial was the first of the five stages of grief, but it had been over a month and she was still stuck firmly at number one. Shouldn't she be starting to come to terms with it by now?

*

Mallory Smith was my best friend in Tansy Falls. We met while skiing on Mount Maverick when we were ten and bonded over a love of puppies and making friendship bracelets. We looked kind of alike too, and used to pretend we were twin sisters—Meg and Mal Carey (in honor of our idol, Mariah). Mallory's now married to a local dairy farmer in Tansy Falls. We're friends on Facebook and exchange Christmas cards, though we haven't spoken in years. If you get stuck with anything, Mallory's who you should go to for help. I just know the two of you will get along—if, of course, you can find her!

Darlene had an old Buick station wagon the size of a hearse that was covered in imitation wood paneling, both inside and out. Anything that wasn't made to look like wood was colored beige. Darlene called it Sue Ellen, after J.R. Ewing's wife on the soap opera *Dallas*, "because they both drink too damn much."

The steering took some getting used to, and reversing the eight-seater out of the space in front of Darlene's store was like maneuvering a ferry inside a bathtub, but by the time Nell was picking up speed on the road out of town, with Fleetwood Mac playing on the cassette deck, she was silently thanking Darlene for insisting she take the car. It was a cold morning, and even walking the short distance from the inn to the store had left her with numb toes. As much as she hated to admit it, Jackson Quaid had been right about her needing better boots.

The shops and businesses of Main Street soon thinned out and were replaced by snow-dappled fields and stretches of woodland, the rolling hills keeping pace with Nell as she flew along the road. There was the occasional house and farm building, but these were few and far between. It couldn't be more different from London, where everyone was piled up on top of each another and only the occasional spindly tree or worn patch of grass was left to remind you what was there underneath all the concrete. Nell had never really questioned why she chose to live in the city—she had moved there for university and simply never left—but the landscape here lifted her spirits in a way that London never had.

The road stretched out ahead of her to the horizon. Maybe, thought Nell, she should just keep driving? It wasn't like anyone would miss her, after all. She could sleep in motels, eat diner pancakes for every meal and drive all the way across America. Just the thought of this brought a surge of happiness, and Nell broke into a grin as she sped along, singing along to "Go Your Own Way" at top volume, accompanied by the throaty hum of Sue Ellen's engine.

All too soon, though, she spotted a sign by the side of the road with a picture of a grazing cow, under which was swirly red script reading HOFFMAN ORGANIC CREAMERY. As Nell took the turn she had a hairy moment worrying whether Darlene's ancient car would be able to handle the terrain, but her apocalyptic vision of mud, potholes and rampaging cattle vanished as she laid eyes on a smooth driveway that wound gently down the valley to what looked like a child's drawing of a perfect storybook farm. There was a cherry-red farmhouse with a deep shingle roof, a duck pond and an old-fashioned gable barn with a cupola on its roof, topped by a dancing cow weathervane. Tendrils of morning mist rose from the pond and snaked around the silver-frosted branches of the orchard. It was so pretty that Nell considered pulling over to take a photo, but she wasn't sure how to work the handbrake, and a mental image of her chasing after Sue Ellen as she rolled down the hill and sank slowly into the pond was enough to keep her from stopping.

Parking outside the farmhouse, Nell spotted a track leading from behind the barns into a thicket of trees, behind which she caught glimpses of what must be the working part of the Hoffman farm: it was a far more industrial (and less bucolic) setup, with metal barns, silos and the gallons of mud that she'd originally been expecting.

"What in the name of Davy Crockett do you think you're doing?"

Nell's head snapped toward the direction of the shouting and saw a woman storming toward the car waving a stick. She was sturdily built with a helmet of cropped gray hair and for a senior person was moving at surprising speed; within a few seconds, in fact, she was close enough for Nell to see that the stick she was holding was actually a gun, and the look on her face suggested she was prepared to use it.

"Why you've got a damn nerve coming down—" The woman stopped abruptly and did a double-take when she saw Nell in the driver's seat. "Who the heck are you?"

Nell's hands were up in the air, which is where they had flown on registering that yes, that was a gun that was pointed at her. "I'm Nell Swift," she stammered. "From England."

"What in blue blazes are you doing in that woman's car?"

So, this must be Darlene's nemesis, Deb Hoffman. The dislike was clearly very much mutual.

"I, um, borrowed it." Nell suspected that the less she said about Darlene, the better. "I'm actually here to see Mallory if she's around?"

"You one of the Fiske relatives? That snooty niece of hers from Hollywood?"

"Oh, no, no, I'm just visiting. From England," she repeated.

"Huh." Deb Hoffman was still squinting at her suspiciously, although at least she had now lowered the gun.

"Would it be possible to have a very quick word with Mallory?" asked Nell. "If that's not too much trouble?"

Deb dipped her head to scan the car's interior, as if expecting to find Darlene crouched behind the passenger seat, then gave a curt nod. "She's in the office, up past the barn."

"Thank you so much, that's very kind," gabbled Nell, attempting to smile the woman into submission. It didn't work, and Nell could feel her glare burning into her back as she made her way toward the barn as quickly as she could without breaking into a run.

Now that Nell was up close to the buildings she noticed that they weren't quite as pristine as she had first thought. Paint was peeling from the clapboard, while a leaky gutter had been dripping water for long enough to have left a slick of green slime down the side of the barn. It looked far more like a working farm than the idyllic view from the driveway had led her to believe.

The office was located in a ramshackle lean-to that had been tacked onto the rear of the barn so it was hidden from sight. Nell knew she was in the right place as there was a printed sign on the door that read FARM OFFICE, and beneath, handwritten in smaller letters, KINDLY SHUT THE DARN DOOR. She took a couple of breaths to steady herself, her heart still galloping after having been at the wrong end of a shotgun, and knocked.

"It's open!" a voice called out, thankfully sounding far more friendly than Deb Hoffman.

Inside, there was a woman sitting at a desk in front of a computer, on the monitor of which was a bumper sticker that read: MY OTHER RIDE IS A TRACTOR. The rest of the cramped space was taken up with filing cabinets, a storage heater noisily blasting out hot air, and an office chair that was occupied by a man in overalls and a baseball cap, his long legs stretched straight in front of him, leaving no space for Nell to actually get into the room.

"Hi, can I help you?" asked the woman, whose dark hair—such a similar shade to Megan's—was scraped into a ponytail. She was dressed in a worn shirt and jeans, but had the steady smile and confident manner of a TV anchor.

"Hello, I'm looking for Mallory?"

"Well, you've found her." She chuckled, spreading her hands in a "this is me" gesture, and Nell could see why she and Megan would have gotten along. They clearly both shared the same easygoing charm that instantly put you at ease. "What's this about?"

"I was hoping I could talk to you about..."

Still hovering in the doorway, Nell glanced at the man, who was picking out dirt from beneath his fingernails. Should she ask to speak to Mallory in private? This was going to be difficult enough without an audience, but she didn't want to be rude. Thankfully, by some miracle, Mallory picked up on her dilemma.

"Mike, could we finish this later? I'll stop by the milking parlor once I'm done here."

"Sure thing, Mal," he said amiably. He got to his feet, touched the peak of his cap at Nell and ambled out.

As soon as the door closed, Mallory gestured to the now vacant chair. "Don't take this the wrong way, but I've got a horrible feeling that you might be Nell Swift."

Nell's head jerked up to stare at the woman. She opened her mouth, but only managed to gawp in reply.

"Your accent," said Mallory, by way of explanation.

"But how did you know...?"

"That you'd be coming to see me? Megan told me."

"But I..." Nell blinked. "I didn't think the two of you were in touch?"

"We hadn't been for years, not really." Mallory rested her arms on her knees. "But she'd been on my mind for some reason, so at Christmas I sent her a message saying we should catch up, and a few days later she called me." Her face softened at the memory. "It was so great to speak to her. Just the same old Meg."

"When was this?"

"Just after the new year."

Nell did a quick calculation: so they must have spoken *after* Megan had written the itinerary, which explained why there was no mention of their conversation.

"She told you about the cancer then?" asked Nell.

Mallory nodded. "She said that she was very sick and didn't have long left." Then she faltered, and Nell saw in her the same battle she'd had so often, the struggle not to let her train of thought be derailed by sadness. "But she was just so darn upbeat about the whole thing! When she talked about having her ashes scattered on Maverick she might as well have been discussing her vacation plans. And, of course, she told me all about your visit, and some surprise she had planned for you. She told me, 'My best friend Nell's had a crappy time and needs some maple syrup and mountain air.'" Mallory gave a flat chuckle. "It was a joke we had when we were kids. She'd call me from Boston, pissed about some boy or school grades, and I'd be like, 'What you need, darlin', is some maple syrup and mountain air…'" She trailed off, then with an effort plastered on a smile. "Well then, I guess if you're here, Nell, that means Megan—isn't."

"She died a month ago. I'm so sorry."

Mallory pressed her lips together to stop the tears. "Dammit," she muttered, wiping her sleeve across her face. "It's just so unfair."

The rattle of the heater filled the silence. Mallory's head was bowed, and Nell wasn't sure whether to put an arm around her or leave her in peace, so she just sat there feeling helpless. Why couldn't she be more like Megan, who would have dived in for a hug without a second thought? In the end, she reached out a tentative hand and laid it on Mallory's leg; at once, Mallory grabbed hold and squeezed like it was a lifeline.

"I'm glad you're here," she said, her voice trembling. "It couldn't be under worse circumstances, obviously, but it's really nice to meet a friend of Megan's."

"Perhaps that's the reason she wanted me to come here? So we could comfort each other and remember her together? She told me that an ending would be a beginning."

"Maybe." Mallory looked up, her eyes bright with tears. "But I reckon there'll be more to it than just that. If Megan's sending you on a tour around Tansy Falls, I'm sure there'll be a very good reason for it."

Later, as Mallory walked Nell back to the car, she peppered her with questions about the itinerary. "I've no idea how Megan has found enough here to keep you busy for two weeks," she said. "This place isn't exactly New York City. Where are you going tomorrow?"

Nell pondered this for a moment. "The Tansy Falls museum, I think?"

"You're kidding." Mallory gave a snort of laughter. "That's literally the dullest place in the entire state! It's basically a roomful of broken pottery and some dead people's letters. I have no idea why she'd send you there." She glanced at Nell. "Still, I'd be happy to come with you if you like."

"Really?"

"Absolutely. Someone's got to make sure you don't choke on the boredom."

Nell smiled. "Thanks, I'd really like that." They walked on a little farther. "Mallory, you mentioned earlier that Megan told you she was planning a surprise for me. Do you know what it might have been?"

"No idea, I'm afraid—unless, of course, she was talking about the itinerary. Yeah, I guess that must have been it?" They had now rounded the barn and Mallory came to a sudden halt, staring at the car. "Hey—is that Sue Ellen?"

"It is. Your mother-in-law pulled a gun on me when she saw her."

Mallory grinned. "Oh yeah. Deb's a sweetheart, though, don't let the firearm fool you."

"What's the problem between her and Darlene?"

"Nobody knows. I've tried to get it out of both of them. It's the mystery of Tansy Falls: why do Deb Hoffman and Darlene Fiske hate each other so much? Lucas, that's my husband, reckons they were both in love with his dad when they were younger, but I can't see those two alpha females falling out over something as silly as a man." She ran her hand over Sue Ellen's fake-wood hood and gave it a fond pat, as if it was a well-loved cow. "Well, I guess we'll find out one of these days."

Chapter Eight

The next morning Nell pushed open the door of Fiske's, the bell on the hinge jangling its greeting, and breathed in the store's scent of coffee, woodsmoke and lavender oil, which she already found as comforting as a dear friend's perfume. She would have happily spent her entire two weeks in Tansy Falls exploring all the nooks and crannies of Darlene's store.

She had come to ask for advice on where to buy mud-season-appropriate footwear, but Darlene was busy talking to a woman who looked like Building Site Barbie. She was wearing lace-up boots and a fashionably oversized parka, both of which served to emphasize the skinniness of her denim-clad legs, while a spotless white hard hat labeled with the initials L.D. perched on the backpack at her feet. Judging by her flawless face, the woman clearly owned a full set of makeup brushes and knew how to use them (even the weird fan-shaped one that always confused Nell) while her tumbling mass of hair, streaked with shades of caramel, coffee and chocolate, was just a cherry and a squirt of cream short of a hot fudge sundae. It was by far the most glamour Nell had seen since arriving in Tansy Falls, and as incongruous as a Lipizzaner stallion at a rodeo.

"Nell!" Darlene looked delighted to see her. "Come over here, I'd like you to meet someone. This is *Ms.* Liza DiSouza, the lady I told you about who's buying the store." From the way Darlene emphasized the "Miz," Nell got the impression she'd had this corrected in this past. "Liza, this is Nell Swift, she's a new friend of mine from England who feels like a very old friend."

With a swish of her delicious hair, Liza flashed a lot of white teeth at Nell. "It's a pleasure to meet you, Nell. And Darlene, strictly speaking it's DiSouza Developments that's buying your store, not me personally."

"Oh, you know, same difference." Darlene waved a dismissive hand.

Liza simpered at her indulgently, then turned to Nell again. "So what do you think of Tansy Falls, Nell? Isn't it the most adorable town? Will you be skiing while you're here?"

"Well, I..." Nell wasn't sure which question to answer first. "It is, yes. Adorable. And muddy."

Liza gave a burst of tinkling laughter. "Oh, you haven't seen mud until you've been up to our site. You should stop by the mountain and check it out. I'd be happy to give you a tour. Any friend of Darlene's..." Her cheeks dimpled into a smile.

"Liza, have you got one of those fancy brochures about the lodge?" asked Darlene. "I'm sure Nell would love to see it."

"Sure!" Liza bent down to look in her bag, swiveling both her knees to one side in a fluid move that made Nell think Pilates. "Here you go," she said, reverently holding out what looked like a copy of *Vogue*. "This is our little project."

"You want a coffee, Nell?" Darlene asked. "I've got a pot going..."

As she headed to the coffee machine, Nell leafed through the Maverick Lodge brochure. It was mostly made up of glossy computer-generated images of what the new resort would look like—basically a

Bond villain's alpine hideout, but with a daycare—set against real-life photos of Mount Maverick, with a scattering of pie charts for added credibility.

"It looks incredible," said Nell, truthfully—although she couldn't help worrying how this mega-resort with its hot-stone massages and "ski concierge" would affect business at the Covered Bridge Inn.

"You must come and stay with us when we open! Our duplex penthouse suites will be the height of luxury, with a VIP entrance, signature dining and a personal butler." Liza tilted her head toward Nell, as if sharing a fabulous secret. "I'm sure I could secure you a special preferred guest rate..."

"Oh, that's so nice of you, but I'm not sure my helicopter would have room to land."

Nell was grinning as she said this, but Liza just stared at her blankly. "We'll have a rooftop helipad, naturally," she said, with a hint of defensiveness.

"Well, in that case, I'll definitely drop by," smiled Nell, deciding it wasn't worth explaining her joke. "When are you planning to open?"

"Next year in the fall, if all goes to schedule. We feel so lucky to be able to realize our vision for a world-class resort in such a wonderful town, and DiSouza Developments fully intends to share the benefits of our endeavors with the wider community of Tansy Falls."

This was delivered so smoothly it sounded like a PowerPoint presentation.

"Speaking of community," said Nell, "Darlene tells me you're planning to keep this place as the town's general store?"

Liza's smile flickered ever so slightly, as if she had a faulty circuit. "That is certainly our intention," she said, her poise regained, although there was a new hardness in her eyes.

"Nell here's an accountant," said Darlene, who had just reappeared with the coffee. "She thinks you're trying to swindle me."

"Darlene!"

Darlene grinned. "Don't you worry, dear, Liza knows I'm joking."

Judging by Liza's flinty expression, though, Nell wasn't convinced that she did. An awkward silence lingered, and Nell had to resist the urge to fill it with inane chitchat.

"Well, I have a 10:30 up at the mountain, so I better get going," said Liza after a few moments. "Darlene, I'll get the valuation report to you by the start of next week. Nell, it was so nice to meet you. How long will you be in Tansy Falls?"

"Just a couple of weeks."

"Well, I'll be sure to keep an eye out for you," said Liza with a fluttery wave, although to Nell's ears this sounded more like a threat than a promise. Or was she just being paranoid?

As soon as Liza had gone, Darlene held up her palms, pre-empting whatever Nell was about to say.

"I know, I know, she's a piece of work, but Liza's also been very helpful. You don't have to worry."

"I won't. But I—"

"But what, young lady?" Darlene planted her hands on her hips, her eyes steely. "As my mother used to say, don't talk unless you can improve the silence."

Nell knew when she was defeated. "But nothing," she sighed, hoping to smooth things over with a smile. "But I would like your advice on something very important." She held up a pink-galosh-clad foot. "I need a sturdier pair of boots. These are definitely not up to the mud round here."

Darlene leaned over the counter and her eyes widened. "You don't say."

"Where can I buy something more suitable?"

"Right here!" Darlene bustled off toward the storeroom. "What size are you, honey?"

While Darlene was rooting around in the back room, Nell replayed the conversation with Liza DiSouza. She had been so sure the woman was trying to cheat Darlene, but doubts were already nibbling away at her conviction. What proof did Nell actually have, after all? And was it really any of her business? Nell had offered to look at the contract; Darlene had told her that wouldn't be necessary: The End. They all lived happily ever after. Or so Nell hoped.

Darlene emerged from the back room, wrestling the lid off a shoe box. "Here you go." She pulled out a yellow boot with a black sole that looked like what you'd get if a bulldozer mated with a rubber duck. "These'll see you right."

What they lacked in style they more than made up for in coziness: it was like slipping on a pair of blanket-lined buckets. Nell checked her reflection in the mirror by the counter. In her padded coat, hiking pants and the gigantic new boots she was now ninety-eight percent manmade fiber and two percent face.

"Well, it's certainly lucky I'm not on the lookout for a husband," she joked, striking a mock-alluring pose.

Darlene just raised her eyebrows in response.

Chapter Nine

The Tansy Falls Historical Society Museum was located in a house just off Main Street. It stood a little way apart from its neighbors, as if it were far too grand to mix with the likes of the bike shop and the café next door, while its flagpole towered over all the others in the vicinity. There was no need for a sign for passersby to know that Very Important Things were housed inside the white clapboard walls, which was lucky because there *was* no sign. Nell couldn't imagine this place got much in the way of passing trade: not only was there no way of knowing it was actually a museum, but with its dark windows and closed-up front door it looked like the last place you'd pick for a fun-filled day out.

Mallory was waiting outside the museum as Nell approached. At first glance she looked like she was wearing a particularly well-padded coat, but as Nell got nearer she realized there was a baby carrier strapped to Mallory's chest.

Ambushed by a jolt of emotion, Nell took a sharp intake of breath—although she had recovered her smile in the few steps it took her to reach Mallory.

"Who do we have here?" she asked.

"This is Anke." Mallory hooked open the front of the carrier a little so Nell could peek inside: the baby was asleep, her dark lashes fanned against her cheek and her mouth shaped into a kiss.

"Oh, she's gorgeous," breathed Nell, feeling her heart twang.

"She's twenty weeks old today," added Mallory.

Nell made a "well I never" face and kept on smiling, but her mind was already spiraling back in time. *Don't go there, Nell*, she told herself firmly. *Don't count the months, don't imagine what might have been...*

"My other two, Bo and Cordelia, are back at the farm," Mallory went on.

"You've got three kids? How old are they?"

"Five months." She sighed wearily. "All of them."

"Triplets?" Nell's voice shot up an octave, making Anke stir. "Sorry," she whispered.

"Runs in the Hoffman family apparently, those crazy Dutch genes." Mallory rolled her eyes. "Not that anybody thought to warn me. That first-semester scan was quite an eye-opener, I can tell you."

"Wow." Nell's eyes bulged. "Just...well done, seriously."

"Thankfully I've got a hands-on husband and a live-in mother-in-law. Deb is looking after the other two, but Anke sleeps through anything, so I thought I'd bring her along." Mallory glanced at the stern-looking facade behind them. "I haven't been to this place since I was a kid, but I can't imagine it's suddenly got interesting in the last twenty-five years."

"Megan wrote in her letter that she used to come here when she wanted a bit of peace."

"Ha! From me and my three quiet, angelic brothers, probably." Mallory peered at the plaque alongside the front door. "Hey, look at this: BY APPOINTMENT ONLY. Well, looks like we'll have to go for brunch instead!"

Nell grinned. "Don't worry, I asked Connie at the Covered Bridge and she phoned ahead to arrange our visit."

She rang the bell, and moments later they heard footsteps approaching the door and then the jangling and thuds of various bolts and locks.

"Fort Knox," Mallory mouthed, shooting a look at Nell.

"May I help you?" The man who had opened the door—side-parted gray hair, ironed fleece, exuberant eyebrows—was speaking in a hushed, slightly aggrieved tone, as if they had interrupted an exam.

"Hello, my name's Nell Swift. I think you're expecting us?"

"Ah yes." He stood to one side, sticking out an arm. "Please, come in. I'm Walt Whipple, curator and chairman of the museum."

Inside, the hallway was dark, lit only by the natural light coming from two rooms on either side of the passage. Specks of dust eddied in shafts of sunlight, stirred up by the unfamiliar activity.

"Welcome to the Tansy Falls Historical Society Museum," said Walt Whipple. "Is there any aspect of local history you have a particular interest in? The development of the railroad? The collapse of the Merino sheep trade in the mid-1800s?"

Nell and Mallory glanced at each other. "Um, just general sort of, uh, historical stuff?" managed Nell.

"I see." Walt Whipple's mouth puckered; he'd clearly been hoping for a more clued-in crowd. "Well, let me help you get your bearings and then I'll leave you to explore."

Mallory was right: it wasn't very exciting. The museum's guiding principle appeared to be that visitors would rather read about something than actually see it. Consequently, there were very few actual artifacts and instead the glass-fronted cabinets were filled with documents and letters, each of which was labeled with a card covered in writing explaining all the other writing. It was the sort of place a child would take one look at and immediately ask to go to the gift shop.

Yet the tranquility of the place, the smell of yellowing paper and the almost-spiritual power of the mass of memories collected here had a narcotic effect on Nell. Some people might have found the place oppressive, but to Nell it was as soothing as the lying-down bit at the end of a yoga class. She knew exactly why Megan had liked it here.

Walt Whipple herded them toward a display at the end of the room. "This is our current exhibition on nineteenth-century toleware, donated by a local benefactor." He gestured to a cabinet containing a few painted tin trays and tea caddies that looked like the result of someone's grandma having a clear-out. "Then over here—yes, follow me please—this is a wonderful traveling exhibition we're currently hosting on the history of pond hockey in Vermont."

Nell and Mallory peered at the black-and-white photos of men with walrus mustaches and pipes clamped between their teeth, whizzing over the ice with what looked like bear traps stuck on their feet.

"I guess the women were busy making halftime appetizers?" murmured Mallory.

"And then, of course, we have our ever-popular permanent exhibits." Walt Whipple swept an expansive arm across the displays along the opposite side of the room.

"And these have been here a long time?" asked Nell.

"Oh yes, many of the items have been on show since we opened back in 1968. The Tansy Falls Historical Society has quite an impressive history!" Walt Whipple beamed, tickled by his joke. "Do you have any questions? No? Well, I'll be in the archives across the hallway if you do. No food or drink to be consumed in here and, please, don't let the child handle anything."

"She can barely pick up a spoon," Mallory muttered at Walt Whipple's retreating fleece.

Nell looked around the room wondering where to start. Judging by what the curator had said, this place had barely changed since Megan's last visit, and Nell wondered if there was a particular reason her friend had sent her here, some clue that she had intended her to find. Or perhaps she was overthinking things as usual, and Megan just thought she might enjoy the hushed atmosphere while learning about eighteenth-century weaving techniques.

"Now *this* is interesting," said Mallory, and Nell turned to find her examining a machine in the Farming in Tansy Falls section. She read aloud from the accompanying label: "'Early twentieth-century tabletop cream separator.' Huh." She gazed at the other farming implements on display. "I wonder if any of this stuff comes from the Hoffman farm?"

"How long has it been going?"

"The farm? Lucas's great-grandfather bought the land when he came to America after the Second World War and it's been in the family ever since."

"And it's always been a dairy farm?"

Mallory squatted down to read the label on an antique milk churn. "Yup. But for how much longer, I'm not sure." She rubbed her chin. "We've only got a hundred cows, and milk prices are so low we can't keep up with the bigger operations. All the other small guys are dropping out or diversifying, but Lucas and I aren't having much luck convincing his parents we need to try something new."

"They want to keep things the way they are?"

Mallory nodded. "And I understand why, we've got a nice little operation up there. The farm is organic, we bottle our own milk and cream in our creamery and sell it direct to local stores, but it's just not sustainable long-term." She sighed. "Small dairy farmers like us are an endangered breed these days."

Perhaps sensing her mom's disquiet, Anke started to grizzle.

"Oh, so you're awake now, are you?" Mallory smiled down at the baby, stroking her cheek. "Nell, do you reckon Walt Whipple would consider breast milk to be 'food and drink'?"

"I don't think Walt Whipple would want to consider breast milk *at all.*"

Mallory grinned. "You're probably right. I better go and feed this one in the car. Back shortly."

Left alone, Nell wandered around the exhibits, dipping into the stories and enjoying the solitude. The atmosphere reminded her of their college library, a sprawling ancient warren of musty rooms and hidden corners, where she and Megan had spent a few nights, though not nearly enough, cramming before their finals.

Nell had moved on from the farming equipment and was midway through the very small Women's History section when a photo caught her eye. It was a black-and-white picture of a young woman, but although it must have been taken a hundred years ago the subject herself looked entirely modern. In an age when most photos, particularly of women, were stiffly posed, she had her head thrown back in laughter. She was sitting on a grassy bank, her arms resting on her knees in the way a man's might, and rather than the high-necked dress you would expect, she was wearing laced-up boots, pants and a scarf knotted bandanna-style about her hair. And at the bottom of the photo, in tiny, faded lettering was written: *Miss P. Swift, 1923.*

Nell's hand flew to her mouth. That was *her* name: Miss P.— Penelope—Swift! Was this the reason Megan had wanted her to come to the museum? To discover this laughing young woman's story?

Her pulse quickening, Nell leaned in to examine the display more closely. The photo was surrounded by letters, press cuttings and maps that told the story of a Miss Polly Swift of Tansy Falls, who in 1923 became the first woman to hike the famous Wilderness Trail "without a male guide." Accompanied by two girlfriends, Polly trekked the mountainous 200-mile trail from Massachusetts up to Canada, a feat that made headlines across a country where women had only just been given the right to vote. According to one of the letters, the reason Polly had decided to embark on this adventure was "to avoid a man who wished to marry her." Nell grinned to herself at this epic instance of early nineteenth-century ghosting. *Go Polly!*

"What's got you so fascinated over there?"

She hadn't heard Mallory and Anke coming back into the room.

"Come and look at this." Nell stepped aside to show her the photo. "'Miss P. Swift.' Like my name!"

Mallory looked at it, scratching her cheek. "Surely you're Miss N. Swift."

"No, my full name's Penelope. Miss P. Swift!" Nell's voice rose to a squeak. "Kind of a coincidence, don't you think?"

"Maybe." Mallory raised a shoulder in a tiny unconvinced shrug.

"Do you know the Wilderness Trail?" asked Nell.

"Yeah, it goes right around Maverick."

Nell turned to look at her. "Do you think this exhibit might be why Megan wanted me to come to Tansy Falls?"

"What, so you'd see this and then go and hike the Wilderness Trail?" Mallory wrinkled her nose. "Seems a bit far-fetched."

"Yeah, I suppose, but..."

Nell was struggling to articulate it, but she was sure that Megan had wanted her to read about Polly Swift. It was certainly the sort of story that would have appealed to Megan, who was always telling Nell to grab the moment, trust her gut and do less looking and more leaping. She pulled out her phone and took a few photos, while Mallory looked on, shifting Anke to her other hip.

"You know, Nell..." she said, clearly choosing her words with care, "this display might not have even been here when Megan was around."

"I know. It's just a little souvenir."

Deep down though, Nell believed that Megan had wanted her to see this, and that was enough for her. She looked at the photo of Polly again. She seemed so happy, but, more than that, she looked free, like she was following her path without a moment's worry about what anyone would think of her. If Polly Swift could do this in a world where everything was stacked against her, shouldn't Nell be able to make a few bold, scary decisions of her own?

Chapter Ten

Now that she was awake, it didn't take long for Anke to decide that she wasn't very keen on the Tansy Falls Historical Society Museum. What started as low-key grizzling quickly transformed into hurricane-grade fury at the absence of colorful plastic things to stuff in her mouth. Unsurprisingly, Walt Whipple then appeared and informed them that the museum was now closing for lunch, and if they'd kindly make their way to the exit—perhaps putting a contribution in the donation box as they passed?—he would be entirely grateful.

After the door had closed behind them, they stood on the doorstep, securing layers of clothing against the chill.

"What are you up to now?" Mallory was jiggling on the spot to try to calm Anke. "Would you like to go for lunch?"

"I would love that," said Nell. "For some reason, since I got to Tansy Falls my appetite has gone through the roof. At first I thought it was the jet lag, but now I reckon it's just greed. Yesterday at dinner I had a bacon cheeseburger and fries *as an appetizer*."

Mallory laughed. "Then let's go eat!" She gestured toward the next-door café, which had MISTYFLIP COFFEE painted on a snowboard hanging over the window. "This place does the best sandwiches in town. And you've got to try the buttermilk fried-chicken grinders."

Nell had no idea what these were, but she knew she was hungry and anything fried was a bonus. "Done," she said.

It was only midday, but the café was almost full. Nell noticed a Hoffman Creamery sticker on the window as they went in.

"We supply their milk," explained Mallory as they picked their way around the busy tables toward the counter, where she greeted the dreadlocked barista who was giving off a strong snowboarder vibe.

"Hey, Shaun, how you doing?"

"Mal! Good to see you." He clocked the baby carrier. "Where's the rest of the team?"

"Home with Deb." Mallory gestured to Nell. "Shaun, this is Nell Swift, a friend of mine visiting from London."

Shaun grinned. "Hey, Nell, good to meet you. What can I get you guys?"

"Well, Mallory's given me the hard sell on your fried-chicken grinders," said Nell.

"You got it. For two?" He jotted down the order. "Grab a table, I'll bring them over."

Once they had sat down, Mallory lifted Anke out of the carrier, removed her little coat and hat and bounced her on her knee. She had lots of dark hair that was sticking up in an Elvis pompadour. "Phew, you're getting heavy, missy," murmured Mallory, rubbing her shoulders while Anke reached for Nell, her hands starfishing across the table toward her.

"Are all three of them identical?" asked Nell, smiling at Anke while her ovaries hammered out a desperate SOS.

"Yup, totally. Once the three of them are old enough to work out that nobody can tell them apart our life is going to play out like some crappy Nickelodeon movie."

Nell grinned. "I've loved having the two of you with me today, thanks for coming along."

"Oh you're welcome, I enjoyed it. Where else have you been on Megan's itinerary so far?"

"Well, I started at Darlene's store."

"Of course. That should be the first stop on any tour of Tansy Falls."

"And then I went to Megan's aunt and uncle's old house."

"The old Philpott place?" Mallory's eyes were on Nell. "So you must have met Jackson Quaid."

Nell nodded, wondering what was coming next.

"He's buddies with my husband, Lucas," said Mallory. "Do you know his story?"

"Darlene told me a little about what happened with his marriage."

"I knew his wife Cindy in high school," said Mallory, grim-faced. "Ex-wife now, I guess. She was one of the cool kids. Blond, pretty, captain of the cheerleading squad. Cute, but kind of a bitch. She didn't improve much after high school either. She disappeared off to LA, telling everyone that she was going to become a famous actress, then came back a few years later with a baby and husband in tow."

"Jackson?"

"Yup, and baby Joe. From what I've heard, Cindy got pregnant pretty soon after they started dating and Jackson, being a decent sort of guy, proposed. Anyway, they moved into the old Philpott house and everything seemed peachy for a while. Cindy taught Mommy and Me yoga classes, while Jackson built up his forestry business. For some reason, a lot of Tansy Falls' female residents started having tree problems after Jackson turned up..." Mallory's smirk dimpled her cheek. "And then one day Cindy disappeared and it turned out she'd been having an affair with this guy who runs some billion-dollar hedge fund in Chicago. Apparently it had been going on even before she met Jackson."

"Does she ever see her son now?"

"Oh yeah, she comes back every now and then." Mallory's expression told Nell exactly what she thought about Cindy's parenting skills. "Turns up with all these gifts for Joe, makes a huge fuss of him, then disappears back to Chicago leaving Jackson to deal with a very upset kid."

"And Jackson's okay with that?"

"Well, I guess he must be, because she stays up at the house while she's here." Mallory lowered her voice, leaning across the table toward Nell. "You know, I wouldn't be at all surprised if he's still holding a torch for Cindy, even after everything she's done."

Just then Shaun appeared with their grinders, which turned out to be sandwiches, and Mallory dropped the subject, but Nell was still processing what she'd just heard. In the tale of the mercenary ex-cheerleader versus the broken-hearted single dad it was difficult not to pick a side, but Nell reminded herself that relationships were always complicated.

"So how about you, Nell?" asked Mallory. "Are you married? Kids?"

"No and no. And zero prospect of either." Even to her own ears, she sounded defeated.

Mallory tipped her head to the side. "I hope you don't think I'm being nosy, but why? It can't be a lack of offers. Mike—that's the guy I was talking to in the farm office when you turned up—was like, 'Who was *she*?' Even Deb commented on how pretty you are. She said you had the exact same color hair as Daisy."

"Daisy?"

"Deb's favorite goat. Cute strawberry blonde, just like you."

Nell gave a snort of laughter. "Uh, thank you, I think."

"Believe me, that's the biggest compliment you could get from Deb Hoffman." Mallory took a big bite of her sandwich. "Come on then," she said, between chews, "what's the story?"

Nell paused, trying to work out how to tidy up the mess of her love life into a few neat words. "I'm just not very good at relationships," she said eventually; as ever, it was the best explanation she could come up with. "I did have a boyfriend until last year. His name was Adrian. We went out for five years, lived together for most of them."

"What happened? Just say if it's none of my business."

"No, no, it's okay." Nell wiped her fingers on the napkin; the sandwich was oozy with guacamole and melted cheese. "Well, as far as I was concerned, everything was fine between us. Better than fine, good. We never argued. We both enjoyed the same things. Adrian told he loved me most days and it felt like he did. But I guess the warning signs had been there. He made it clear when we first got together that he never wanted to get married, said he 'didn't believe in it.' And"—Nell took a breath—"he was never sure about having children either."

"And you were okay with that?"

Nell's instinct was to say yes, she was absolutely fine with it, just as she had told everyone else (and herself) on numerous occasions. Only Megan had known the truth. And, for some reason, that was what she now wanted to share with Mallory.

"No, I wasn't okay with it," she admitted. "But I told Adrian that I was, because I was scared of being on my own. But in the end, it didn't actually matter what I thought anyway..."

Chapter Eleven

Fifteen Months Ago

Nell had taken the pregnancy test on Christmas Eve. She had gone a bit crazy with the decorations that year: even their bathroom had a giant model Santa on top of the toilet tank and a line of prancing reindeer under the sink. Adrian had complained, saying it was off-putting sitting on the toilet with an audience, but Nell found it entirely appropriate that the world's greatest giver of presents was there to witness the exact moment she found out she was going to be a mother.

While Nell was sitting in the bathroom watching that magical blue line appear, Adrian had been in the kitchen making mulled wine. Convinced it was going to be a false alarm, she hadn't told him that she was taking the test, so it didn't take too much additional willpower to keep the results secret for a little while longer. But later that night, after Adrian had gone to bed, Nell slipped an extra gift underneath the tree.

When he had unwrapped the pregnancy test the next day Adrian had been shocked; actually, horrified would be a better word to describe his slack-mouthed, wide-eyed, "how the hell did this happen?" expression as he stared at the stick in his hands. He had tried to laugh it off—"well, I thought this was going to be a Montblanc pen!"—and had given Nell a quick kiss, but he'd spent the rest of Christmas Day looking like he'd just been fired and had no idea why.

Nell told herself his reaction was perfectly understandable; after all, they hadn't actually been trying for a baby. They had talked about it, of course. After five years together, with both of them in their mid-thirties and Nell being invited to baby showers virtually every week, the subject had come up. Every time it did, though, Adrian was always ready with a perfectly good reason why the time wasn't right—he wanted to wait until he'd gotten a promotion, or they'd paid off some of their mortgage—and so Nell put her dreams of motherhood on hold, along with her fears about how long she had left. Adrian was so good with their friends' kids she felt sure he'd come around to the idea given time.

By that New Year's Eve, Adrian was still skulking around with the air of a condemned man. He didn't want to talk about it, insisted he was fine; nevertheless, Nell tried her best to reassure him. "This is just the universe taking charge," she'd told him, gripping his hands as tightly as if she could squeeze just a fraction of her excitement into him. But his terror (because really, that was what it looked like) was starting to unnerve her. For the first time in their relationship, Nell wondered how well she actually knew him.

And as it turned out, the universe quickly had a change of heart; a few weeks later Nell had lost the baby. It was still early enough not to be too physically traumatic, but Adrian had insisted on taking time off work to look after her. He had always been at his best in an emergency—he worked in crisis management, after all—and he made her stay in bed while he brought her hot drinks and magazines and cooked all her favorite meals. But he was so happy and upbeat it was like he was acting as if she had just made an against-the-odds recovery from a deadly disease, and while positivity is always nice, Nell wished he could be a little bit sad too, because to her it felt as if her whole world had collapsed. Adrian didn't appear to have been affected by the loss of their child at all.

With hindsight, though, he *had* been affected, just not in the way that Nell had hoped.

It was a sunny spring Friday a couple of months later, and Nell was working from home as usual. She was having a sandwich at her desk in the bedroom when she heard the front door open and Adrian call out a greeting. In the moments it took him to put down his keys, take off his coat and walk to the bedroom, Nell had concluded that his surprise arrival home must be a good thing. If he was sick, he would have called her first, and there was no way he would have been fired as he'd recently gotten his long-awaited promotion; he even had his own office and "executive assistant" now. That left the prospect of either an afternoon snuggling at home on the sofa, or perhaps—she felt a shiver of excitement—a surprise weekend away? It was their five-year anniversary in a few days, after all.

But when Adrian appeared in the doorway, his expression had proved her wrong. "Nell," he said gravely, "we need to talk." Which is never something people say when they're about to whisk you away for a romantic night in a luxury hotel.

Sitting at the kitchen table, Adrian explained to her that their "baby scare" (his words) had made him see that their relationship wasn't what he wanted long-term. Or short-term. Or basically any term, ever. He had also realized that he didn't want children, so had decided to give her the chance to find happiness with someone else; the way he put it, he made it sound like he was very generously doing her a favor. For a man of generally few words when it came to their relationship, it seemed as if Adrian had suddenly dredged up a whole lot of them from somewhere.

To Nell, sitting in appalled silence as her world was carefully dismantled, brick by brick, it felt as if she was listening to a slick, focus-group-approved presentation, and knowing Adrian, it may well have been. Ever the PR professional, he lived and breathed his five golden rules of crisis management, the first of which, as he had told Nell on many occasions, was to "get ahead of the story," which clearly was what he was doing now with this little speech.

He was careful to shoulder the blame, repeatedly assuring Nell that it wasn't her, it was him (rule number two: "take responsibility"). He told her that he wished things could be different, and he was truly sorry for hurting her, but it was for the best if he moved in with his workmate, Giles, that very evening (rule three: "apologize, then take immediate action"). He assured Nell that he would always love her, but he felt he had no choice but to "live his truth" (rule four: "be human"). And then there was rule five: "prepare for the backlash." In the days that followed, Adrian actioned this with typically flawless efficiency by blocking Nell's number, ignoring all her emails and refusing to see her, thus neatly avoiding any backlash at all.

This wasn't quite the end of the story, though. There was one final twist, which was what led Nell to conclude she was better off staying single forever, because honestly, how could she have been so wrong about someone she had been with for five years? Seven months after Adrian had so smoothly crisis-managed his way out of their relationship, one of his Facebook posts popped up on Nell's feed. He had long since unfriended her, but a mutual friend had commented on one of his posts: "Awesome news, mate, congrats!!"

It turned out that Adrian had just gotten engaged to his new executive assistant, a pretty graduate called Molly, and they were expecting a baby together the following spring.

Chapter Twelve

The Covered Bridge Inn is named after the town's actual covered bridge (built in 1847—just call me Meg-ipedia) which spans the Wild Moose River a little way out of town. You'll find the turning a couple of miles along Birdsong Hill, then you follow the road through the woods a little farther until you get to the gorge. The bridge is closed to cars, but you can still cross it on foot. It's one of those magical places where time feels like it's stood still for a hundred years. Stepping across the boards, you can imagine a pair of lovers meeting in secret, the young woman's long skirts swishing in the dust as she runs into the arms of her handsome beau for a kiss. Go there, feel the history, take a breath. You'll need it if you've kept to my itinerary so far!

Nell had woken that morning to fresh drifts and a white sky, heavy with the promise of more snow, but the sun was now shining as Sue Ellen rumbled along the mountain road toward Birdsong Hill. The last time she'd traveled this way it had been on foot; Nell now eyed the boggy ditch running along the side of the road and boggled at the tenacity (or stupidity?) that had kept her going for as long as she had. It was bizarre to think that had only been two days ago. Now, here she was with a car borrowed from a new friend, the correct footwear and a better grasp of local gossip than she'd had even after 15 years of living in London. Before setting off this morning she had stopped at Mistyflip Coffee to get a takeout cappuccino, and the barista Shaun had greeted her like an old friend; back home she didn't even know the names of her neighbors in her apartment block.

It was amazing how quickly you could feel at home in a new place, mused Nell, as she whizzed past the red barn. Just five days ago all this was new to her, but now there was a cheering familiarity to the muddy fields and snowy hills, the honking of geese overhead and the pungent farming smells that sneaked up and punched you full in the face. Maybe it was the caffeine, or perhaps the sunshine, but happiness was bubbling up inside her like a mountain spring. Today's itinerary was set to be the easiest yet: no talking to strangers, no deciphering of clues, just some leisurely sightseeing, after which Nell planned to go back to the Covered Bridge Inn, take a bath and eat a large slice of the triple-layer sour-cream coffee cake that Connie had told her earlier was the day's special. (She'd also told her that Piper had trained as a pastry chef before marrying Spencer, which explained why the Covered Bridge's daily cake offering was so spectacular, and why Nell would be heading home with more than a little excess baggage.)

Nell had a moment of panic trying to change gears on the steep initial stretch of Birdsong Hill—at one point the car slowed almost to a halt, like a stubborn horse—but as the road flattened out Sue Ellen got her groove back. As she approached the turning to the old Philpott house Nell punched the accelerator, shrinking into the seat until it was safely behind her. Just seeing the driveway stirred up an unsettling cloud of feelings inside her. On the one hand, she hoped she'd never see Jackson again: the amount of detail she knew about his personal life made her feel guilty, even stalkerish, plus of course there was the not-insignificant fact that she'd made a total fool of herself when they last met. Yet for some reason over the last couple of days her thoughts had kept returning to him. It was, Nell decided, the same sort of compulsion as when you see a gorgeous but ludicrously expensive and impractical pair of shoes: even though you know you can't afford them, you still wonder if they could have been the shoes that might just have changed your life.

As Nell turned off Birdsong Hill toward the covered bridge, the car bounced and jolted as she found herself on a dirt road. Her hands tensed on the wheel as she remembered Connie's warnings about cars getting stuck in mud season, but the rutted surface seemed firm enough beneath the tires, plus she didn't have too much farther to go. It was even quieter up here and, for a city girl, it felt to Nell as if she were forging a path through the wilderness. The ribbon of the road dipped and curved through the woods, the trees packed so tightly it looked as if it would be impossible to pick a path between them—although someone obviously had, because some of the trunks had pairs of metal buckets attached, giving them the look of bizarre fairy-tale milkmaids.

Intrigued, Nell was wondering whether to pull over to find out what the buckets were for when up ahead she saw a tractor approaching at surprising speed. She was pretty sure the road was too narrow to accommodate both of them and the tractor didn't show any intention of stopping; spooked, Nell swerved hard to the side of the road, slamming the brakes just in time to stop Sue Ellen's front wheels tipping over the edge of the shoulder. The tractor driver saluted in thanks as he chugged past, seemingly unconcerned that he had nearly forced Nell off the road and into the ditch.

Her heart racing, Nell sat in the stalled car for a few moments, making herself take some deep breaths. Once again, she felt a flash of that same anger she'd had during her encounter with Jackson, an irrational fury at Megan for putting her through this, but it faded as quickly as it had flared. She was okay, wasn't she? Just a bit shaken, that's all. No harm done.

Muttering apologies to Megan, Nell turned the key in the ignition, automatically checked her rearview mirror and flicked on her blinkers (which made her smile, because what exactly was the point way out here?) then put Sue Ellen into reverse and eased off the clutch.

The car didn't move.

Nell tried again, pressing the accelerator harder this time, but the back wheels just spun in the mud while the car bucked and slid beneath her. Ignoring the rumblings of fear in her belly, she gave it one more go, really punching the pedal now. The engine roared and the wheels skidded, sending mud splattering over the sides of the car, but Sue Ellen was stuck fast.

Grasping onto the hope that there was just a rock in the way or something easily fixed, Nell got out of the car to check and discovered that the back wheels had been sucked into the ground as if it were quicksand. Nell gritted her teeth, fighting the urge to kick at something. *Don't panic*, she told herself firmly. *This happens a lot around here.* She would simply call Connie and ask her to arrange a tow truck to pull her out. But when she looked at her phone, she discovered she had no coverage, the "no service" message a final, taunting blow.

"Dammit!" muttered Nell, throwing the phone back in the car. She scanned the road in both directions, but the only other vehicle she'd passed had been the tractor, and that was long gone. In the stillness, Nell was unsettlingly aware of just how alone she was out here.

So—she would wait: someone else would come this way again, surely? Ten minutes later, though, nobody had passed, the woods silent except for the dripping of melting snow and a very persistent bird that sounded like it was calling for "Phoebe."

If you're up there, Meg, thought Nell, resting her folded arms on the steering wheel, *now would be a good time to send someone this way.*

She gave it another few minutes, just in case miracles do happen, then got out of the car and started trudging back the way she came.

Her first thought, of course, had been Jackson. It was probably only a twenty-minute walk back to the old Philpott house and she knew he had a truck, plus she was pretty sure he had something that looked like a tractor in the garage too. At the very least he'd have a landline she could use to call for help. But the thought of turning up on his doorstep unannounced and asking a favor for the second time made her feel sick. No, she would just flag down a passing car on Birdsong Hill and ask for a lift back to town. Tansy Falls folk seemed like a helpful bunch, it shouldn't be too hard.

Now that she was taking positive action rather than just waiting to be rescued, Nell felt the tension that had been gripping her chest start to ease. It was a beautiful day for a walk: the trees muffled the chill and the sunshine warmed her face, its brightness bouncing off the patches of snow and making even the mud sparkle, while just breathing in the mountain air was as refreshing as drinking a glass of ice-cold water. The wet woods had that very distinct verdant smell that Nell could only describe as green.

Soon she was back on Birdsong Hill and the road started to climb again, her breath puffing in the stillness. Another ten minutes passed, but still nobody drove past. Was Birdsong Hill always this quiet? She was sure she'd passed other vehicles when she came this way last time.

Well, if she had to walk all the way back to the mountain road, then so be it: she could do with breaking in her new boots.

To her left, the ground fell away steeply toward a ravine, and Nell was just admiring the way a beam of sunlight lit up a clearing, making the wet rocks look as if they had been painted silver, when out of the corner of her eye she spotted something moving in the undergrowth. Nell froze, instantly on alert; she was sure she saw a large dark shape—some sort of animal perhaps?—just on the edge of the clearing. Her pulse racing, she scanned the area, but everything was now still.

Could it have been a wolf? *Unlikely*, she decided, so close to human habitation, if indeed they even had wolves in Vermont. But Nell's imagination, clearly in the mood for taunting her, then came up with the suggestion of bears. She swallowed awkwardly, as if her throat were being squeezed. Yup, she was pretty sure there would be bears around here—but what kind of bears? Well, they weren't going to be cuddly little koalas, that was for sure.

She should try her phone again: perhaps she would have some coverage here? But as Nell patted down the pockets of her coat, an image flashed into her mind. Her phone lying on Sue Ellen's back seat, where she had thrown it in frustration.

Nell wasn't one for unnecessary panic, but in light of this new information—no phone, a possible grizzly sighting—she decided it would be wise to get help sooner rather than later. She broke into a run and hadn't gone more than twenty yards when she realized she was right opposite the driveway to the old Philpott house. Nell slowed to a halt again and tipped her face up to the sky. *Oh come on, Meg, is this your idea of a joke?*

She hesitated by the mailbox, her resolve wavering. Compared with a bear, Jackson was most definitely the lesser evil. Besides, he already thought that she was crazy, what did it matter if she cemented that opinion? Raking her fingers through her hair and looping her shoulders, Nell set off down the driveway. At least this time she wasn't covered in mud.

Chapter Thirteen

Nell hadn't gotten very far when she spotted Jackson and a little boy crouched together on the driveway, staring at what looked like a muddy puddle. Nell hesitated, expecting the dog, Simba, to appear in a flurry of barks and alert them to her presence, but he was nowhere to be seen. A thought popped into her head: *that's probably because he's currently sniffing around the ravine pretending to be a bear.* Nell groaned. Of course, it had just been the dog she'd seen! Well, it was too late to turn back now. Odds are Jackson would spot her before she made it back to the road, and then what would she say? "So sorry, I was just going for a walk and took a wrong turn?"

Jackson and the boy—his son, Joe, Nell presumed—were still scrutinizing the ground, a bucket and assortment of tools sitting beside them. Joe was pointing, asking questions, while his dad listened. At one point, Joe said something that made Jackson's face light up and he leaned over and ruffled the little boy's blond hair, which was glowing in the sunlight like a fluffy golden halo. Nell was acutely aware that she was about to blunder into the middle of a special father-and-son moment. It seemed as if she had a knack for picking the worst possible times to intrude on Jackson's life. Well, she supposed she might as well get the blundering over with.

"Hello there!" she called out, with forced heartiness.

Both of the Quaid boys, one dark and one blond, looked up with identical frowns. After a moment, Jackson got to his feet, a polite smile on his face although his eyes were saying: *what the actual heck?* He was wearing a baseball cap and his square jaw was lined with a few days' of golden-brown stubble; a ripple in Nell's belly confirmed this was a very good look on him.

"Hello again," he said. "Back to have another shot at the tire swing?"

"Ha! No, I'm so sorry to bother you again, you're not going to believe this, but I was on my way to see the covered bridge and my car got stuck."

Joe tugged at Jackson's arm. "Dad, who's that lady?" he asked in a loud whisper.

"I *think* her name is Nell," said Jackson, eyes narrowed. "Did I get that right?"

"Yes! That's me. I wasn't sure if you'd recognize me without all the mud."

"Yeah, you do seem a bit—cleaner."

She'd forgotten how intense his gaze could be. She was so uncomfortable at having intruded again that she could barely look at him, yet his eyes were fixed on her with an unsettling steadiness.

"I don't think we were ever properly introduced," he said. "I'm Jackson Quaid, and this is my son, Joe."

"Hi, Joe." Nell crouched down to get on a six-year-old level. "It's a pleasure to meet you."

"Are you a friend of my dad's?" Joe looked suspicious.

"Um, well, no, not friend exactly, more like his"—Nell fumbled for the right word—"stalker."

She cringed. It was meant to be funny, obviously, but for all she knew Jackson might not have a sense of humor. She stole a panicked glance at him, but to her relief the corners of his mouth were twitching upward.

Encouraged by this, Nell straightened up so they were back on the same level. "Look, I really am sorry to barge in on you again, but I wondered if I could use your landline to call someone to help?"

"No need. I can pull you out."

"Are you sure?"

"No problem, it happens a lot round here. I'll go get my keys."

Already bored of the adult conversation, Joe had crouched back down and was prodding at one of the puddles with a stick. He was wearing heavy-duty work gloves that were far too big for him; probably Jackson's. Nell studied him for a moment.

"What are you up to down there?"

"I'm grading the driveway. It's a very important job." He looked up at her. "You can help if you like."

"Sure. What shall I do?"

"See that bucket? I'll show you where, then you need to pour out some gravel. Okay? But only put it where I say so. Because I am the boss."

"Sure thing." She pushed up the sleeves of her jacket. "It's my first time grading a driveway, you know."

Joe frowned at Nell, clearly wondering whether he should trust an amateur, but after a moment pointed at a hole. "Here, please. But you have to do it slowly."

"Okay, boss." Nell picked up the bucket and began shaking out the gravel. "Wow, there's a lot of water in these potholes."

Joe wrinkled his nose at her. "You say 'water' funny."

"That's because I'm English."

Joe processed this information for a moment. "Say it again."

"Wah-tah."

Joe laughed like this was the funniest thing he'd ever heard.

"I say other words differently too," said Nell, tickled by his amusement.

"Like what?"

"Tomato."

Joe giggled. "To-mah-to! That's weird."

"I know," said Nell, smiling. "But I'll let you into a secret: weird is what makes things interesting..."

It took her a moment to realize that Jackson had returned and was standing watching them. As she looked up, Nell caught the warmth in his expression and something stirred deep inside her.

Nell, no, she warned herself. *Not a good idea.*

Jackson had a rope looped over his shoulder. "You guys ready? Joe, I promise we'll finish the driveway when we get back, okay, buddy?"

The little boy gave an exaggerated huff of frustration, but he pulled off the gloves and reached for his dad's outstretched hand. Together, the three of them walked toward the truck parked a little further down the driveway.

"Nice boots," said Jackson, glancing at Nell's feet.

"Oh, thank you. They're not really that nice, are they? But they do the job."

"Well, that's really all you need boots to do."

Having Joe with them in the back of the truck made Nell more relaxed than if she'd been alone with Jackson, and once they were on the move she decided to raise a question that was still bothering her. She was 99.9 percent sure it had been Simba she'd seen down in the ravine, but it would be good to know whether she should pack mace spray next time she ventured into the woods.

"Bears?" said Jackson. "Unlikely at this time of the year. They'll still be hibernating."

"And what kind of bears do you get around here?"

"Black bears." He glanced at her, half smiling. "Not the English-woman-eating type."

Joe piped up in the back, "You must always make sure you put your trash in the garbage can because otherwise the bears will make a mess and chase Simba."

"Very wise," said Nell. "You know, I think Simba looks quite like a bear himself." She felt she'd already embarrassed herself enough without revealing her earlier mix-up. "What kind of dog is he?"

"A Leonberger," said Jackson.

"He's beautiful."

"You've met Simba?" asked Joe. "My mommy doesn't like him. She says his *damn hair gets everywhere.*"

"Joe," Jackson reprimanded him. Nell glanced at him; his eyes were fixed on the road, but she could see the tension in his jaw, and she thought again about Mallory's assertion that Jackson still had feelings for his ex-wife.

Keen to lighten the atmosphere, Nell dug around for the puppy photo she carried in her wallet. "I have a dog too, you know," she told Joe, handing him the picture. "His name is Moomin." In the photo, he looked like a puffy little cloud with black dots for his eyes and a nose.

Joe pulled a face. "That's a dumb-looking dog."

Nell let out an amused grunt—her "laugh-oink," as her ex, Adrian, had called it. Once upon a time she had assumed this was meant to be cute, but looking back now the term sounded rather less flattering. Not for the first time, she wondered if Adrian had liked her much at all.

"Well, I suppose Moomin is quite dumb because he thinks he's a cat, but he's very sweet."

Up ahead, Sue Ellen loomed into view; Nell flinched at the sight of the car's back end, which was entirely covered with mud.

"That's me, just over there," she told Jackson.

He stared at Sue Ellen for a moment. "Is that Darlene Fiske's car?"

"Yes, and I am *definitely* going to have to get her cleaned up before taking her home."

"There's a car wash in town," said Jackson, turning to help Joe out of his seatbelt. "I can point you in the right direction."

Nell looked at the road ahead: a little way past Sue Ellen it curved and disappeared into the trees, and she wondered how close they were to the covered bridge. She hadn't even thought about it since getting stuck, but she felt like she'd be letting Megan down to have come this far and not even have taken a quick look.

"Is the bridge near here?" she asked Jackson.

"About a five-minute walk. Do you want to check it out?"

"Yeah, let's go to the bridge!" Joe was bouncing in the gap between the front seats, his hands resting on the headrests. "We need to attack the enemy's hideout!"

"Well, in that case," she said with a smile, "we should definitely go."

They got out of the truck and Joe ran ahead, grabbing a stick from the roadside and using it as a gun, dodging between the trees and taking aim at an invisible foe, while Nell and Jackson strolled behind.

"It's so beautiful out here," sighed Nell, tipping back her head and taking a deep breath. "It's a novelty for me to be somewhere that has so many more trees than people. In London it's most definitely the other way around."

"It suits me, for sure," said Jackson. "For a start, I find trees a heck of a lot easier to talk to."

Nell laughed. "Oh, you're not doing all that badly."

"That's because I'm pretending you're an oak," said Jackson, with one of his lopsided grins.

Nell narrowed her eyes. "You know, I think I'd prefer to be something a little less, well, *sturdy*."

Jackson thought for a moment. "How about an American mountain ash? It's a small ornamental tree that can live in the city, but prefers the mountains, and has bright red berries that are irresistible to birds and animals. That better?"

Nell grinned—"I'll take that"—but inside, her mind had instantly zeroed in on the word "irresistible." Had Jackson used that deliberately? Or was she reading too much into what was probably just a description of a tree?

She glanced at him, as if she could find answers in his face, and discovered that he was already looking at her. Flustered, she flashed him a quick smile then immediately looked away. Up in the trees, the bird with the Phoebe song started calling again, filling the gap that had opened up in their conversation, but as they trudged on Nell could occasionally sense Jackson's eyes on her.

"So if you're driving Sue Ellen," he said, after they'd gone on a little way, "that must mean you're friends with Darlene. And here was I thinking you were just a tourist."

"I guess I'm just a tourist who's become a friend of Darlene's. She's been really kind to me since I arrived."

Jackson nodded. "She's a remarkable woman. There are loads of crazy rumors about her in town—my favorite is that she once had an affair with JFK."

"Ha! Do you know, I can actually believe that."

"How did the two of you meet?"

Nell paused; this was obviously the point where she should tell him about Megan. It was a natural progression in their conversation, and would help him understand why she'd been so weirdly obsessive about having a go on his swing. But just as she was readying herself to say the words, Joe suddenly burst out of the undergrowth nearby.

"Troops, prepare yourselves for battle!" he yelled, waving his stick over his head. "We've reached the enemy headquarters!"

Megan was right: when Nell set eyes on the covered bridge it felt as if she had been whisked back in time a hundred years. The wooden sides were bleached and splintered with age and it was all too easy to imagine a horse and buggy flying out of the darkness toward her, the driver cracking his whip as the wheels rattled over the boards. Under the bridge, the Wild Moose River meandered peacefully along the rocky bed, its banks narrowed by jagged margins of ice. Nell presumed the river had been named after a different stretch of water because this tranquil trickle was anything but "wild."

Joe had gotten there ahead of them and Nell could hear his feet thundering across the bridge and his excited whoops echoing under the gabled roof.

"Pretty cool, huh?" Jackson gazed up at the entrance. "We don't have many covered bridges back in California, so this is still a novelty for me. Come on, let's go inside."

It was, Nell decided, like walking into a medieval English church. The covered bridge had the same dimly lit interior, the same small, high windows that splashed pools of light across the floor, the same air of dust and age that makes you automatically talk in a hushed voice. Joe had already disappeared out the other side, so Nell was alone with

Jackson again, the only sounds the river chattering over the pebbles beneath and their footfalls on the wooden boards. Midway along, Jackson turned to her, the angles of his face sharpened by shadows. They were standing so close that Nell caught his scent, like freshly washed cotton bedsheets after they've been slept in for one night, and her heart beat a little faster.

"So, what do you think?" he asked, as softly as if they were in Sunday service.

"It's so peaceful," she said, looking around at the bridge to avoid making eye contact; being in such close proximity to Jackson was whipping up all sorts of emotions inside her. "Do you know why they built these bridges with a roof?"

"To protect the wooden boards from the elements so they'd last longer. But you can see why so many myths and folk stories grew up around covered bridges—they've got a kind of... magic to them, I always think."

"What kind of stories?"

"Well, they're often known as wishing bridges, because apparently if you hold your breath for the entire length of the bridge, you'll have your wish granted." He tilted his head, smiling. "Shall we give it a try?"

Turning now to face Jackson, Nell noticed a tiny crescent-shaped scar on his cheekbone; they were so close she could have reached out her hand and traced the pale jagged line it formed on his olive skin.

"I'll have to think of something to wish for," she said, her heart thumping so loudly she worried he might be able to hear it.

Jackson's eyes were fixed on hers, his full lips slightly parted, and Nell felt herself shiver under the steadiness of his gaze. She had a sudden vision of Megan's image of the lovers meeting here in secret for a kiss; for a moment, she wondered what it would be like to—

Blushing, she quickly looked down at the floor. She always did have an overactive imagination.

Jackson took a breath. "I—"

"I guess we should really be getting back," she blurted, and then turned toward the light at the end of the tunnel without even waiting to see if Jackson followed her.

In the end, rescuing Sue Ellen wasn't the big deal Nell had feared: one pull from Jackson's truck and she slid out like a wallowing hippo emerging from a mud bath. The only awkward moment came when Nell had to turn the car around to face back in the direction of Birdsong Hill. She was a confident driver, but with Jackson watching from the truck, her three-point turn was more like a thirty-two-point turn.

She pulled up alongside his truck, grimacing at her driving prowess.

"All set?" he asked, his hands ready on the wheel.

"Yup. Thank you so much for your help with the car, I really appreciate it. And the tour of the bridge too."

"You're welcome. Anytime."

That "anytime" gave Nell pause, and she hesitated, wondering if Jackson might suggest she stop by his house to see the backyard. That moment on the bridge when their eyes had met something had passed between them, she was sure of it, a mutual spark of—well, what exactly? Interest? But now Jackson just seemed desperate to get away from her, and she was confused by what had changed.

"Well, I'd better go and find that car wash," she said, after it became patently obvious he had no intention of inviting her over.

Joe stuck his head out of the back window. "Will you come and see us again?"

"Nell's going back to London next week," replied Jackson, before she could answer.

Taken aback by the sharpness of his tone, she smiled to cover her unease. "I am. And your dad's already had to rescue me twice, three times would be really weird."

"But you told me weird was what makes stuff interesting," pouted Joe.

"I did, yes, but—"

Jackson put the truck into gear and turned to Joe. "Okay, buddy, that driveway isn't going to grade itself." He shot a throwaway smile at Nell—"enjoy the rest of your trip"—and then sped off.

Watching him go, Nell felt her chest tighten in irritation. Clearly, it was too much to ask that he'd allow her a quick peek round the back of the house. What was he doing back there: growing marijuana? Her eyes still drilling into the place where the truck had disappeared from view, she realized she was clenching her jaw and rubbed it to ease the tension. Why on earth was this thing about the backyard bothering her so much? Jackson had already put himself out several times to help her, he owed her nothing. It must be because she was upset at the thought of letting Megan down. Nell put Sue Ellen into gear and eased off the clutch. Yes, that was it, it was simply the responsibility of the itinerary weighing on her. Nothing to do with Jackson Quaid at all.

Chapter Fourteen

Today, my darling, you are going to have lunch at the Black Bear, which in my day was the best bar in town. (It was also the only bar in town, but even if that hadn't been the case, it would still have been my favorite.) You'll find it up near the mountain: it's where all the skiers and boarders hang out after a day on the slopes, although it's quieter at lunchtime. To enjoy the full Megan Shaw Nostalgia Experience™ you must follow these precise steps:

Sit at the bar. (Only tourists use the tables at lunchtime.)

Order a bottle of Coors Light.

Order a Black Bear Burger and fries.

Put the song "Jump Around" by House of Pain on the jukebox. Dancing optional but encouraged.

Eat, drink, enjoy.

If it hadn't been for the roadside sign—an immense slab of wood, over ten feet tall, engraved with a design of a bear looking up at the moon—Nell would have missed the Black Bear as she wound up the mountain road toward Maverick. The wooden cabin was tucked a little way back from the road, set among the trees and behind a broad parking lot that was currently operating at just a fraction of its capacity, but then it was still early, just after midday.

Nell rolled into a space near the road, turned off the engine and stayed sitting in the car, Sue Ellen settling into stillness with her usual of groan of relief, while she gave the Black Bear a once-over. First impressions were not good. It had the look of a place that a stranger would walk into and every head would turn—and not in a friendly way. The sign over the door was missing a "B" (it now read: WELCOME TO THE BLACK EAR) and there was a chalkboard on the porch heralding Taco Tuesday, even though today was Saturday. Nell reckoned the place must have gone downhill since Megan's time and she found herself hoping they were no longer serving burgers so she could have a quick beer, cross it off the itinerary and then go back to the Covered Bridge for lunch instead.

As Nell was trying to gather together the motivation to get out of the car, she saw the door to the bar swing open and a woman emerge from inside. She was dressed in a tight-fitting black ski suit and padded snow boots, looking ready for a day's skiing in Aspen with Paris Hilton. Her visor-like sunglasses covered much of her face, but Nell instantly recognized her glossy haystack of hair. It was Liza DiSouza, and she was smiling to herself as if she had just said goodbye to a very close friend.

Surprised, Nell's first instinct was to get out and say hello, but she hesitated, feeling a little awkward after their last encounter, and by the time she'd decided that yes, she should definitely take the friendly option (because if Darlene trusted her, then surely she should too) Liza had already climbed into her black Escalade, which was as miraculously shiny and mud-free as its owner, and swung out of the parking lot toward the mountain. Nell watched her go, wondering what she was doing here. At least this bit of intrigue gave her the push she needed to get out of the car.

Perhaps it was because her expectations had been at rock bottom, but when Nell stepped inside the bar she felt a moment's giddiness, as if she'd just been whisked off to a parallel universe. Instead of the gloom and shabbiness she'd been expecting, the Black Bear was an excellent lesson in never judging a book by its cover. With lots of pale-colored wood, cozy booths and wall mirrors, the place had an air of polished wholesomeness that was a million miles from what its dive-bar exterior had promised, although judging by the live-music posters and the stage at the far end of the room, there was probably a grittier vibe at night.

There were a few free stools at the bar and Nell chose the one closest to the TV, which was currently showing an ice hockey game, so she had something to occupy her while having lunch. She was used to dining alone now, but it still made her feel a little self-conscious, not that the tables of friends and families dotted around the room were paying her any attention. Megan would be pleased to see this place, thought Nell, glad that her friend's favorite hangout hadn't lost its mojo.

She caught the barman's eye and he came straight over.

"What can I get you?" Despite his heavy metal T-shirt and the tattoos covering his arms, he looked like the sort of kid who called his mom at least once a week.

"Hi, do you have Coors Light?"

"Afraid not." He stepped aside to show her the run of fridges, which were packed with dozens of bottles with brightly colored labels, while above them reclaimed wooden planks had been turned into shelving and draped with lights, the packed ranks of liquor bottles reflecting their glow.

As Nell's eyes widened at the choice, the barman grinned and pulled out a bottle. "This is a local pale ale. Citrusy, not too strong. Really good."

"Perfect, thank you. And can I please order a Black Bear Burger?"

"Sure. Fries?" He popped the lid of her beer and handed it over.

"Yes, please."

"You got it." He shot her a smile. "Enjoy."

Nell took a swig of the beer and scanned the room, wondering if she could work out who Liza DiSouza might have been meeting, but she didn't see any obvious candidates, though short of Kim Kardashian or a posse of mafia dons she couldn't imagine what the uber-groomed New Yorker's associates would look like. Spotting a pool table in the corner, Nell felt a rush of nostalgia for the countless nights she and Megan had spent playing pool in their college bar. It was the only sport that Nell had ever been any good at, although she hadn't played for years. What she wouldn't give right now to spend the afternoon here with Megan, drinking bottles of this really excellent beer and shooting pool.

With this thought, Nell remembered Megan's instructions. "Excuse me," she called to the barman. "Is there a jukebox in here?"

"No, sorry," he said, frowning as if this was an odd thing to ask, which it probably was.

"It's just a friend of mine used to come here, and she mentioned there was one."

"How long ago was that?"

"Maybe fifteen years?" Nell realized the barman would have probably been in kindergarten back then and felt ancient.

"Hold on," he said, looking toward the far end of the bar. "Brody? Did there used to be a jukebox in here?"

A man's voice answered. "Yeah, Tanner got rid of it about ten years back. Why?"

Nell tried to see who was speaking, but her view was blocked by the other people sitting at the bar.

"This lady here says a friend of hers remembered it."

As Nell watched, at the far end of the bar a man's head emerged from behind the row of other customers, leaning back to look in her direction. Her first impression was of lots of messy sandy-blond hair, tanned skin and white teeth, and Nell couldn't help returning the man's smile.

"Hey there," he said, getting up and sauntering toward her with the confidence of someone who owned the place, or at least spent a lot of time there. He was dressed for skiing and, judging by his build, was very good at it. He stopped next to her stool. "If you don't mind me asking, who's this friend of yours?"

"Megan Shaw," said Nell. She was doubtful he'd have known her, as she reckoned he was younger than she was, but at the mention of her name the man's eyes grew wide.

"Well, I never. Now that's a name I haven't heard for a long time." He held out his hand. "Brody Knott. Your friend Megan and I used to"—a smirk hovered about his lips—"hang together."

Brody Knott. Why was that name familiar? Nell had definitely heard it before.

"Nell Swift," she said, shaking his hand.

"It's a real pleasure to meet you, Nell." Brody held onto her hand, and her gaze, a little longer than she would have expected with a stranger. "D'you mind?" He nodded at the empty stool next to her.

"Go ahead," said Nell. Now that they were up close, she noticed the fine white lines in the tan around his eyes and realized they were about the same age after all, although he had the sort of surfer-dude good looks that would probably keep him unfairly youthful for many years.

Just then an older guy came up and greeted Brody with a complicated handshake that was clearly familiar to them both. Nell noticed both men were wearing the same red-and-white ski jacket. While they chatted, she racked her brain to work out how she knew Brody's name. Had Mallory mentioned it, perhaps?

"You on duty this afternoon?" the newcomer asked Brody.

"Yeah, I'll see you up there in a bit."

When he'd left, Brody turned to Nell, gesturing to her almost-empty bottle. "Do you want another beer?"

"I'm driving, so I better not, but a Coke would be great, thank you."

Brody paused, scrutinizing her with unnerving frankness. "Where are you from?"

"London."

"Man, gotta love an English accent," he said, chuckling to himself, then signaled for the barman. "Jay? Another beer for me, and a Coke for Miss Nell here."

Brody leaned his forearms on the bar and turned to look at her again, flashing another of his laid-back grins that would have looked flirtatious on most people, but seemed to be just his regular expression.

"So tell me, how's Megan?"

Nell took a breath. It wasn't getting any easier. "I'm so sorry to have to tell you, but Megan died recently."

Instantly, the life drained from Brody's face. "Oh my God. What happened?"

"Cancer."

"Oh jeez, that's...I heard she'd moved to England, but..." He looked shell-shocked, deeply emotional. "Man, I'm so sorry. You two were good friends?"

"Yes. I'm here because she wanted me to scatter her ashes on Mount Maverick."

At the mention of this, Brody flinched. Nell understood why: she too was struggling to accept the notion that Megan, such a brilliant, shining rainbow of a human being, had been reduced to nothing but dust.

Brody sighed, dragging a hand over his face, then turned to Nell with a new intensity in his eyes.

"Nell, I'd really like to help you, for Megan's sake. I'm part of the mountain rescue team here and I know Maverick like my own backyard. I'd be really happy to take you up the mountain, show you the best views, maybe help you find an appropriate place to..."

He trailed off, unable to say the words, but Nell knew exactly what he meant.

"Thank you so much, that would be fantastic. I can't ski and—well, I wouldn't really know where to start."

As he smiled at her acceptance of his offer, a group of girls in ski gear wandered past. One of them, a willowy blonde who was looking at Brody like he was lunch, called out: "Heyyy, Brody," and he raised his bottle in reply with a wolfish grin.

"So how about the day after tomorrow?" he asked, his attention fully back on Nell. "Monday's my day off."

"I'm meant to be going on a tour of the Thundersnow ice cream factory that day," said Nell, and explained to him about Megan's itinerary. She'd been looking forward to visiting the local organic ice cream factory, especially the tasting room that Megan had told her was the final stop of the tour.

But Brody was shaking his head. "Sorry, you can't visit the factory anymore. Thundersnow's been bought by some big multinational and they put a stop to the behind-the-scenes visitor tours. Probably because they're spiking the ice cream with chemicals." He grimaced and rolled his eyes; this was clearly a sore point. "So how about I take you on a tour of the mountain instead?"

Nell didn't even need to think about it. "That would be great," she said, smiling. She'd only known Brody a few minutes, but, as with Darlene and Mallory, the fact that he knew Megan made her feel an instant connection to him.

"Great. Where are you staying?"

"At the Covered Bridge."

He gave a single, decisive dip of his chin. "I'll pick you up from there at 9 a.m. on Monday. See you then, Nell from London."

Brody put some money on the bar, saluted to the barman and walked toward the door still carrying his beer. Nell watched him go: as he sauntered through the room he was greeted by a couple of the other customers, but just before he reached the door he glanced back at Nell again. She returned his grin, glad that she'd bumped into him. At times like these it really felt like Megan was up there looking out for her.

Chapter Fifteen

When Nell arrived back at the Covered Bridge after lunch at the Black Bear, she came across Piper in the lobby, dressed up in outdoor clothes, fixing a leash to Boomer's collar. Nell eyed Piper's puffer jacket and woolly beanie enviously; next to her, she felt like someone's dowdy great-aunt in her Gore-Tex windbreaker (borrowed from her mother, who had bought it to go on a hiking vacation in Scotland years ago), ancient pom-pom hat and Darlene's monstrous yellow boots, but then Nell supposed that if you lived in a state that was snowy for almost half the year you'd probably have better wardrobe options.

Piper seemed pleased to see her and they chatted for a while, with Nell making her laugh with her account of Sue Ellen getting stuck, which, now that it was twenty-four hours behind her, she was starting see the funny side of. Piper then told Nell about her first mud season in Tansy Falls, when she too found herself headlights-deep in a bog up in the hills.

"Luckily I had coverage on my phone, so I called Spencer and he arranged for a tow truck to pull me out, but while I was waiting for them to arrive this freak blizzard suddenly blew in, making driving impossible, so I had no option but to sit in the car and wait it out."

Nell made a face. "You must have been freezing!"

"Right? But it's a risk up here in the winter, getting stuck in a snowed-in car, which is why we tend to carry emergency blankets in the trunk. For some crazy reason, though, I decided that instead of wrapping myself in the blankets, it would be wiser to run the car heating on full blast. It got so hot I had to take my coat off. I even remember feeling quite smug about it! Anyway, the tow truck eventually managed to reach me and pulled me out, only for the car to break down a split second later because the heating had drained the tank of gas." Piper shook her head, grinning at the memory. "Not my finest hour."

Nell laughed. "I would have done the same thing."

"I think everyone around here has a mud season horror story," said Piper, bending down to pet Boomer, who was straining at the leash, clearly anxious to get moving. "We were just heading out for a walk, do you want to join us?"

Beyond eating a large slice of cake (today's special was grasshopper pie) and writing postcards to her parents and Megan's daughters, Nell had zero plans, and she eagerly accepted. She enjoyed Piper's company, and, of course, Boomer was a bonus. She was already missing Moomin and their daily outings.

They headed out of the hotel, crossed over the road and then took a narrow path between the drugstore and bank that Nell had assumed just led to a parking lot, but after a short stroll down a series of wide steps they wound up on a path that led alongside the river. Thrilled by all the smells, Boomer zigzagged along with his nose fixed to the gravel. On both banks the trees leaned inward as if trying to reach across the water and touch each other's branches. Nell could well imagine the lush leafy green tunnel that must appear here in the spring, but today the bare branches formed patterns like lace against the gray sky.

"Isn't it beautiful?" said Piper, as if reading Nell's thoughts. "Sometimes I can't quite believe I've ended up somewhere as magical as this."

"It must have been quite an adjustment, though, moving from New York to a little town like Tansy Falls."

Piper squinted, thinking this over. "You know what, it really wasn't. It was like coming home."

Nell glanced at her, and Piper held up her hands. "I know, it's a cliché, but that's exactly how it felt. Nowadays I can't imagine living anywhere else."

"You don't miss New York at all?"

"Oh sure, there are some things of course. Fiske's is great and all, but I do miss the shops. Plus, of course, New York's restaurant scene. For a cook, the range of cuisines and ingredients was a total inspiration, but I can go back and stay with friends whenever I need a city fix." Boomer suddenly caught the scent of something down the riverbank and dashed after it, bouncing like a rabbit where the snow still lay in knee-deep drifts. "It's funny," Piper mused, as they paused to watch him, "but you don't know what it is you've been missing until you actually have it." She furrowed her brow. "Does that make sense? I thought I was perfectly happy living in the city, but Tansy Falls has given me so much more than I could ever have imagined."

"Like what?"

"Well, to be honest, I get a buzz simply from the all the space we have here."

"I get that," said Nell, recalling the rush of happiness she'd felt when she'd first driven Sue Ellen through the countryside. "It's kind of like when you're a kid and you see a big stretch of grass and you can't help running or doing cartwheels over it. It's that same feeling—like you've been set free."

"That's a nice way of putting it," said Piper. "I think all the people and buildings in the city were kind of—crushing my soul, if that doesn't sound overly dramatic. I'm just happier here with all this room to breathe." Boomer reappeared, his tail wagging furiously, and they set off again toward a footbridge that spanned the river. "How about you, Nell? Do you think you could ever move out of London?"

It was a question that hadn't even occurred to Nell to ask herself before coming to Tansy Falls, but for the second time since her arrival here she found herself considering it, and the answer came surprisingly easily.

"Yes," she replied. "Yes, I think I could." She glanced at Piper. "I don't suppose you need a sous chef at the inn? I can just about boil an egg."

Piper laughed. "Honey, the job is yours."

A gust of icy wind blew up as they crossed the bridge, making Nell turn up her collar against the sudden chill. On the other bank, the path traced around the edge of a broad meadow, its snowy borders pitted with animal and human prints.

"This is known as the Tansy Loop," explained Piper. "In the winter it's really popular with snowshoers and skiers. Have you tried cross-country skiing before? It's so wonderful, gliding along in the cold air and sunshine. You should come back next year and give it a try."

"I'd love to," said Nell. "Cross-country sounds far more my style than downhill skiing."

"You're not a fan?"

"To be honest I've never actually tried it, but the idea of balancing on a pair of thin planks and chucking yourself down an icy mountain while dodging loads of other people doing the same thing doesn't exactly appeal." She gave a theatrical shudder.

Piper grinned. "It's better than it sounds, I promise."

"Well, I'm very happy to take your word for it."

Nell glanced at the horizon where Mount Maverick kept watch over Tansy Falls; today the summit was concealed in cloud, but she could still visualize its jagged peak. For some reason the image unsettled her—and with that thought the new resort popped into her mind.

"Piper, have you had much to do with DiSouza Developments, the company behind Maverick Lodge?"

"A little. The boss came to talk to me and Spencer. What was her name, um…"

"Liza DiSouza."

"That's it. She was very friendly and kept saying she wanted us all to work together, although in what capacity she didn't really say." She shrugged. "I think the visit was more of a public relations exercise really, just to make sure we were on board."

"And are you? On board, I mean."

It took a moment for Piper to answer. "It's complicated. On the one hand, the lodge will bring lots more visitors to the mountain, which will obviously be great for our tourism industry, but at the same time I do worry about the impact it will have on Tansy Falls. I couldn't bear the thought of our home losing its small-town charm and turning into just another soulless, corporate playground for millionaires." Piper looked up at the mountain. "I really hope the Lodge will be good for Tansy Falls, but I know a lot of folks round here are yet to be convinced."

"Do you worry it will take business away from the Covered Bridge?"

"I'm sure there'll be an impact, although I think we'll be catering to different markets. Hopefully there'll be room for both of us."

While they had been talking, Boomer had disappeared into the undergrowth again, but now he bounded back with a slobbery, soppy smile that made Nell desperately miss Moomin.

"Good boy," said Piper, bending down to brush the snow from his coat.

Nell decided to broach a subject that was still nagging at her.

"Piper, you know that Liza DiSouza is buying the store from Darlene..."

"Uh-huh." She straightened up. "She's made offers to some of the other store owners in town too. A friend of mine, Jessica, owns the beauty salon on the mountain road, and one day Liza DiSouza dropped in for a mani-pedi. While she was there she asked if Jess had ever considered selling up and mentioned such crazy amounts of money that Jess felt it would be stupid to refuse, so she agreed to meet with her again."

"What happened?"

"Well, let's just say that Liza DiSouza's initial promises in no way met up to the eventual reality. Jessica pulled out, although not before Ms. DiSouza had turned quite nasty."

A cold finger of fear traced down Nell's spine. "She's promised Darlene that she'll keep Fiske's as a general store. It's really important to Darlene."

"I know. And it's important to Tansy Falls too, Fiske's is a local landmark." Piper bit her lip. "Maybe Liza DiSouza will keep her word. I can't imagine it would be easy to pull the wool over Darlene Fiske's eyes. She's stubborn as a mule, that one."

"But you don't trust Liza."

Piper didn't reply outright. "She's running a business," she said eventually. "Darlene's store is one of the few original historic buildings in town, and it sits on a good-sized plot of land right in the middle of Main Street. From a moneymaking perspective, I can see exactly why Liza DiSouza wants it, but her primary motivation is never going to be preserving the unique character of Tansy Falls." Piper plunged her hands in her pockets. "So, we'll have to take care of that ourselves."

Nell walked on beside her, taking this all in. Piper had just confirmed her worst fears; now she had to decide whether she was going to do anything about it.

Later, when they got back to the hotel, there was a note waiting for Nell in the cubbyhole along with her room key.

Lunch tomorrow at the farm? I can promise you plentiful local gossip, Deb's famous Dutch beef stew and way too many Hoffmans to number. It will be chaos, but it would be really good to see you. 12 p.m.?

Mallory

Chapter Sixteen

You've made it to the halfway point—congratulations! As Sunday is the day of rest, that's exactly what you'll be doing today. My only instruction is to take it eeeeeasy, y'all. I'm dying (oops, lousy choice of words there) to know how you're getting on in Tansy Falls. Perhaps you've already made some friends? Please don't worry if you haven't, though. I know you, Nell Swift, and I can just imagine you telling yourself that you're antisocial or "bad with people" or some other garbage when you are truly one of the sweetest, most lovable people it has been my pleasure to know. After all, why do you think I chose you for a best friend? So have faith in yourself, Nellie. Other people see the same person I do—how about you give it a try too?

Nell was giving today's note from Megan some serious thought on the drive over to the Hoffman farm. Throughout their friendship Meg had always been so supportive, Nell's biggest cheerleader, but for some reason this particular message had struck a chord with her. Perhaps it was because over the last few days she had actually met some people in Tansy Falls whom she now considered friends, and it had happened so naturally that it made Nell wonder if she wasn't quite as lackluster a person as she had started to believe over the past few years. It helped she was actually feeling pretty good about how she looked today: her grooming regimen, not the most high maintenance at the best of times, had gone fully back to basics since she'd arrived in Tansy Falls, but today she was wearing the one dress she had brought with her and had even put on some makeup. Making a final assessment in her bedroom mirror, Nell had been amazed by how a bit of mascara and some blush could make such a difference. She looked—well, "pretty" wouldn't have been entirely out of the question, she thought, smiling at her reflection, and she was surprised how much more confident that thought made her feel.

Nevertheless, after her last encounter with Deb Hoffman, Nell was anxious at the prospect of seeing her again. She'd stopped by the store yesterday and Darlene had given her a hard stare when Nell told her she'd been invited to Sunday lunch at the Hoffmans', muttering, "Rather you than me, sweetie." At least Darlene was happy for Nell to borrow Sue Ellen again to drive there.

"I'm just pleased she's being used," she had said, when Nell apologized for monopolizing the car. "The old girl is seeing more action than either of us have in years!"

Nell presumed that Deb would be expecting to see Sue Ellen this time, so hopefully there wouldn't be a repeat of last week's standoff; nevertheless, as she rolled down the driveway toward the farm she was relieved to see that there were already a couple of other vehicles, including quite a sizable truck, in the parking circle outside the farmhouse. She couldn't exactly hide Sue Ellen—she was the size of a pregnant whale, after all—but she could at least park behind the other vehicles so that she wasn't front and center, waiting for Deb to use for target practice.

As Nell walked up to the farmhouse door, nervously smoothing down her dress, she heard the clattering of pans and singing coming from inside: a woman's voice, deep and powerful, belting out show tunes like she was trying to reach the cheap seats. Taking a deep breath, Nell knocked; a voice sang out: "*Nobody is gonna rain on my paraaaaade*... Come in, it's open!"

The kitchen was long and low-ceilinged and dominated by a vast wooden table that stretched the length of the room like something out of a medieval banquet hall. If you were sitting at one end you would have had to shout to make yourself heard by the person at the other. Although the flagstone floor was rubbed to a shine and the table beautifully presented, set with blue-and-white patterned china and sparkling glasses, the rest of the room looked like a tornado had just blown through it, which was hardly surprising when you considered the number of people clearly expected for lunch. Not that their hostess appeared in the least bit flustered: Deb Hoffman was standing at the stove, pans bubbling away on every burner, stirring a pot with the serene air of someone who knocked out a three-course lunch for twenty people every week. She was wearing a floral apron over a floral dress and her hands were encased in floral oven mitts; it was a curiously girlish look for Deb, whose cropped gray hair and thickset frame put Nell in mind of a five-star army general.

"Well, hello there!" she boomed. "Nell, isn't it? I'm Deb Hoffman, Mallory's mother-in-law. She's told us all about you."

No mention of the gun incident, then. Perhaps, thought Nell hopefully, they could just pretend it had never happened.

"It's a pleasure to meet you, Deb. Thank you so much for having me over for lunch."

She held out the bottle of wine she'd bought for the occasion from Fiske's (Darlene had grudgingly admitted that red would be more gratefully received chez Hoffman).

Deb wiped her face, which was beet purple and sheeny from the heat, and took the bottle in an oven-mitted hand. "Mmmm, very nice," she said, peering at the label. "You're a sweet girl. Thank you, Nell. Just put it over there, will you?"

She gave a vague wave in the direction of an antique dresser, the wooden shelves of which were groaning with decorative plates, ornaments, candlesticks and framed photos. Whatever their differences, Deb and Darlene evidently ascribed to the same school of maximalist interior design. Nell was tentatively attempting to shuffle things around to make a space for the bottle when a man loomed in the doorway next to her. He was a huge bear of a man, with a bushy white beard that gave him a decidedly Santa-ish air.

"Ah, so you must be the lady my wife pulled a shotgun on the other day." He made a big show of looking over Nell. "She don't look so scary to me, Deb."

As he roared with laughter—both Hoffmans seemed to communicate at twice the normal volume—Deb flapped at him with a tea towel. "I thought she was a *Fiske*," she muttered darkly, as if that was explanation enough.

Still chuckling, the man offered Nell his hand, clasping hers in both of his.

"It's Nell, isn't it?" he asked, beaming. "I'm Dewitt, or Mr. Deb Hoffman as I'm known around these parts. Or Mal Hoffman's father-in-law." He leaned toward her as if about to tell her a secret and raised his eyebrows. "These days I answer to either."

"Dewitt, make yourself useful and get our guest a drink," yelled Deb, disappearing into a billowing mass of steam as she drained a saucepan over the sink.

"A drink for the lady! Of course. What would you like, Nell? Beer? Whiskey? Wine?"

"Well, I'm driving so..."

"Beer it is then!" Dewitt rubbed his hands. "Why don't you head on through to the living room, Nell, Mallory is in there with the ankle biters." He gestured to the doorway he'd just appeared from. "I'll bring your drink through. Go on ahead."

Nell made her way down a narrow stone passageway and emerged into a cozy room with a fire blazing in the grate and a patchwork quilt hanging on one of the walls. Mallory was sitting on the floor next to a rainbow-colored padded ring, inside which three little Ankes dressed in identical white rompers were propped up, wobbling and chewing on toys.

"Hey!" Mallory jumped up and gave Nell a hug. "I didn't hear you come in. These three appear to have inherited the Hoffman loud gene."

"It's so good to see you, and these gorgeous little ones." Nell was astonished by how alike the babies were; she couldn't imagine how you could possibly tell them apart. "Which is which?"

"Anke, Bo, Cordelia," said Mallory, pointing to each in turn. Bo chose that moment to start to wail, which immediately set off the other two. "Uh-oh, looks like it's time for a nap."

Just then Nell heard footsteps behind her and turned to see a handsome dark-haired man come into the room.

"Hi there," he said, raising his voice over the crying. "I'm Lucas."

"My husband," added Mallory.

"It's good to meet you, Nell," he said. Compared with the other Hoffmans she'd met, Lucas had a gentler, more thoughtful air. "I was so sorry to hear about Megan's passing. We never met, but I know how special she was to Mal."

"Thank you," said Nell with a smile, warming to him instantly. "And also for inviting me for lunch."

Lucas broke into a grin. "You're a brave woman. As you're about to find out, Hoffman family gatherings are not for the faint-hearted."

As Mallory had warned her, lunch was chaos—albeit a delicious, entertaining chaos. Deb had cooked great vats of beef stew, braised red cabbage and mashed potato, and kept discreetly topping up the serving dishes so they seemed to refill miraculously like the fairy tale about the magic porridge pot. It felt entirely possible that if they stopped eating for a moment the stew would overflow and flood the room, so it was fortunate there were enough guests present for a modestly sized wedding reception, all of whom clearly had hearty appetites. As well as Mallory and Lucas, they were joined by the other three Hoffman brothers with their wives and various children of assorted ages, a handful of farmworkers and a very frail, very elderly man who Nell got the impression was someone's great-uncle. Everyone talked over each other and, apart from the softly spoken Lucas, all of the relatives had most certainly inherited the Hoffman "loud gene." One of the grandkids had just announced she was going vegan (not a winning move in a dairy-farming family) and Deb spent most of lunch berating the teen. "But what are you going to *eat*?" she boomed, as the girl glared sullenly at the plate of beef stew placed in front of her. "Potatoes with a side of darn potatoes?"

Nell was sitting next to Dewitt at the head of the table with Mallory on her other side.

"Nell, what do you think of Tansy Falls?" Dewitt asked. "Best place on God's green earth, don't you agree?"

Mallory rolled her eyes. "She's only been here a week, Dew."

"Oh, I think it's wonderful," said Nell. "All the space and fresh air—you're so lucky to live here."

"Let's hope it's still just as wonderful once those Maverick Lodge cowboys have finished trampling all over it," said the youngest of the many Hoffman brothers, whose name Nell had instantly forgotten, although to be fair there were an awful lot of names to remember. Badges would have been useful.

"Have you heard about the new resort, Nell?" asked Dewitt.

"Yes, I met the woman in charge of the project when I was at—" She stopped before making the mistake of mentioning Darlene's store. "When I was in town," she said quickly.

"You know, I still think they must have bribed someone to get a construction permit," said Deb, who was stopping by their end of the table with a bowl of mashed potatoes. "It's going to be a complete and utter eyesore. And all those thousands of visitors overrunning the town!" She tutted, shaking her head. "And Lucas, you can keep your thoughts to yourself."

Lucas, who had been quietly eating his lunch, looked up. "I didn't say a word!" he protested, but once Deb had moved on, he leaned over the table to Nell. "I've tried to explain to my parents that the resort might actually be good for Tansy Falls, and that we should fix up a meeting with the Maverick Lodge people to see if there's any opportunity for us, maybe even to supply them with Hoffman

Creamery products, but will they listen?" His expression made it quite plain that *no, they most certainly will not.*

Mallory put her hand over his and squeezed it; it was clear that this was well-trodden conversational territory in the Hoffman house.

"So, Nell," said Mallory, deliberately changing the subject. "What have you been up to since I last saw you?"

"Well, the other day I managed to get the car stuck in the mud on the way to see the covered bridge."

Dewitt gave a bark of laughter. "Happens to the best of us, my dear. Who pulled you out?"

"Jackson Quaid." Nell was mortified to feel her face growing hot at the mention of his name.

"Lucky you," joked one of the other Hoffman brothers' wives.

"Shame he's never got over that crazy ex-wife of his," said another, to general mutters of agreement around the table.

"Come on, Jackson's a good kid," said Dewitt, forking stew into his mouth—but then he paused mid-mouthful, his eyes narrowing, as if something important had just occurred to him. "We should have invited him and young Joe over for lunch today." And then, with barely a pause, he went on, "Are you married, Nell?"

"Dewitt. Don't." There was a note of warning in Mallory's voice.

He held up his hands. "What? Just finding out a little more about our delightful guest."

"Dad fancies himself as our local matchmaker," Lucas chipped in. "Tansy Falls' one-man *off* line dating service."

"I just like to see people happy, that's all." Dewitt heaped more stew onto his plate. "And you know what, I do think there's something to be said for arranged marriages. Take all the guesswork, uncertainty and silly romance out of it, and let someone sensible and levelheaded decide for you."

From all the way down at the other end of the table there was an incredulous bark of laughter: there was clearly nothing wrong with Deb's hearing. "Dewitt Hoffman!" she boomed. "I know you're a very old and very foolish man, but surely you remember that the guesswork, uncertainty and silly romance is the best part about getting married?"

"You're not wrong there, old woman..." Then Dewitt suddenly pushed back his chair, making the glasses on the table wobble, stood up and blew Deb a theatrical kiss. "And I wouldn't have missed any of it for the world," he bellowed, arms spread wide.

Deb swiped her hand at him, a girlish smile dimpling her cheeks, while Dewitt sat down chuckling to himself. "Come on, Nell," he said, his voice low, "*is* there a Mr. Nell waiting for you back in London?"

"No, I'm afraid not. Just a dog."

"Well, I've got to say that's a damn waste."

"Dewitt!" Deb thundered at him from the other end of the table. She was clearly a highly skilled lip-reader too.

"What?" Dewitt was the picture of wide-eyed innocence. "It's true! If I were forty years younger, I'd marry her myself!"

After dessert, which was a choice of maple cheesecake, apple streusel or chocolate mousse (Deb insisted Nell have all three, and she happily surrendered), the party broke up, with Dewitt and Lucas heading off to the dairy with the farmhands and some of the grandkids—although not before Dewitt had cornered Nell and whispered, "Give my best to Darlene, won't you?" with a twinkle in his eye that made Nell wonder if there had actually once been something between the two of them after all.

The triplets had now woken from their nap: there had been a sudden wail over the baby monitor during dessert, and although Mallory had leapt from her chair like she'd been electrocuted and sprinted to the triplets' room to extract whoever it was before she woke her sisters, she had reappeared with a baby tucked under each arm and had muttered wearily to Lucas, "You'll need to go and get Bo."

Nell and Mallory were now playing with the girls in the living room, excused from dishwashing duties, which gave Nell a chance to brief Mallory on her latest Tansy Falls encounter.

"Mallory, do you know a guy called Brody Knott?" asked Nell, bouncing a giggling Cordelia in front of her.

"Sure, I went to school with him. Why?"

"I met him yesterday. At the Black Bear."

"That figures. The mountain rescue guys treat that place as their canteen, it's right next to their headquarters. What did you think of Tansy Falls' most eligible bachelor?"

Nell looked at her quizzically, sensing a tinge of cynicism in her tone.

"Oh, Brody's fine, if you're into extremely charming, extremely handsome, extremely untrustworthy men." Mallory grinned. "Just don't go falling for him. That would be boringly predictable and very unwise."

Nell laughed. "Honestly, it hadn't even crossed my mind," she said truthfully. His good looks were undeniable, but Brody Knott was the type who dated twenty-something party girls who liked dancing on tables, not thirty-seven-year-old accountants who liked reading historical fiction. Besides, it wasn't as if he were Nell's type either. "He's a sweet guy, but I certainly wouldn't want to date him," she told Mallory. "I get the impression you'd be fighting for space in front of the mirror."

"I'm glad to hear it, because a lot of women seem to find him irresistible. Megan, for instance. You know, I think she had her first kiss with Brody, up on Maverick."

And then Nell suddenly remembered. That was where she had seen his name before: on Megan's original letter! What was it that she'd written? "Man, he was trouble..." For the umpteenth time, Nell wished Megan were still alive so that she could tell her about bumping into him: she would have found it hilarious.

"So did he try to seduce you?" asked Mallory, in a matter-of-fact way.

"Of course not! I told him what I was doing in Tansy Falls and he offered to take me up Maverick tomorrow. He seemed nice. Besides, I'm definitely not his type."

"He *is* nice, and you're sure to have fun." Mallory leaned over to grab a dust bunny from Anke's fist before she stuffed it in her mouth. "Just keep an eye on him, Nell. As my grandma used to say, Brody Knott could charm the dew off honeysuckle."

Chapter Seventeen

Nell's Monday morning began the way of so many Monday mornings: clouded in gloom. She had made the mistake of checking her emails when she first woke, to be greeted by an irate message from her least favorite bookkeeping client, the boss of a small chain of coffeeshops. Nell could never understand how this woman had managed to build a career in a service industry, as her people skills were questionable at best. Her email message had been the digital equivalent of someone standing outside her window yelling abuse at her: the woman demanded Nell get back to her AT ONCE about her query, scolded her for being tough to get hold of and threatened to take her business elsewhere if she didn't hear from her in the next three hours—a deadline that had already passed, as she'd sent the email at 8 a.m. London time, which was 3 a.m. in Tansy Falls.

Still sitting in bed, Nell bashed out an apology, assuring the woman that she'd look into the matter and get back to her as soon as possible, but she hesitated before pressing send. Nell had emailed all her clients before leaving for America, explaining that she was taking a vacation (her first ever, in fact, since starting the business) and assuring them that although she wasn't in the office, she would be happy to help with any emergencies. The coffeeshop owner's query was not an emergency, however. In fact, it was something she could have easily found out for herself, and Nell's initial panic about losing a client gradually changed into indignation at her unreasonable demands.

Nell had mixed feelings about her job. She had built up a profitable business from scratch, which was clearly something to be proud of, but the work was dull and repetitive, and she missed having colleagues. In fact, she hadn't realized quite how reclusive she'd become until this past week in Tansy Falls. Over the last few days it had been as if she'd emerged from a long hibernation to discover a world that was far brighter and filled with possibility than the one she'd known before, and right now the idea of returning to her cramped London apartment to stare at spreadsheets all day made her body slump as if she were a hundred years old.

Trying to shake the melancholy, Nell got out of bed and opened the drapes. The sun reflected off the scattering of snow that had fallen overnight, making it look as if light were pouring from every direction, and the sky was a wash of unbroken blue. The dazzling sight before her couldn't be more of a contrast to the view from her apartment back home, which was flat, gray and unchanging with the seasons.

Gazing out of the window, Nell ran her fingers down the heavy fabric of the drapes.

I don't want to go back to my old life, she thought suddenly, with a ferocity that shocked her.

Build yourself a new one then, a voice in her head replied.

It came as no surprise that the voice sounded very much like Megan's. Nell closed her eyes, trying to imagine what it would be like to run away and make a fresh start in Tansy Falls—but the idea slipped away like the flight of fancy it so obviously was. Nell leaned her forehead wearily against the window frame. Nobody wanted to go home when they were on vacation, she told herself. Everything would feel fine and normal again once she had settled back into her life in London.

With that thought, Nell glanced at her phone, which stared back at her accusingly from among the bedsheets. She found herself thinking about Darlene and Mallory, and what their response to this shouty, grouchy client would be—and she was certain it wouldn't be the groveling apology that she had just drafted. With a decisive nod, Nell deleted the message, turned off her phone and then showered, dressed and headed downstairs for breakfast. It was a very small act of rebellion, but it made Nell feel as giddy as if she were skipping school for the day.

"Morning, Nell!" Connie greeted her cheerily as she passed through the lobby. "You going skiing today?"

Nell was wearing a ski jacket and pants she'd borrowed from Mallory at lunch yesterday for her trip up the mountain. They fitted her perfectly, and—compared with her mum's shapeless hiking castoffs—at least hinted at the suggestion of a figure underneath.

"I'm visiting Maverick," explained Nell, "although I'm not yet sure if I'll get on skis." (This wasn't actually true: she was 100 percent *certain* she wouldn't get on skis, but she didn't want to admit this to Connie.) "I'm going up there with Brody Knott—do you know him?"

"I most certainly do," said Connie, and Nell was reassured by the warmth in her smile. "You'll be in very safe hands then. Nobody knows Maverick better than Brody."

At 9 a.m., Nell stood outside the inn and scanned the street for Brody. She spotted his car instantly, even before she knew it was his: a bright yellow Jeep with knobby wheels and the sort of underbody armoring you'd find on a light-infantry vehicle—basically a sixteen-year-old boy's dream car. Sure enough, the driver's door opened, letting out a blast of rock music, and Brody Knott's shaggy blond head poked out.

"Yo, Nell from London!" He was wearing mirrored Ray-Ban aviators and waving a gigantic ice cream at her. "You better hurry, your breakfast is melting!"

She jogged up to the car and climbed into the passenger seat. Brody treated her to a dazzling grin of the sort more commonly seen on Hollywood red carpets, although his cool was slightly ruined by the fact that his hand was dripping with melted ice cream like a toddler's mom.

"Ma'am," he said, presenting the cone to her with a bow of his head. "This is for you, to make up for missing the Thundersnow factory tour. I didn't know what flavor you liked, so I got three: butter pecan, snickerdoodle and"—frowning, he licked his hand—"rocky road."

Nell laughed. "Well, I've only had a cinnamon roll, a smoothie and a stuffed omelet with a side of bacon so far this morning, so this gigantic triple-decker ice cream is *extremely* welcome, thank you."

"Excellent, we've gotta keep your energy up. I've got coffee here too. Wanted to make sure I had all bases covered." He cranked the Jeep into gear and the engine roared. "Okay then, let's go and introduce you to Maverick."

He swung into the traffic on Main Street and soon they were speeding along the mountain road. Brody drove like someone who enjoyed adrenaline sports, keeping one hand on the wheel and the other dangling out the window. She tried to imagine what the Nell of a week ago would have made of herself today: sitting alongside the town heartthrob in his pimped-up Jeep, eating ice cream for breakfast. She honestly wouldn't have recognized herself.

"So, what's it short for?" asked Brody, interrupting her thoughts.

"What?"

"Your name, Nell." He waved at a passing car that had just honked in greeting.

"Oh, right. Penelope."

"Ooh, very *Downton Abbey*." Brody put on an English accent. "Would you care for a cup of tea, Lady Penelope?"

Nell laughed, and Brody glanced sideway at her, grinning. "You don't look much like a lady though."

"Gee, thanks."

"That's a good thing! With that hair, you're more like some wild Scottish lassie." Brody yelled out of the window in a broad Scottish accent, "They may take our lives, but they'll never take our freedom!" He chuckled to himself. "That was *Braveheart*, by the way."

"Well, I hope you're good at rescuing people off mountains, because you're terrible at impressions."

Brody gave a snort of laughter. "Dang, that's harsh, girl! But, you know, probably fair."

They flew past the turning to Birdsong Hill, which made Nell think of Jackson, and she felt a prickle of irritation about the fact that she still hadn't managed to cross the old Philpott place off the itinerary. Why on earth wouldn't he let her take a quick peek at his backyard? Why did he have to make himself so hard to reach? She was more angry at herself, though, for allowing Jackson Quaid to still have a hold over her. After all, it was plain he couldn't get away from her fast enough after their visit to the covered bridge.

Then out of the corner of her eye, Nell saw Brody glance at her. "You look different today," he said, thoughtfully.

Nell was aware that she was blushing, which of course made her cheeks even pinker. It hadn't been for Brody's benefit, but after realizing yesterday how much of a boost a little makeup had given her, she had decided to make it a daily habit.

"Different in a good way?" she asked, batting her lashes coquettishly.

"Oh, for sure," said Brody, grinning. "Hey, I almost forgot, I've got something to show you. In the glove compartment."

It was a sheaf of old photos. Nell looked at the first one and let out an involuntary "oh!" of delight. It showed a teenage Megan, her grinning face surrounded by a dark haze of curls, with her arm around a younger, even blonder Brody, who was pouting and pointing at the camera like one of the New Kids on the Block, a plaid shirt knotted around his hips.

"I dug them out last night. Pretty cool, huh?"

Nell flicked through the photos, each one featuring Megan among an assortment of unknown teenagers, although to her excitement she did spot a familiar face.

"Is that Mallory?" she asked, peering at the photo in which a dark-haired teen had been caught mid-eye-roll at a clowning Brody.

Brody looked over. "Yup. You know her?"

"I do."

"That figures, Mal was pretty tight with Megan. Who else have you met in town?"

"All the Hoffmans, Darlene Fiske, Piper Gridley and Connie at the Covered Bridge. Oh, and, um, Jackson Quaid." As ever, she handled his name with care, as if it might explode.

"Yeah? I was at high school with his ex-wife, Cindy."

"Are you friends with him?"

"I know the guy, but I wouldn't say we're that close."

He shrugged as if to dismiss the subject, so Nell carried on flicking through the photos. The last one was of Megan sitting cross-legged on the grass, her head thrown back in laughter as if the photographer had just told her a joke. Nell couldn't believe how similar it was to the photo of Polly Swift she'd seen in the museum. Both girls looked happy and carefree, yet you could see a steeliness in them, a determination to achieve whatever they put their mind to. It had been some comfort to Nell knowing that at least Megan had lived her brief life to the absolute fullest, never shying away from any emotion or experience, and she had a feeling Polly Swift would have been the same. Would she be able say the same thing about her own life, wondered Nell, staring at the image in front of her.

"Man, she was special," said Brody, glancing over. "I still can't get my head around the fact she's gone." He clocked the way that Nell was looking at the photo. "You can have that one if you like."

"Thank you," she said, forcing herself to shake off the grief that was at risk of smothering her again. She tucked the photo in her pocket and forced herself to focus on the scene outside the Jeep's window.

They whizzed past the Black Bear and then Nell's pulse quickened as they headed into what was, for her, unexplored territory. Following the road as it wound upward through the woods, Nell caught glimpses of the mountain through the ranks of tightly packed trunks, and then they rounded a final bend, emerged from out of the trees and suddenly Mount Maverick was right there in front of them, looming upward like a wall at the end of the world.

The parking lot was dead ahead, but instead Brody took an abrupt right-hand turn, nearly taking out a ROAD CLOSED sign, and bumped along a rough track that looked like it had been slashed through the trees by an army of machete-wielding giants. It opened onto a vast clearing, and there, crawling with hard-hatted workers and noisy with the squeals and rumbles of machinery, its vast bulk making the diggers look like toys, was Maverick Lodge.

The building was covered in scaffolding, clearly still months away from completion, but the scale of it was jaw-dropping. Nell reckoned it would be able to house all of the residents of Tansy Falls and still have room for a few visitors. The design of the main building appeared to have been based on an alpine ski lodge, with stone walls, shutters and plenty of weathered timber, yet all blown up to Disney World proportions.

Brody put the Jeep into park and turned to Nell with an expectant smile. "What do you think?"

"It's..." She shook her head. "Just—wow."

"Right? Impressive, huh?" Brody misread Nell's expression. "This place is going to seriously transform the mountain."

"For the better?"

Brody made a "duh" face at her. "Of course! DiSouza Developments is going to pump money into the mountain, which will mean we can replace the ski lifts, improve the restaurants, upgrade the snowmaking system. It's gonna be the best thing that's happened to Maverick since they first cut ski trails here back in the 1940s." He opened his door, as excited as a kid at Christmas. "Come on, let's take a look."

Nell wasn't even sure if they were allowed to be here, but Brody strode around the site as if he were an honored guest. They picked their way through the mud to the front of the main building, where there was an enormous glass and timber hexagonal structure that Brody told her was going to be the resort's new sports center. Set against the backdrop of Maverick's quiet majesty, Nell thought it looked as incongruous as if it had been dropped off by a passing spaceship. It was like a billionaire's idea of a humble vacation home.

"Some of the locals seem worried the lodge will change the character of Tansy Falls," said Nell, attempting to be tactful.

"What, by dragging it into the twenty-first century?" Brody looked incredulous. "This town runs on tourism, we can't afford to be romantic about the past. The lodge will bring a new golf course, restaurants, a pool complex: it'll be a hundred percent positive for Tansy Falls." They stopped to let a dump truck rumble by in front of them. "The lodge is also buying up some old businesses in town, so Main Street will see the benefit as well."

"Yes, Darlene Fiske told me she's selling her store. I met Liza DiSouza when I was there." She glanced at Brody, interested to see his reaction. "You've met Liza, I presume?"

"Oh, she's had meetings with everyone," he said dismissively. "Anyway, it will be a fantastic opportunity for Darlene," he went on. "I'm sure DiSouza Developments have made her a good offer, and besides, everyone knows the store is too much for her to cope with on her own. She must be nearly ninety by now."

They had now arrived at the mountain parking lot, having circuited the entire building site, and Brody gazed up at the slopes of Maverick with something close to adoration.

"Okay, Lady Penelope," he said. "Let's get you up my mountain."

Chapter Eighteen

As it was a weekday near the end of the season there were only a few skiers and snowboarders milling around at the base of the mountain. Compared with its glamorous new neighbor, the resort's current sports center looked more like a tumbledown shack, yet Nell was enchanted by its folksy charm. A pair of antique wooden skis hung crisscrossed over the entrance, while inside there was a closet-sized boutique offering handknitted ski hats and souvenirs, ticket windows selling mountain lift passes and the Maverick Café, outside of which was a sunlit terrace that looked out over the main ski trail. If she hadn't been so full of ice cream she would have asked Brody if they could have stopped off to enjoy the sunshine and one of the café's delicious-sounding cinnamon-cream hot chocolates.

Her hand shielding her eyes against the glare, Nell watched as skiers flew down the mountain toward where they were standing at the bottom, swishing to an elegant halt in a flurry of snow that sparkled like handfuls of glitter thrown in the air. Well, most of them looked elegant: some barreled past, arms flailing, as if they had been picked up and chucked down the mountain (which was exactly how Nell imagined she would have looked on skis).

It was quite an experience walking around the resort with Brody, because virtually everyone they passed seem to know him. Every few steps, somebody would stop to say hi—and he was charming to all, doling out smiles and high-fives like Tom Cruise at his latest premiere, and she felt a prickle of pride at being squired by a local celebrity.

They paused at the bottom of a gentle hill that even Nell felt she might be able to get down, watching as a line of preschoolers with bright helmets and pizza-wedge legs snaked down behind their ski instructor.

"How do you feel about getting on skis?" asked Brody. "I'd be very happy to give you a lesson."

Before she could answer one of the kids fell facedown in the snow, while the rest of the class just wove around him like a procession of clockwork toys. After a moment he got up and bombed down to the bottom where the others were now waiting; he clearly had no idea how to stop and crashed into them, taking out half the line in a bowling strike.

"Maybe another time," said Nell, grimacing. "I'm not sure I'm a mountain person."

"Okay, but I think you'd enjoy it. I think you'd be a natural at skiing—you're the right build for it."

Nell wasn't sure what he meant by that: plenty of padding around her lower half, in case she fell? She got the impression, though, that it was intended it as a compliment; after all, Brody's default setting was "charming."

They were now approaching the quad chair lift and Nell watched, horrified, as the waiting skiers were scooped up into the air by what looked like a bench on strings, their skis dangling beneath them as they rocked and juddered over the treetops. Nell's legs felt wobbly; *is this how they were going to get up to the top of the mountain?* If it had been a fairground ride, it would have been instantly shut down due to health and safety concerns.

"So we, um, line up over there, do we?" she asked Brody, trying to keep the tremor out of her voice.

"Oh no, we'll be getting the gondola up."

To Nell's immense relief, he pointed to where a procession of red cabins was traveling sedately up the mountain. Each cabin had a floor and a roof and looked much more her style than the high-speed benches of doom.

"Right this way, ma'am," smiled Brody, offering her his arm, and together they trudged up the slope toward the small brick building that housed the gondola station. Once inside, Brody cut ahead of the waiting line and went straight up to the kiosk, waving at the guy inside.

"Hey, Mike, we're just heading up for a quick look."

"Sure thing, Brody, go right ahead."

Brody helped Nell into the next available cabin, sliding the doors closed before anyone else could join them, and seconds later they swung out of the gloom and into the sunshine. They really had lucked out with the weather today: the sky was such an intense color that Nell found herself wondering what actually made it look blue, a question she'd never even considered before—but then this place seemed to have a knack of making her look at the world through fresh eyes.

Although the gondola was moving at a steady speed, its height varied dramatically as they climbed the mountain: in some places they barely skimmed the tops of the trees, while in others they left the ground far below, giving Nell a bird's-eye view of the skiers and snowboarders as they arced down the slope. Brody too seemed transfixed by the view, one hand pressed up against the window like a delighted child, even though he must have made this trip thousands of times before. He caught Nell's eye and grinned, widening his eyes as if to say: "Pretty cool, huh?"

At the top, they emerged from the gondola onto a snowy plateau, the highest point on the mountain, with the rest of the world spread out below. Perhaps it was because the air was thinner up here, or maybe she was dizzy from the ride up, but it felt as if Nell's senses had been cranked up to maximum intensity. Everything seemed startlingly vivid: the brightness of the sky and dazzling snow, the bite of cold on her face, the crunch of the snow beneath her feet. She gazed around her, enthralled, as if being able to see for the first time. She didn't even want to breathe in case she broke the spell.

"So what do you think?" asked Brody. "Still think you're not a mountain person?"

Still dazed, Nell could only manage a slight shake of her head.

He grinned, clapping a hand on her shoulder. "Come on, mountain girl. Let's go."

Nell reluctantly dragged herself out of whatever trance she had been in, only now becoming aware of other people milling around them on the plateau, and followed after Brody.

They passed what looked like a cannon shooting a stream of mist up into the air, which had left the branches of the spruce trees on the slopes below them thickly crusted in white.

"Snowmaking machines," explained Brody. "They come in particularly useful at this time of year when the snowfall is slowing down."

At various points around the plateau, color-coded signposts indicated the trails where skiers were vanishing over the edge. Nell had already noticed blue and black runs, but then she spotted one marked with two black diamonds. The sign read: GOOSE GULLEY. WARNING: EXPERTS ONLY.

Brody observed her interest. "Do you want to take a look? It's a double-diamond run. Pretty gnarly."

He led her to the edge and as they peered over. Nell's stomach plunged into her boots. From what she could see, there was a sheer drop for about forty feet leading to a narrow crevasse, jagged with rocks, that disappeared off into the dense woods at a gradient of somewhere near vertical. If the rocks didn't get you, the trees most definitely would. This was a ski run? The thought of standing at the top of this and deciding, *yes, I'd very much like to make my way down this, but on a pair of skis so I'm extra out of control*; it was insanity! Like throwing yourself off a skyscraper with only a bunch of party balloons for support.

She turned to Brody, who was fiddling with his gloves, unfazed by the horror below them. "You can ski down this?" asked Nell.

He rolled his eyes. "Babe, I was skiing down this when I was in diapers." He turned away from the edge. "Come on, I want to show you something."

With the horrors of Goose Gulley safely behind them, they walked on a little farther, passing a blue run that Nell thought looked *almost* manageable, and then they were tramping through the virgin snow away from the main ski area toward some orange netting, draped between metal rods, that was clearly intended to stop you from going any farther.

Without pausing, Brody swung his legs over the netting and headed straight for the edge.

"Where are we going?" asked Nell, grinding to a halt.

"Well, I've been giving this some thought, and I think I've found the perfect spot for Megan's resting place."

"But where?"

He looked over the precipice. "Down here." And then he disappeared over the edge.

Nell hesitated, her legs feeling wobbly. From where she was standing it looked like there was nowhere to go but certain death. But Brody worked in mountain rescue: there was no way he would put them in any danger, would he? Even if, judging by Goose Gulley, he did seem to have a wildly different understanding of the word "danger" than she did. Swallowing her fear, Nell climbed over the barrier and followed his tracks to where he'd vanished. Looking over, she saw him edging down a steep but not terrifying slope a little way below, setting off a tiny avalanche of tumbling snow as he went.

"You might need to do some of this on your butt," he called up to her.

Nell took a deep breath. From the look of the slope, she anticipated doing *all* of it on her butt. Ignoring the voice inside that was telling her this was a really bad idea, she took a wobbly step into the unknown.

It wasn't anywhere near as hairy as Nell had feared. She slid a bit of the way, but there were trees to grab hold of to slow her descent, and when she got to where Brody was waiting she realized they had only gone about twenty feet below the main plateau.

They were standing on a shallow, rocky outcrop, on which a single spruce tree had managed to take root, its snowy needles adding a flourish of Christmas cheer to the remote spot. Even though they weren't in any danger—the slope below fell away sharply, but Nell thought you could probably roll down without serious injury—by some geological trickery it appeared as if they were on the very edge of a precipice with nothing beneath them but sky. Far below, the Tansy Falls valley was spread out in a patchwork of browns and greens, overlaid in places with patches of white and woven through with the glittering silver ribbon of the Wild Moose River.

Brody stared out at the horizon, his hands on his hips. "Megan would have loved it here. She was wild about this view."

It took Nell a moment to answer. "Yes, she would," she managed eventually, still transfixed by the sight below. Somewhere down in the valley the sun hit the roof of an invisible car, flashing like a lightning bolt. "It feels like we're standing at the very top of the world," she murmured, shielding her eyes.

Nell glanced at Brody, wondering whether to say more, and then decided she had wasted far too much time in her life worrying about saying the wrong thing. "This is going to sound weird, but I feel so alive right now. Like—I've been asleep all my life, and now I've finally woken up."

She was expecting Brody to laugh, but he just nodded. "Maverick will do that to you. There's something very special about this mountain, some primitive, elemental force. It has the same effect on me, too. It's why I always knew I wanted to work here."

"Before today, I thought the mountain looked threatening, but now—well, it's the complete opposite. It's the most life-affirming place I've ever been. I can see exactly why Megan loved it here. And this spot"—Nell gazed around, shaking her head in wonder—"it's perfect."

Brody looked pleased. "We'll christen it Megan's Point. I'll make it official, write it on a map someplace at Maverick HQ." He glanced at Nell. "I'll visit her often, I promise."

She smiled at him. Even though they were only a few feet below the main plateau, it was perfectly quiet down here, with just the sound of their breath to lift the silence, and Nell was suddenly conscious of how alone they were.

"You remind me of her, you know," said Brody, softly.

"Megan?" Nell was stunned; as much as she had loved her, she'd never seen any of her friend's wonderful qualities in herself. "In what way?"

"She was just...nice to hang out with. I liked the way she looked at the world. And there was no pretense, no trying to be cool or whatever. She had a sweet soul."

"And that's how you see me?"

"Yeah. You're..." He cocked his head, thinking. "What's the opposite of cynical?"

Nell thought for a moment. "Innocent?"

"Nah," said Brody, flashing a wicked grin and fixing her with a knowing look. "Definitely not that."

Then Nell laughed, remembering Mallory's warnings about Brody. She'd spent enough time with him to be well aware that he flirted with everyone; still, it was nice to be the focus of his infamous charm.

"How long are you in Tansy Falls for?" he asked.

"Another week."

"I'd really like to get together again, maybe join you for some more of Megan's itinerary—if you don't mind me tagging along. Can I take your number?"

"Sure, that would be fun. As long as you make sure you bring ice cream again."

Brody put a hand on his heart, bowing his head. "I promise."

"Well, in that case, you're on," said Nell with a smile.

Chapter Nineteen

I'm not sure exactly what time of the year it will be during your stay in Tansy Falls, but if I've managed to time my death perfectly, then I'm hoping you'll be here during sugaring season (which also coincides with the infamous mud season—or perhaps I should have mentioned that earlier?!). Anyway, if that is the case, today you're going on a tour of the Lazy Knoll Sugar Shack. I'm sure you've realized it by now, but this little corner of the country runs on maple syrup, which suits me because I absolutely love the stuff. I'd go as far as to say that if you don't agree that pancakes and bacon with maple syrup is the breakfast of the gods, then you're pretty much—again, unfortunate choice of words—dead to me. At the sugar shack you can see the syrup being made, which is a pretty interesting process in itself, but the main reason I want you to visit is to try the local delicacy, Sugar on Snow. This is the stuff of my childhood dreams, and my eight-year-old self is FURIOUS she's not joining you.

Nell had missed her morning coffee with Darlene the previous day, so she stopped off at the store on her way to visit the sugar shack. When she arrived, Darlene was busy with a customer: a tourist, judging by her quilted Chanel bag and spike-heeled boots that had never met a speck of mud in their lives. The woman was peppering Darlene with questions about the display of llama-wool socks, and from the look of Darlene's tightly folded arms and thunderous brow, the old adage about the customer always being right was being severely tested.

Steering clear, Nell went to check out the shelf of secondhand books at the far end of the store, although as she passed she heard the tourist ask, "But is the flock of llamas organic?" Darlene caught sight of Nell and shot her a covert eye-roll.

The books were housed in the quietest part of the store, tucked well away from the displays of local produce that drew the tourists with liberal use of the magic word: "artisan." It was dimly lit back here, the air musty with the pages of third-hand thrillers; at some point Darlene had obviously tried to make this area more of a feature, putting in an armchair for browsers, but this was now hidden under a collapsing heap of books. With better lighting and more shelving, perhaps a cozy rug to cover the floorboards, Nell could just imagine how inviting this spot would be. If this store were hers, she would expand this whole area, maybe start selling new books as well as secondhand: as far as she knew there wasn't another bookstore in town, and if you moved this enormous stack of boxes (*what on earth was Darlene storing in these?*), you could cover the whole back wall with shelves, perhaps put in a special section for kids too, with puzzles and . . .

Nell's daydream was interrupted by a soft noise nearby, and she turned to find that the most enormous ginger cat had jumped up on the pile of boxes next to her and was regarding her through half-closed green eyes. When she put out a tentative hand to stroke him, he pressed his tiger-striped head up to meet her and began to purr with such rumbling intensity that she could feel it vibrating through her like a road drill.

"Aren't you're a handsome boy. Why hasn't Darlene mentioned you before, I wonder?"

Just then Nell heard the click of the front door closing and moments later Darlene appeared, tutting to herself. "A *flock* of organic llamas," she muttered, her jewelry rattling out her irritation. "Of all the—" She stopped. "Ah, I see you've met Cat."

"That's his name? Cat?"

"Well, he doesn't really have a name—he's not mine, you see. He just comes to stay every once in a while."

"Who does he belong to?"

"Oh, Cat doesn't belong to anyone but himself. He just appeared in town, years ago, and never left." Darlene rubbed the patch of silky white fur under his chin, and the purring increased to the decibels of a jet engine. "You like it in Tansy Falls, doncha, Cat?"

"He's clearly very well looked after."

"That's because everyone in town feeds him. He probably has twelve meals a day. He's already had two here this morning." She tipped her head to the side, scrutinizing him. "I guess we really should decide on an official name for him. I'll raise it at the next town meeting and we can vote, although personally I think Cat suits him just fine." With that, she strode off, asking over her shoulder: "Coffee, sweetie?"

"Yes please."

"What did you get up to yesterday?"

"I went up Maverick."

"Oh, that's nice," said Darlene, bending down to retrieve a couple of mugs.

"I had a look at the building site for the new lodge too. Brody Knott took me round."

Darlene's head snapped up. "What were you doing with him?"

"I met him at the Black Bear a few days ago and he offered to take me up the mountain." Nell noticed Darlene's expression. "Is there a problem? He's been very nice to me."

"Oh yes, Brody Knott is very nice to everyone as long as it suits Brody Knott. You watch him, Nell. He might fool most people around here, but I see right through Brody Knott's pretty-boy charm. His father was the same. A liar and a cheat."

Darlene uttered these last words with such vitriol that Nell wondered if she was speaking from experience. She wasn't unduly concerned, though—after the dire Deb Hoffman warnings, she was learning to take Darlene's pronouncements with a hefty pinch of salt.

"Don't worry, I doubt I'll see him again while I'm here," she said.

"I'm very pleased to hear that. Where are you off to today, honey?"

"The Lazy Knoll Sugar Shack. D'you know it?"

"Huh." Darlene looked surprised. "Well, I guess it must have changed hands since Megan was last here."

"What do you mean?"

"Oh, it's no big deal. It's just there are other sugar houses I would have recommended before that particular one. The lady in charge is kind of a windbag, but you'll have fun, I'm sure of it."

At that moment, the bell over the door jangled and Nell turned to see a very elderly man enter the store, leaning on a stick. He paused by the door and took off his woolly hat, leaving his white hair sticking up in wispy tufts, then began a painstaking shuffle toward the counter.

"Ted!" Darlene swept over and took his arm, steering him into a chair. "How are you, my dear?"

"Oh, I'm just fine, thank you, Darlene," he said, beaming up at her as he sat down.

"Nell, meet a very old friend of mine. This is Ted Libby, my attorney."

This was Darlene's attorney? Nell eyes widened and she stuck on a smile to hide her shock.

"It's lovely to meet you, Mr. Libby. I'm Nell."

"Good morning, Belle, I'm delighted to make your acquaintance."

Darlene patted his hand. "It's *Nell*, dear," she murmured. "Ted and I have known each other—ooh, how long is it now, Ted?"

"Well, I opened my office here in the summer of 1966. Do you remember, Darlene?" He leaned both hands on his stick in front of him. "Hottest July on record, it was. Turned the slopes of Maverick to hay and the Wild Moose was left bone-dry for nigh on six weeks."

Darlene beamed at him indulgently, then turned to Nell. "Liza DiSouza's bringing over the paperwork for the store sale later this morning and Ted is going to check it over for me. Isn't that right, Ted?"

He frowned in her direction. "What's that?"

Darlene raised her voice. "You're going to take a look at the valuation report for me, remember? For the sale of Fiske's?"

"Oh, yes indeed, ma'am. I'm gonna make sure they've dotted those t's and crossed those i's. Ab-so-lutely."

He gave her such a delightful smile, his pale eyes twinkling, that Nell couldn't help but return it; nevertheless, the prospect of Ted Libby being the sole line of defense between Darlene and the razor-sharp Liza DiSouza gave her palpitations. Before she could change her mind, Nell followed Darlene over to where she was making the coffee, hoping the splutters of the machine would allow them to speak in private— although she got the impression Ted's hearing wasn't the sharpest.

"Darlene, I know you've said there's no need, but I'm concerned that Liza DiSouza is not being completely straight with you and I really would like to take a look at the valuation report, just to make sure everything's in order."

"Nell, I've already told you, Ted is taking care of it. He may be old, but he knows his stuff."

"I'm sure, but—oh!" Cat had jumped up onto the counter in front of Nell. "It's just, this is what I used to do for my job," she went on, as Cat butted up against her, demanding affection. "I've had a lot of experience with these sorts of deals. I only want to make sure Liza DiSouza is being fair and abiding by your wishes to keep Fiske's as a general store."

While Nell had no idea what DiSouza Developments had planned, she was damn sure it wouldn't include a lovely new book area.

"Like I've said, I'm grateful for the offer, but Liza and I have been over this and she's given me her word."

"But Piper Gridley at the Covered Bridge told me that—"

"Young lady." Darlene pulled herself to her full five-foot-nothing, although she may as well have been twice that height—she really could be quite terrifying. "Ted and I will be taking care of this matter, and that is that."

"Is this a bad time?" cooed a silky voice.

They swung round to discover Liza DiSouza standing on the opposite side of the counter, clad head-to-toe in white Lycra, a sickly smile on her flawlessly contoured face. Nell had no idea how long she'd been standing there, but she must have heard at least some of their conversation.

"I just stopped by with the valuation report," Liza went on, placing a glossy document on the counter. "And also to get some of your delicious coffee before my run. I have no idea what you put in there, Darlene, but I swear I go twice as fast after a cup!"

She gave a tiny ladylike sneeze and noticed Cat, who was sitting on the counter twitching his tail at her. "Oh, I'm sorry, Darlene, my allergies. Would you mind...?"

"Not at all." Darlene plonked Cat on the floor, then picked up the report from the counter and clutched it to her, as if to underline her determination to keep it out of Nell's hands.

Nell knew when she was beaten. "Well, I'd better be going. Nice to see you again, Liza."

Liza gave her a gracious nod, but her eyes were granite hard.

"Bye, Mr. Libby," said Nell, waving at him.

"Going already, Kelly dear? I thought you were going to show me some paperwork?"

"No, Ted, that's this lady—Ms. DiSouza, remember?" said Darlene, tersely, then hurried after Nell to the door, pressing a takeout coffee into her hands. "We'll speak later, okay?"

"I'm sorry, Darlene," muttered Nell, wishing she'd kept her mouth shut.

"Don't be silly. I know you're just looking out for me, but you gotta trust me on this one." She gave her a hug. "This is my business and I'll deal with it my way. As the saying goes, an ounce of experience is worth a pound of theory. I've managed on my own for sixty-odd years, after all."

Chapter Twenty

Having left Sue Ellen in the parking lot, Nell picked her way through the maze of silver birch trunks toward the Lazy Knoll Sugar Shack, a sunshine-yellow cabin with a chrome chimney that was belching out clouds of toffee-scented steam. Together with the delicious smell, a sign outside reading FRESH DONUTS—HOT CIDER—PICKLES—SUGAR ON SNOW made Nell's stomach start shouting for food, although even that couldn't distract her from the conversation she'd just had with Darlene. Nell wasn't sure why the issue of the store's sale was bothering her so much: she barely knew Darlene, after all, and if she didn't want her getting involved in her private business, then that should surely be the end of it. It couldn't be, though, partly because Nell had no doubt that Megan would have wanted her to look out for Darlene, but also because she genuinely cared: for the old lady, for Tansy Falls and, she was beginning to realize, for Fiske's itself. This morning when she had dabbled in her mental makeover of the store, Nell had been surprised by how passionately she'd felt about it, and since then other ideas had been popping into her head: how she could rearrange the layout, start selling freshly baked sourdough bread, expand the range of hot drinks, maybe move the sales counter nearer the front of the store where it would catch the morning sun. This last thought was accompanied by an image of herself, standing behind the till, wearing

a smart new custom-made Fiske's apron in navy or spruce green...
but no, in another life perhaps. Instead, Liza DiSouza was going to
turn it into a soulless chain-store 7-Eleven, and Nell was going to go
back to her spreadsheets in London. She sighed, brushing her hair off
her face. As much as it bothered her (and just thinking about it made
her body scrunch up) this wasn't a battle she was required to fight.

The door to the sugar shack creaked on its hinges and Nell was hit by
a wave of stifling warmth as it swung open. Inside, the small room was
crammed full of people—families with kids, a couple wearing matching
Tansy Falls sweatshirts, a small party of seniors—all of whom seemed to
be waiting for the tour. Hushed conversations and the scent of maple
blended in the muggy air, soothing away the tensions of Nell's morning
so far. The walls were lined with shelves carrying every imaginable
maple-based product: alongside bottles of syrup there was maple butter,
cream, cookies, mustard, even maple liqueur. Nell was just examining
a bar of maple soap, wondering whether it would taste as good as it
smelled, when a sharp clap snapped her out of her sugar-drugged stupor.

"Good morning, everyone!" A woman stood at the front of the
room wearing a pair of large round glasses and a pink sweatshirt
emblazoned with the words MAPLE SYRUP SNOB, holding her hands
aloft as if she were preaching. "My name is Franny Cooper, my
husband, Coop, and I have owned the Lazy Knoll for ten years, and
I'll be leading your tour today to show you how we make our famous
Lazy Knoll maple syrup. I was the Maple Syrup Federation's Maple
Advocate of the Year in 2012, so what I don't know about syrup ain't
worth knowing!" She treated the room to a sickly smile. "I would
please ask that you save your questions until the end of the tour, so
as we don't miss any fascinating maple syrup facts. Alrighty then,
this way please."

She began herding the group through a side door, and Nell let herself be carried along by the tide of the group when she heard Franny saying: "It looks like we have a latecomer! Hurry along, sir, we don't want to hold everyone up now, do we?"

And then Nell glanced behind her and found herself looking straight into the dark eyes of Jackson Quaid.

Nell's breath caught in her chest and warmth rippled through her insides. He was wearing work clothes, his hair as rumpled as if he'd just pulled off a hat. He looked—*dammit*—as attractive as ever. But what on earth was he doing here?

Jackson ran his fingers through his hair. "I'm sorry, I just need to speak to..."

Then Nell's belly turned somersaults as Jackson pointed straight at her.

"As I said to the rest of the group before you arrived," Franny said, "there will be ample opportunity for questions at the end of the tour."

"But I—"

Franny raised a warning hand. "Sir, you are holding up the entire group. You can ask anything you want later, but right now you do the walking and I'll do the talking!"

She twinkled at him, threateningly.

Jackson hesitated, glanced over at Nell once more, and then, his shoulders slumping, joined the back of the group.

"That's right, off we go," said Franny, as if talking to a naughty child. "Straight through the door, please, no dawdling, we have a lot to get through."

As they filed outside, Nell's mind raced with questions about Jackson's surprise appearance. Perhaps he was here for the tour? He'd seemed quite excited about the covered bridge, after all, and she didn't think they had maple trees in California; perhaps it was simply a coincidence that they were here at the same time? But no, he had made it clear he needed to speak to her—although she couldn't for the life of her imagine why. Nell glanced back at Jackson again, but he was looking at his feet, his hands stuck in his pockets, staring at the ground.

Franny herded the group toward some trees that had metal buckets attached to their trunks, just like the ones Nell had noticed up by the covered bridge. In any other circumstances she would be keen to solve the mystery of what they were, but right now Jackson Quaid was taking up most of her brain's real estate.

"Does anyone know what these are for?" asked Franny, pointing to the buckets.

A little girl piped up: "To collect the maple sap to make the syrup."

"Well done! See this little tap here, stuck into a hole in the trunk? The sap runs out of here and into the bucket. And over here—everyone follow me, NO TALKING—this is where we store the sap once it's collected."

As she steered them toward a large tank, Nell noticed Jackson starting to edge his way through the group in her direction; unfortunately, she wasn't the only one who saw him.

"No pushing, sir, please!" yelled Franny, bustling over to him. "My goodness, you are a troublemaker," she simpered, looping her arm around his. "Looks like I'm going to have to keep a very close eye on you!"

Once they were all gathered around the tank, Franny launched into a long-winded explanation about, well, Nell wasn't sure exactly. She caught the odd word—something about "hydrometers" and "sap viscosity"—but it was impossible to focus on the details as she was too busy sneaking peeks at Jackson, who was clearly mortified to have been hauled up next to Franny yet too well mannered to complain. He looked like he had caught the sun since they last met, the skin across his nose and the ridge of his cheekbones a flash of dark gold. Nell imagined she wasn't the only female member of the tour group admiring Franny's reluctant new assistant.

The tour continued back in the sugar shack, where Franny led them around a bewildering system of pipes, pans and tanks, explaining the process of how the sap was boiled down to become syrup. With a different guide it would have been fascinating, but Franny's long-winded lecture was PhD level in complexity: the facts flowed as thick and fast as syrup, but with none of its sweetness. Some of the younger kids started muttering about being bored and were tetchily shushed by their parents. It didn't help that the room was sweltering and clouded with steam: Franny's face was sweaty and her glasses had completely misted over in the heat of the room, and when Nell caught a glimpse of Jackson through the network of pipes and steam she saw that he'd taken off his outer layers, the sleeves of his T-shirt clinging to his biceps as he clutched his jacket to him. As much as she tried to fight it, Nell felt a flicker of desire.

Finally, after what felt like hours, Franny announced that they were now going back outside to get a taste of Sugar on Snow and if everyone would *please* line up in an orderly fashion, she would be *most* grateful. Nell wondered just how frizzy her hair had gone in the steam, because everyone else looked like they'd stepped out of a sauna. Franny waddled along in front of the group, chattering away at Jackson as they headed toward a food stand with a red-and-white awning that sat photogenically among the maples.

Sugar on Snow turned out to be just that: boiling maple syrup poured over a cup of snow, which transformed the syrup into a shiny, chewy caramel. Its smoky sweetness contrasted perfectly with the sour pickles and buttery donuts that were served alongside, and Nell piled her paper plate up high. The combination of flavors was addictive and almost worth the tedium of Franny's lecture; so delicious, in fact, that Nell momentarily forgot all about Jackson, and she had just stuffed a particularly chewy nugget of syrup into her mouth, along with a chunk of donut, when she looked up and there he was, standing right in front of her.

"Nell, hi."

She attempted a smile, but her mouth was so full it came out as more of a grimace. Holding up a hand in a "give me a moment" gesture, Nell angled herself away from him and chewed furiously. Why did Jackson always seem to catch her at her worst? The thought of how she must look right now made her skin itch: frizzy-haired, covered in donut crumbs and pickle juice, chomping away like a guinea pig on a carrot. Meanwhile, Jackson was standing there looking as cool and unruffled as James Bond. Finally, after what seemed like long minutes, she managed to swallow.

"Hello there!" she blurted, as breathless as if she'd just finished a workout. "It's great to see you! Would you, um, like a pickle?" She retrieved one from her plate and brandished it at him.

Jackson smiled, holding up a hand. "No, I'm good, thank you."

"No? Well, you're missing out, this is delicious." Nell could tell she was babbling and took a bite of the pickle to force herself to shut up, which of course led to another awkward silence while Jackson waited for her to finish chewing again. "So what did you think of the tour?" she mumbled behind her hand.

"Well, it was certainly long." He grinned. "But, full disclosure, I didn't actually come for the tour. I was looking for you."

"How did you know I'd be here?"

"Darlene told me." He winced. "Sorry, that makes it sound like I'm following you."

"Not to worry. I stalked you, now you're stalking me. Fair's fair."

"I guess we're even then." Jackson grinned, his eyes flashing with amusement. "Shall we?" He gestured to an empty picnic table amid a cluster of trees, set apart from the rest of the group, and Nell could only nod her reply, her mind buzzing with possibilities about why Jackson Quaid had gone to all the trouble of tracking her down and her body tingling at the prospect of being alone with him again.

They took a seat opposite each other, Jackson lacing his fingers together on the table in front of him in a businesslike fashion, and despite the easy banter of a few moments ago Nell felt a strangely stiff formality descend over them, as if they were sitting down for a job interview.

"So what's this about?" asked Nell, trying to keep her voice level.

"It's about me apologizing. I went to Fiske's this morning to grab a coffee, and Darlene told me about your friend Megan. She explained about this itinerary she's sent you on, and why you came to my house the other day." Jackson took a breath, slowly letting it out. "I had no idea. I'm sorry, Nell. You must have thought I was so rude, not inviting you to have a look around. I wanted to, it's just I get so protective of Joe—maybe too protective sometimes. He's had a lot to deal with in his young life, and I like to keep things as stable as I can for him at home." He rubbed his cheek. "I don't know if you're aware of my personal situation..."

"Darlene's told me a little." Nell looked down, but could feel herself flush at how much she really knew about Jackson's private life. "Sorry, she mentioned about your marriage in passing."

"Don't worry, it's impossible keeping secrets in Tansy Falls—the curse and blessing of living in a small town. I grew up in one back in California, so I'm used to it. Anyway, I wanted to find you to tell you that you must, please, come and see the backyard. I'll show you around the house, too, if you'd like. Heck, you can even have a ride on the tire swing!"

She laughed with him, touched he'd come out of his way to find her and tell her all this; he was clearly a good man, just as Darlene had said. Yet Nell couldn't ignore a pang of disappointment that his motive for tracking her down was entirely noble. Deep down, she'd been hoping that Jackson was here to declare that he couldn't stop thinking about her and was hoping she'd join him for dinner tonight.

"Thank you," she said, smiling away the little ache of rejection in the pit of her stomach. "You really didn't have to come all the way out here, though."

"It wasn't a big deal. I was coming this way to see a client. Plus, thanks to you, I now have my master's degree in maple syrup production." He grinned, glancing down at his watch. "I better get going, I'm over an hour late as it is. When are you going back to England?"

"At the end of the week."

"Oh." Jackson's brows knit together. "Well, how about you come over the day after next? I'm in pretty much all day. I may even make you a coffee if you're very lucky."

"That would be perfect," said Nell.

"Great." Jackson stood up to leave, but then hesitated. His eyes were full of some unreadable emotion, and she got the impression he wanted to say something more—but then the clouds lifted and he broke into a smile.

"See you then, Nell," he said, and strode off to the parking lot without a backward glance.

Chapter Twenty-One

You remember me telling you about Cyclops, don't you? Of course, there's no way you could forget my old family dog, our beloved terrier-poodle-hyena cross with a squeaky bark, one eye and a heart the size of Texas. What I don't think I ever told you, though, is the story of how Cyclops came to live with us.

When I was eight, the years of badgering my mom for a puppy finally paid off and we paid a visit to the Wild Moose Animal Shelter in Tansy Falls. I knew exactly what sort of dog I wanted—a huge mutt, big enough to rest my head on like a pillow—but then I spotted this scrappy little one-eyed puppy, no bigger than a rabbit, who jumped into my arms and licked me all over my face as if to say: "I choose you." Cy came home with us that day, and from then on I'd volunteer at the shelter whenever I could while in Tansy Falls. It was an important place to the teenage me, and I know you'll be missing Moomin by now, so enjoy getting your puppy-petting fix at the shelter today!

Nell could already hear the barking as she headed up the path toward the redbrick building, and her spirits plunged at the thought of the heartbreaking stories she'd no doubt discover behind the deceptively cheery cornflower-blue door. She'd never been to an animal shelter before, but was imagining dark rows of overcrowded cages occupied by cowering abandoned dogs. The thought of people mistreating animals stuck a boulder to her throat and a twist of fury in her guts.

Behind the door, though, wasn't the gloomy dog prison she had feared. The walls of the sunny reception area were covered with photos of pets, both the shelter's current residents and those who had now gone onto their "forever homes," and it had the air of a happy place run by caring people. At the front desk a college-age girl wearing a T-shirt in the same vivid blue as the front door greeted her with a smile.

"Hey there, welcome to the Wild Moose Animal Shelter. How can I help you?"

"Would it be possible to have a look around the shelter?"

"Sure. Are you interested in adopting a pet?"

"I'd love to, but I live in England. Would it still be okay to meet some of the dogs?" Nell glanced at the charity box sitting on the counter. "I'd obviously be happy to make a donation."

"Well, that would be very kind of you, thank you." The girl held out her hand. "Carlee Spring, animal care associate."

"Nell Swift," she said, "dog obsessive."

Carlee grinned. "Well, you'll fit right in then. Come this way."

Nell followed Carlee outside to another building where the dogs were housed. As they walked along the row of pens most of the occupants bounded up to greet them, tails wagging, their bright eyes trained on humans that they were learning meant food and love, rather than violence and neglect. There were a few, though, that still cowered at the back of their pens, and Nell's heart broke a little more with each of them that they passed; she would have taken every one of them home with her if she could.

As they approached the final pen, its occupant, which Nell was delighted to see was a Maltese terrier like her own dog, struggled to her paws and padded over to say hello. She was clearly quite elderly, her eyes foggy with age and her movements stiff.

"Hey, honey," murmured Nell, petting her through the bars, then looked back at Carlee. "I have a Maltese back home. His name's Moomin."

"This here is Maggie," said Carlee. "She's what we call a lifer. She's been here over three years. She's a sweetheart, but she has a lot of health problems."

Maggie was now licking Nell's fingers and making excited little whimpering sounds.

"Would you look at that! She really likes you."

"Can I go in to see her?"

"Sure thing," said Carlee, and unbolted the gate.

As soon as Nell sat on the floor, Maggie placed her front paws on her leg and started sniffing her face.

"Hopefully we'll find someone who can take her on," said Carlee. "She was an ex-breeding bitch and had never known any love or kindness until she came here, poor girl. It would be so wonderful if she could live out the rest of her life in her own forever home."

Maggie had now rolled onto her back for a tickle, gazing adoringly up at Nell. Nell's heart lurched at the sight of the little dog's stomach, which was stretched and slack from overbreeding, and her eyes brimmed with tears.

"Oh, I'm sorry!" said Carlee. "I didn't mean to make you feel bad. It's just so nice to see Maggie showing so much interest in a new person. It's taken her a long time to trust us."

"I'm fine, honest," said Nell, wiping her face with a sleeve. "If only I lived here, I—"

Carlee smiled. "I understand. And don't worry about Maggie, she's very happy here. Way better than your old home, right, honey?"

Nell sat in Maggie's pen for nearly an hour, playing with her and then petting her as she curled up and went to sleep. She knew very well that the longer she stayed, the harder it would be to say goodbye, but she couldn't help it; the little dog had captured her heart, and she couldn't bear the thought of her being left alone again. When Carlee came back to get her, Nell had to fight back more tears. Maggie woke up as the bolt on the gate slid shut, her tail drooping as she watched Nell walked away; it took every ounce of Nell's resolve not to scoop her up and smuggle her out inside her jacket.

As they made their way back to the front office, Nell wrenched her thoughts away from Maggie (who she had resolved, somehow, she would give a home to) and instead found herself thinking about Megan, and how she must have walked this very same route all those years ago. She gazed around the shelter grounds—at the exercise yard, the brick building that housed the cattery, the grassy area where a volunteer was walking a pack of dogs—as if hoping to see some sort of evidence that Megan had once been here. Ridiculous, Nell knew, although a second later a rather less ridiculous idea occurred to her.

"Carlee, do you keep records of past animal adoptions?"

"We do. They go right back to the 1980s when the shelter opened."

"My friend adopted a dog from here when she was a child, about twenty-five years ago. Would it be possible to check if you still have the file?"

"Sure," said Carlee. They had now gotten back to reception, and she gestured to a door behind the desk. "Let me have a look out back. What was the family's surname?"

"Shaw. And the puppy was called Cyclops."

"Give me a moment."

Carlee disappeared into the back office. Through the open door, Nell could hear the clank and slide of filing cabinet drawers being opened, and a few minutes later Carlee returned carrying a slim cardboard file.

"You gotta love the filing system in this place," she said, holding out a photo. "Is this your friend?"

The picture was faded, its colors dulled with age, but the little girl in the picture was unmistakably Megan. She was sitting cross-legged on the floor of a pen and on her lap was a tiny scrap of a puppy: all black, except for a white forelock and a flash of his pink tongue. Seeing the delight on Megan's face, Nell broke into a smile, her fingers tracing her friend's familiar curls. She marveled at how she could come halfway around the world and still find traces of Megan; it was amazing how a life left its mark in all these tiny ways. Nell found this thought strangely soothing: Megan had gone, but she would live on—in people's memories, and in hidden treasures such as this photo.

Carlee glanced over Nell's shoulder. "Aw, look how happy she is! Do you know how it worked out with the puppy?"

"They adored each other. And Cyclops lived to a grand old age."

"Well, that's what makes this job so great! I'm really pleased it ended happily."

Nell looked back at the photo again. The month since Megan's death had been anything but happy—at times, Nell had even wondered if there was any point to life when it could be so cruelly snatched away—but seeing the joy lighting up the young Megan's face, it struck Nell that just because sooner or later we all die it doesn't cancel out the moments of happiness that come before, or make them any less important. In fact, it actually makes them more important. And she suddenly realized, with the passion of a eureka moment, that this was exactly the point Megan had been making in her original letter, but that Nell had been too grief-stricken to grasp at the time: that life can be glorious, and you need to grab hold of every moment and squeeze all the joy out of it while you can.

At once, she turned to Carlee. "Do you know if it would be possible for me to adopt Maggie and take her back to London?"

The young woman sucked in a mouthful of air. "I'm not sure, I know there are all sorts of regulations. I can check with the shelter's director and get back to you. Can you leave your phone number?"

Nell did so. "You've been incredibly helpful, thank you," she said.

"You're very much welcome. I hope we'll meet again."

As Nell walked back to the town, she wondered when exactly that might be. The idea of adopting the little dog seemed far-fetched, but perhaps, somehow, they could make it work. Feeling something soft against her cheek, she looked over her head. The pale gray sky had been threatening snow all morning and was now making good on its promise, but it was the perfect type of snow: not the spitty wet stuff that stung your face and hit the ground as rain, but voluptuous flakes like fat soft moths fluttering down to earth. The sort of snow that made powder for skiers and snow angels for children. Nell tipped her face up to the sky, enjoying the softness of the snowflakes brushing her skin. *Only three more days left in this magical place*, she thought sadly. Nell hadn't appreciated that you could fall in love with a place just as you could a person, but she knew for sure that the way she felt about Tansy Falls wasn't a passing flirtation. For some reason, she had a sudden memory of Sara, the woman she'd sat next to on the flight, who had been so enthusiastic about the idea of leaving your comfort zone. Had it really only been ten days ago that Nell had flatly dismissed that notion? Because, she realized, Sara had been absolutely right: out of your comfort zone *is* where the magic happens. So much had changed since that conversation it was as if Nell was a different woman living an entirely different life.

She came to a halt on the sidewalk as she saw she was right outside Fiske's: only three more days of being able to drop by on a whim for a coffee and a chat with Darlene! Without a second thought, Nell strode up the steps, but as she reached for the door it opened from the inside, and she came face to face with none other than Dewitt Hoffman.

Chapter Twenty-Two

"Well hello there, Miss Nell!" he boomed, in a voice that was, as ever, stuck in upper case. "How wonderful to see you!"

He didn't seem in the least bit uncomfortable at being spotted on enemy territory. Nell, however, was as flustered as if she were the one caught leaving the store of his wife's archenemy.

"Morning, Dewitt, how are you?"

"I'm just fine, thank you, ma'am." He beamed at her through the fuzz of his beard. "I better be getting on though. Damn milking machine's playing up, and I need to go down to Burlington to get a part. Will you be stopping by the farm again soon? Deb and I would love to see you."

"I'd love to, but I'm going home at the end of the week."

"Well, that's Tansy Falls' loss, for sure." Then he dropped his voice and grinned, his bushy white brows twitching as if to punctuate his point. "And certain other people's loss too..."

Nell could only smile and nod. Was he talking about Mallory?

"Now, I'm counting on you to come say goodbye before you go," Dewitt went on, waggling a finger.

"Of course, Dewitt."

"Excellent, excellent. See you then, my dear."

He stomped off, singing "Fly Me to the Moon" to himself (and to everyone else in a one-mile radius), and Nell watched as he hauled himself into his truck and puttered off. What on earth had Dewitt been doing here? The mystery of Tansy Falls just got a little more mysterious.

"Hey there, honey!" From behind the counter, Darlene gave Nell a wave that made her stack of bracelets and bangles drop down her arm with a heavy clunk. "Your timing is perfect. Chief Watkins's fly rod has finally arrived and I said I'd drop it by the station. Would you mind looking after the store? I'll only be five minutes."

"Of course, but—" Nell hesitated. "What was Dewitt Hoffman doing here?"

Darlene straightened up and flicked her long braid over her shoulder. "Shopping," she replied, an edge to her voice. "What did you *think* he was doing?"

"Well, I just wondered, because of the situation with you and Deb…"

She was also thinking of the rumors about Darlene and Dewitt, but knew better than to mention this.

"Last thing I heard, missy, it was a free country, and people can shop where they please." She fixed Nell with a stern look, indicating that the subject was most definitely closed. "Now, what do you say about minding the store for me? It'll save me having to shut up shop and throw out these customers." She gestured over to where a group was clustered around the display of local preserves. "They're most likely just rubberneckers but you never know."

"Of course. Mind if I help myself to coffee?"

"Absolutely. Have a cookie too," said Darlene. "I baked them at four a.m. this morning when I couldn't sleep."

Nell looked at her with concern.

"It's just age, sweetie. The closer you are to death, the less you need a preview. Anyway, I'll eat them all myself if you don't help me."

Darlene picked up the chief's rod and headed for the door, blowing a kiss over her shoulder. "Back soon!"

After pouring herself a coffee and taking two of the cookies, Nell sat on Darlene's stool. It felt odd being on this side of the counter for a change, and, taking a moment to have a look around, she was astonished to discover that from this vantage point you could see every part of the store, every hidden nook and secret cranny. Nell smiled at the old woman's ingenuity: as much as this place looked like a higgledy-piggledy labyrinth with zero logic to its layout, Darlene evidently knew exactly what she was doing—but then Nell really should have learned not to underestimate her by now.

She took a large gulp of coffee, and almost spat it out again. It was scalding hot and burned her lips. Sucking the tender skin and cursing her stupidity, she looked around for something to rest the mug on while it cooled, so as not to risk marking the wooden countertop. There was a stack of papers next to the till and she reached for whatever was on top to see if she could use it as a coaster. It only took a second for Nell to recognize the bound document with its laminated cover emblazoned with the familiar corporate logo. It was the DiSouza Developments valuation report.

Nell froze, staring at the document that had somehow found its way into her hands—through absolutely no fault of her own!—and her breath caught in her throat. *Put it back right away. This is none of your business.* Nevertheless, the shiny cover with its gold logo of two entwined letter "D"s lured her in, like a magpie eyeing up a shiny trinket, and before she could stop herself she lifted the corner of the cover and peeked at the first page. It was a list of contents. She glanced up at where the customers were still busy examining the preserves, and then over to the front door; Darlene had already been gone a couple of minutes; if she was going to do this, she would need to work fast.

Pulling out her phone, Nell worked methodically through the report, photographing each page in turn. She kept looking up to check if she had been caught—at the door, at the browsing customers—but nobody seemed to notice her crime. She was doing this for the right reasons, she kept telling herself, although she knew all too well that this wasn't the point; she was going against Darlene's wishes and she would be rightly furious if she found out. Still, it wasn't enough to stop her, and when she had finished Nell slipped the report back among the papers, feeling as guilt-ridden as if she'd pocketed the takings from the till.

Mere seconds later, the bell over the door jangled and Darlene reappeared.

"Well, the chief was very happy with the rod, and it's arrived just in time for the start of the trout-fishing season." She stopped to neaten up some bottles of salad dressing as she passed by. "Thank you so much for minding things here, Nell dear. Anything happen I should know about?"

Nell fiddled with her ear; she was not a good liar. "No, not really," she said.

Just a massive, outrageous betrayal; no biggie.

"I can't believe you'll be going home soon. You're becoming part of the furniture! I'm going to miss you very much, young lady." Darlene patted her hand, her eyes bright with emotion. "Would you come and have dinner with me on your last night here?"

Nell felt her heart sink, disloyalty crushing down on her like a physical weight. "I'd love to, thank you," she muttered, staring at her feet. She had to get out of there before she crumbled and ended up confessing everything to Darlene, which, judging by the whirlpool currently whipping up her insides, seemed highly likely. "Well, I better get going, lots to do," she said, with a chirpiness that even to her ears sounded fake. "See you later, Darlene! Have a great day!"

Then she scuttled out, head dipped, before Darlene could notice her red cheeks and trembling hands.

Back at the Covered Bridge, Nell vaulted up the stairs two at a time in her haste to look at the photos. Housekeeping had already been around and her bed was made, the candy-colored scatter cushions arranged perfectly across the pillows. Nell wrenched off her boots and coat, threw herself among the pile of cushions and, her heart thumping away in the stillness of the room, opened the file on her phone.

It took nearly an hour to read and process all the pages: the report was dense with information, most of it, to Nell's expert eyes, completely irrelevant. She got the impression that the authors were trying to bury the important stuff under an avalanche of waffle, so that neither Darlene nor Ted Libby would notice that the wool was being pulled over their eyes—which, as Nell had feared, it most certainly was.

It wasn't that Liza DiSouza was doing anything illegal. She had detailed all the necessary information in the report, providing a valuation of the store based on its assets (the store and its resources) and another valuation based on cashflow, reflecting Fiske's future prospects. As Fiske's was clearly quite a successful business, the cashflow valuation was far higher than the asset value: again, all perfectly standard and above board. The problem, and it was a big one, came on the very last page of the report, on which was listed the final figure DiSouza Developments was offering Darlene to buy the store. Rather than a fair combination of the two valuations, as would be expected, they had based their offer solely on the net asset value, thereby undervaluing Fiske's by almost a half. Worse still, if they were only offering what it was worth in terms of real estate, Nell felt certain that this confirmed they had no intention of keeping Fiske's trading as a store.

Nell threw the phone on the bed and put her head in her hands. She was in an impossible position. Darlene had made it crystal-clear that she didn't want Nell getting involved, it was a point of principle for her. She had run the store by herself for decades—and done an excellent job of it too, judging by the details of the report—and so of course she didn't want some jumped-up know-it-all Englishwoman pushing in and bossing her about.

On the other hand, could Nell really stay silent about what she'd found? Not only did it look very much like DiSouza Developments was planning to close the store, it was trying to cheat Darlene out of a large amount of money that was rightfully hers.

Nell nibbled on her thumbnail, her brain ping-ponging back and forth between the two options, neither of which were attractive. Perhaps, she thought, with a sudden surge of hope, Ted Libby would step in and save the day after all? Sure, he was a little doddery, but Nell had spotted what DiSouza Developments was up to as soon as she opened the final page—hell, even a high school business major would have noticed it—so hopefully Ted would see it too. The problem was, though, when it came to Ted Libby, the sweet old attorney's questionable eyesight was the least of Nell's numerous concerns.

No, it looked like it was going to be down to her to make sure Darlene discovered what was going on.

Chapter Twenty-Three

On your marks, get set, go: today is sports day! Honey, I can see you rolling your eyes at me so forcefully right now. I get it—you're not sporty; I have loved you long enough to know that. But you can't come to Tansy Falls and not at least get on a pair of skis. Or a snowboard. Hell, even a sled will do. The important thing is that you get out and enjoy the slopes of the best mountain in North America—if not the world—Mount Maverick. And maybe while you're up there, enjoying the rush of the wind as it whips your hair, and the smoosh of your face as it hits the snow (Haha! Just kidding!), you can have a little recon and find a final resting place for me. Somewhere cozy and quiet with a stunning view, if you please...

"Would you like a top-off, Nell?"

She looked up from her day's itinerary to see Shae, the waitress who was always on duty at breakfast, standing at her table with a jug of pink grapefruit juice. Nell had met Shae on her first morning in Tansy Falls, when she'd given her directions to Darlene's store, and every day they'd spoken a little more, until she had told her all about Megan's itinerary.

As she topped off her glass, Shae gestured to the sheet Nell was holding. "So what's she got you doing today?"

"She wants me to go skiing on Maverick."

"Ooh, fun!" Then Shae registered Nell's expression and frowned. "Not fun?"

Nell shook her head. "I'm not very good at sports."

"Me neither." Shae glanced around, then leaned toward Nell and quietly confessed: "I've worked here all winter and haven't been on skis once."

Nell took in the girl's sculpted arms and slender figure. "Well, you certainly look sporty."

"I teach Pilates and yoga at the rec. I prefer my activity without a risk of life-changing injury." She tapped her chin. "Didn't you go to Maverick the other day? Surely that counts, even if you weren't actually on skis."

Nell gave this some thought. "Yeah, perhaps you're right."

Thanks to Brody she had already found Megan the perfect resting place; besides, there was something else she had to do today, something she had a feeling Megan would agree was infinitely more important than getting a bruised butt on the slopes of Maverick. Today was the morning of Nell's date with Jackson.

It wasn't really a *date* date though, she told herself, heading back to her room after breakfast. Jackson had made it clear that he had invited her around simply so that Nell could fulfill her promise to Megan. He was a kind man doing the decent thing—that was all there was to it. As much as she'd like to fantasize otherwise, there was zero chance of any actual first-date stuff occurring. No prospect of one of those wonderfully sprawling conversations where you're discovering everything about the other person and it's all so fascinating you feel as if you could talk all night. No hope of any lingering glances where your eyes meet and you can literally feel the electricity crackling between you. And definitely no chance of all the talking and glances and anticipation building up to that delicious moment when you realize you're about to kiss...

Nell paused, her hand gripping the banister of the staircase, waiting for the effects of this particular thought to fade. Dragging herself back to reality, she continued trudging up the stairs, giving herself a talking-to about not losing her head over Jackson. Still, this time when they met she was at least going to be looking her best: no muddy cheeks, frizzy hair or her mother's hand-me-down hiking gear today, that was for sure.

After a long shower, Nell blow-dried her hair until her arm ached and her rumpled bob was tamed into sleek strawberry-gold waves that caught the morning sunlight pouring in through the window. She sprayed clouds of the musky rose-heavy perfume that had lain ignored in her suitcase for the past ten days, then applied enough makeup for it to look as if she weren't wearing any. After deliberating for a solid half hour, she dressed in gray skinny jeans and a black turtleneck that struck just about the right balance of practicality and sexiness. It was a shame about the yellow boots, but it was either those or white sneakers, and she didn't want Jackson to think she was a city girl who didn't know how to dress for the outdoors, even though he'd probably already worked out that was exactly what she was. Besides, Nell reckoned she would probably leave her boots at the front door when Jackson invited her in. Rifling through her socks to find the least holey pair, she imagined padding across the polished floorboards of his hallway, following him into his kitchen where she'd sit at the counter while Jackson (who, in her vision, had his sleeves rolled up, revealing his strong, tanned forearms) busied himself making coffee with the confidence of a man who knows his way around a kitchen just as well as he does a circular saw.

Nell shook her head, dislodging the daydream. She needed to get a grip: Jackson was doing a favor to a bereaved woman, and that was all there was to it. After taking one final look in the mirror, she grabbed the jacket she'd borrowed from Mallory and the bottle of whiskey she had bought as a thank-you gift for Jackson and headed for the door.

Downstairs, Connie was sitting at the wooden reception table talking to a young couple who appeared to be checking in. Judging by their entwined fingers and gooey-eyed smiles it was their first trip away together. At one point the man leaned over and brushed his fingers on the woman's cheek, looking at her in such a tender way that it wrenched Nell's heart. *Would anyone ever look at me like that again?* she wondered. It was almost a relief when the lovebirds got up and wandered, hand-in-hand, toward the restaurant.

"Morning, Nell, how are you?" Connie's brown eyes shone with genuine pleasure as she greeted her. "Goodness, don't you look lovely? Off someplace special?"

"Oh, just to see a friend," said Nell quickly, embarrassed to admit the reason she'd gone to so much effort.

"Well, you have a great day," said the manager.

The drive to the old Philpott house seemed to go more quickly every time she did it, and within minutes Nell was turning off Birdsong Hill at the red mailbox, her insides alive with butterflies. She piloted Sue Ellen carefully down the narrow driveway (now pothole-free, thanks to Joe's grading efforts) and parked near the outbuildings, planning to walk the rest of the way to calm her nerves. Nell noticed green shoots poking through the blanket of fallen pine needles under the trees and splashes of pink and white flowers where the sunlight had made its way to the ground through the canopy of branches. Spring was stirring; the snow and mud would soon be gone, and this little piece of paradise would soon be lush and bursting with life. A sudden noise made Nell turn to see a large white bird slowly lifting into the sky nearby, its wings beating the stillness. Watching it go, she took a deep breath, savoring the smell of woodsmoke and wet earth saturating the air, and the powerful effect this ancient woodland seemed to have on her soul, which currently felt as if it was soaring over the trees like the white bird.

Ahead of her, the house sat in a clearing among the spruce and maple trees, opening out onto a broad meadow bordered by the dark line of the creek. At her first proper look of the house, Nell let out a gasp of delight. The walls were the soft silver-gray of cygnet feathers, while the ornate pilasters and embellishments decorating the gables and wraparound porch looked like they'd been plucked straight off a gingerbread house. It certainly wasn't the sort of place you'd expect to find a man like Jackson Quaid—it had more of a Little Red Riding Hood vibe—but he clearly took excellent care of it. Pots planted with spring flowers sat under the porch and a swing-bench hung outside one of the side windows, offering the perfect spot to sit and gaze at the slopes of Maverick, while a thread of smoke curled from the peach-colored brick chimney, fueled, no doubt, by the stack of perfectly chopped logs near the door. It couldn't have looked more welcoming if there had been a banner reading WELCOME NELL! draped over the shingle roof.

As she climbed the front steps Nell smiled to see the pairs of boots, both big and small, lined up outside. She hesitated at the front door, brushing her fingers through her hair and smoothing down her clothes, then she swung open the screen and knocked. At first, she didn't think anyone could have heard, as she'd tapped so gently, but moments later there was the sound of footsteps from inside and then the door opened—to reveal a woman Nell had never seen before, but recognized instantly. She was tall and slim, probably in her midthirties, but with the long blonde hair, freckled cheekbones and cute little nose of the high school cheerleading captain Nell remembered Mallory telling her she had once been.

"Can I help you?" she asked.

So this must be Cindy: Joe's mom and the woman who apparently had broken Jackson's heart—and was now at risk of trampling over Nell's too.

"Um, hello!" Nell stammered. "Is Jackson in?"

Cindy rested her hand on the doorframe. "He's in the office working." She glanced at the whiskey Nell was holding and her brow raised slightly.

"Would it be possible to have a quick word with him?"

"He's busy, I probably shouldn't disturb him."

Just then Joe's voice called from somewhere inside. "Mommy! Are you coming?"

"Be there in a minute, honey," Cindy replied, turning her head slightly, but with her gaze still fixed on Nell, as if to make sure she wasn't going to attempt to sneak inside the house. With a jolt, Nell noticed she was still wearing a wedding band, and she remembered what Mallory had said on the day of their museum trip: "I wouldn't be at all surprised if Jackson's still holding a torch for Cindy, even after everything she's done…"

"I'm sorry," said Cindy, looking far from it, "but I need to go and help my son. Would you like me to pass on a message to Jackson?"

"Um, maybe just tell him that Nell stopped by."

"Nell? Sure, I'll mention it." Judging by her blank face, Jackson hadn't told Cindy she was coming; he'd probably forgotten all about it, thought Nell miserably.

"Thank you," said Nell, but the door had already closed.

She turned and headed back toward Sue Ellen, her heart sinking a little further with every step. In a gap through the trees, she glimpsed the tire swing hanging over the creek; well, at least she could tick that off, she thought, with an attempt at cheerfulness, although even that didn't stop the rapidly descending gloom.

Back in the car, Nell sat with her hands on the wheel, unable to bring herself to drive away. This was the last time she would be here, she realized, an ache in her chest; she didn't want to think too hard about whether it was the place itself she was going to miss or the man who lived here. She eyed the bottle of whiskey, tempted to take a medicinal swig even though she hated the stuff.

"Damn you, Jackson Quaid," she muttered, a lump squeezing her throat. Nell gripped the wheel, taking breaths to compose herself. It wasn't Jackson's fault that she couldn't distinguish between fantasy and reality. He'd done absolutely nothing to make her believe he was interested in her, after all.

She caught her reflection in the rearview mirror: the makeup she'd been so proud of earlier now looked fake, as if she was trying to turn herself into someone she could never be, and she rubbed her hand across her mouth, smearing the lipstick across her cheek. This wasn't her life: Jackson, the mountain, Mallory, Darlene—they were nothing to do with her. The past few days had simply been a break from reality, and in a few days' time she would be back in London and it would be as if Tansy Falls and its inhabitants didn't even exist.

Nell squared her shoulders and turned the key in the ignition. She was fine, she told herself, as she drove back up the driveway too fast, the wheels skidding on loose dirt. For the two days she had left in town, she wouldn't let any stupid fantasies distract her from what was important: finishing Megan's itinerary, which, after all, was the reason she was here in the first place. And then she would go back home to her job, and her not-quite-right apartment, and her life would carry on exactly as it had before. And that, thought Nell, gritting her teeth, would be absolutely *fine*.

Chapter Twenty-Four

Nell woke early the next morning, her head throbbing and mouth as parched as if she'd spent a night dancing on tables and downing tequila, rather than going to bed at 9 p.m. with a hot chocolate and Robyn Carr on her e-reader, which is how she'd actually spent last night. Staring at the ceiling, she tried to remember the last time she'd danced on a table; she had a vague recollection of a dark club and thumping music, giggling with Megan over a spilled vodka, but it had been so many years ago she couldn't recall the exact details. Perhaps she was imagining it.

Nell sighed, dissatisfaction prickling at her insides; she really should have done more dancing on tables when she was younger, and less worrying about what other people would think if she did. Well, it was too late now, she thought, rolling over to retrieve her phone, where to her surprise she discovered a text message from Brody Knott—well, not a message, so much as an exclamation.

Yo.

Nell frowned at the screen. Was that it? Well, she could do brevity too. She typed a similarly snappy response—*Hey*—and threw the phone among the bedsheets, stretching out so that her fingers touched the headboard and her toes stuck out the bottom of the duvet. It felt good, and her grumpiness began to recede a little.

From somewhere within the duvet, there was the muffled beep of another new message.

What are you up to today?

Nell rubbed her eyes; what *was* she up to? Ah yes, that was it.

I'm visiting the Tansy Falls waterfall.

There was a sequence of dots on the screen, showing that Brody was typing a response. Five minutes later they were still there. Was he writing an essay?

Eventually, a reply appeared.

Cool.

And then, seconds later:

Can I come too?

Nell stared at the message, trying to assess how she felt about this. After yesterday, she had vowed to focus on the itinerary without any distractions, but there was no denying that Brody had been very useful finding a place for Megan's ashes. Surely there was no harm in letting him tag along for the morning; he would probably make the trip more fun, and perhaps he'd take her mind off Jackson Quaid.

Sure. 10 a.m.?

This time, Brody's response was immediate.

Great. I'll meet you in the gorge parking lot. It's about a half-hour hike up to the falls. See you then, Lady Penelope.

*

The town of Tansy Falls gets its name from a waterfall in the woods near Mount Maverick, where the Wild Moose River meets a rocky hillside and takes a spectacular running jump. It's known as Smugglers Leap and is a popular spot on hot summer days when the foot of the falls is like a natural whirlpool spa and the rocks around the pool are draped with sunbathers. My favorite time to visit, though, is in the colder months: the hike up through the gorge is beautiful, and you'll probably have the place to yourself. Just make sure to wear sensible footwear!

Nell glanced down at her yellow boots in Sue Ellen's footwell and smiled. *One step ahead of you, Meg,* she thought, as she pulled off the road and into a parking lot that was empty apart from a shiny egg-yolk-yellow Jeep.

Brody got out while she parked and leaned against his car, arms folded. He was wearing a woolly beanie, his blond hair poking out haphazardly beneath, and Nell was struck again by the golden-boy good looks that seemed to be catnip to most women. It was almost a relief to know she'd never be the target of his famous seductive powers, because she imagined that if he put his mind to it Brody Knott could be quite hard to resist.

"Nice wheels," he said, as she got out of the car.

"She belongs to Darlene Fiske."

"Oh yeah, you and Darlene are friends, right?" Brody said, rubbing at an invisible spot of dirt on his car with his elbow. "She's not my greatest fan," he added, although judging by his grin this didn't trouble him overly much. He walked round to the back of the Jeep and popped the trunk.

"Any idea why?" asked Nell.

"She had a falling-out with my dad years ago over some land, and Darlene isn't one to forgive and forget. The sins of the father and all that." Brody shrugged, rummaging in the trunk. "It's not a big deal. I'm sure she loves me really." He pulled out a large backpack and slammed the trunk. "Are you ready to go?"

Nell put her hands on her hips. "I am. But haven't you forgotten something?"

Brody frowned, looking at his rucksack. "I've got binoculars, a compass, penknife, a flask of coffee, emergency flare and a sleeping bag in case we get stranded—although I've only brought the one, so I guess we'll have to squeeze in together and share body heat."

He gave his best smoldering look, and Nell tried not to laugh.

"We had a deal, Knott." She folded her arms, mock stern. "The ice cream?"

"Oh, that!" He rummaged in his rucksack. "Well, I figured ice cream wouldn't last the drive, so I took a gamble and brought these instead: Mistyflip's peanut-butter-banana donuts." He held up a brown paper bag. "Can I still come with you? Please?"

Nell thought for a moment. "I suppose donuts will do, just this once."

"Excellent!" Brody shouldered the rucksack and nodded toward a gap in the trees. "Come on, city girl, let's go."

The trail through the forest was carefully marked and well maintained; in some parts, logs had been sunk in the earth to mark the path's border, while in others planks had been propped up to create raised walkways over boggy areas. There was a kaleidoscopic assortment of trees here: squat spruce sat among the gray-brown trunks of sugar maples and elegantly slender beech, while the white pines, with their fluttering tassels of needles, soared high overhead, making Nell feel pleasingly tiny and insignificant.

They walked on in companionable silence, Nell tracking Brody's footsteps; he always knew exactly where to tread to avoid ending up knee-deep in a bog or trampling the pale green blades of new growth. Although the forest felt like a welcoming place, bright with birdsong and sunlight, Nell was glad that Brody was with her. It was a remote spot—in fifteen minutes they hadn't passed another soul—and she would have spent a lot of time mistaking innocent trees for serial killers if she'd been here on her own.

Up ahead, Brody took a sudden detour off the path. "Look at this," he said, crouching down near a tree and beckoning Nell over. "I promised you a nature walk," he said, and pointed to a splay of young foliage in the middle of which a strange mottled brown-and-purple leaf was unfurling. While Nell watched, Brody rubbed the leaf between his fingers, and she caught a sudden whiff of a foul smell that made her hand fly to her mouth. "What is that?" she asked, eyes bulging.

"Skunk cabbage. Also known as clumpfoot cabbage, polecat weed and swamp cabbage."

"Wow," Nell boggled. "Its mother must have really loved it. Couldn't she have just gone with 'Bob'?"

Brody chuckled. "It's actually a fascinating plant. It can generate heat, which means it can melt its way up through the icy ground, so it's one of the first to flower in spring. That smell is to attract pollinating insects."

Nell looked at him, impressed. "You know an awful lot about young Bob here."

"This place was like my backyard when I was growing up and you pick things up over the years." Brody stood up, stretched, and headed back to the path. "Not too far now," he said over his shoulder.

The path started to climb more steeply and the ground underfoot became muddier. In most places there were rocks they could use as stepping stones, but at one point Brody had to offer Nell his hand to help her jump over a particular squelchy bit. She slipped as she landed, but Brody's grip kept her from falling, and she got a sense of just how strong he was.

"You okay?" he asked, his blue eyes fixed on hers.

"Yes, thank you, sir," she replied, bobbing a curtsey, smiling to herself at the thought of all the women who would love to play at being the helpless maiden to Brody Knott's knight in shining armor.

"Hey, check this out!" Like a dog catching a scent, Brody had bounded off into the undergrowth again. When Nell finally caught up with him, she found him cradling clusters of dainty white flowers. "These are Dutchman's breeches," he told her, with the sort of enthusiasm most men reserved for sports and beer.

"You're making these names up," said Nell.

"I'm not, honestly! Take a closer look."

She leaned in and sure enough the flowers looked exactly like tiny white pairs of pants hanging from a washing-line of twisty green tendrils.

"They're beautiful!" She glanced up at him, beaming, their faces just a few inches apart. "Brody, you are an excellent nature walk guide. Thank you."

"You're very welcome. I'll have a think about how you can pay me back." He shot her a jokily suggestive wink; laughing, Nell bashed his arm.

They set off again, still tramping steadily upward. Between the slalom of tree trunks, Nell could now see the river: the Wild Moose ran a little wilder here, tumbling over large rocks, the dark water crested with white as it crashed downhill.

"You're actually supposed to stay off the Wilderness Trail until after Memorial Day," said Brody, hopping over a fallen branch, "because the snowmelt can make it so muddy."

"Hang on, this is part of the Wilderness Trail?"

"Yeah." He turned to look at her. "Do you know it?"

Nell's face lit up, a warm glow spreading through her insides: she was following in the footsteps of Polly Swift! She looked at the forest with a renewed sense of wonder; these may well be the exact same trees that Polly had hiked past nearly a hundred ago.

"I read all about it in an exhibit at the Tansy Falls museum," she said, still gazing around.

"Whoa, Megan sent you there?" He screwed up his face. "What did you do to piss her off?"

Nell laughed, remembering Mallory's similar reaction. "It was actually pretty interesting."

"Yeah," muttered Brody, turning back to the trail, "if you're into dust and dead farmers."

Nell heard the waterfall long before she saw it. As they followed the river up through the gorge, the rushing sound got louder, until the trees gave way to a clearing and Nell found herself standing at the foot of the falls. It was no Niagara—you could have sat underneath the cascading water and just got a vigorous massage—but Mother Nature had clearly gone to a lot of trouble to make the scene picture-perfect. The falls tumbled down into a rocky grotto, at the bottom of which was a large pool, emerald green in the center, crystal-clear in its shallows, surrounded by large smooth boulders and overhung by branches that were bare now, but would be bowed down with garlands of green in less than a month's time.

"This is Smugglers Leap, the lower tier of the falls," explained Brody, gazing up at where the water tipped over the rim. "The rocks are too slippery at the moment, otherwise I'd take you up and show you the other cascades." He shrugged. "Still, a decent place for coffee, right?"

Nell nodded, bewitched by the view. "It's beautiful," she murmured.

Thank you, Meg, she added silently. *And thank you, Polly, too. Have you guys bumped into each other up there? Because I really think you'd get along . . .*

Brody had already hopped onto the largest of the boulders and pulled out a tarpaulin from his backpack, which he spread over the damp surface.

"Ma'am," he said, holding out a hand to help Nell jump across and join him.

They sat together in easy silence, drinking coffee and eating donuts, which felt like more than a fair reward for the hike up there.

The rushing sound of the water was hypnotic, and Nell felt a blissful heaviness in her limbs and a lightness in her spirits as she leaned back against Brody's bag.

Her eyes had drifted shut and she was in that lovely floaty trance that comes just before sleep, when Brody spoke, jolting her back to consciousness. "How many more days have we got you for?" he asked.

"Two," she replied, opening her eyes.

Brody stared into the water, deep in thought. "Well, that's a damn shame." He picked up a pebble and threw it in the pool.

Surprised by the emotion in his voice, Nell struggled up to sitting and looked at him, but his eyes were fixed on the circular ripples spreading across the pool. Unsure how to respond, she turned back to watch them too, the churning of the falls filling the silence.

After a moment, she sensed Brody shift his position and then take a breath. "Nell," he said, carefully, "I really want see you again."

Nell tensed, her chest tightening; not just at Brody's words, but at his tone, which was unusually serious.

Risking another glance, Nell discovered Brody was now looking directly at her. Holding her gaze, he moved his hand from where it had been resting on his knees and placed it over hers. Nell realized she was holding her breath; she was no longer sure if the hissing sound in her ears was from the water or the emotions churning inside her. Brody brushed his thumb across the back of her hand, and her skin smarted as if it were raw.

"Would you come to dinner with me tonight?" he asked. "As my date?"

Nell was lost somewhere between shock and confusion. She had been so certain that Brody had zero interest in her romantically that she had no idea how to respond. Her first instinct was to refuse: she liked him—he was fun, great company and, of course, unarguably attractive—but she hadn't thought about him in *that* way at all. Her mind had been too full of Jackson Quaid. Besides, she'd seen the way other women who came into Brody's orbit looked at him, the hungry eyes and hair flicks. She had no interest in becoming another notch on Mr. Maverick's undoubtedly notch-heavy bedpost. But (and it was a very persuasive "but") perhaps an evening of fun with Tansy Falls' most eligible bachelor was exactly what her bruised ego needed. She was going back to London in two days' time, and it wasn't as if Jackson was likely to phone up to pledge undying love anytime soon. In fact, Nell was beginning to wonder why she was even hesitating.

"Okay," she said, relieved her voice didn't sound as shaky as she felt. "That would be fun, thank you."

He broke into a grin. "Excellent. You know, I think Megan planned this all along—us meeting up and getting on so well. She's probably up there making it happen."

Nell thought back to what Megan had written about Brody in her letter: "Man, he was trouble..." Would she have approved of her going on a date with him? Nell wasn't at all sure, and she knew for a fact that Mallory would have something to say about it. But then she had a flashback to lying in bed that morning and remembered the regret she'd felt at opportunities she'd missed over the years, all because she'd been too worried about what other people might think. With a nudge of stubbornness she jutted her chin, her mind made up. Brody had proved himself to be a good friend over the past few days, and you'd have to be one of these boulders not to fall for his blue-eyed charm just a little. And who knows, she might just end up dancing on tables tonight after all.

Chapter Twenty-Five

Just before 8 p.m. that evening, Nell pulled up outside the Black Bear. She had decided she would drive to prevent herself from doing anything stupid after one too many drinks; not that she was discounting the possibility of doing something stupid, but she wanted to have chosen to do it, rather than being talked into it by a friendly tequila.

It was a cold and clear evening, and as Nell got out of the car she could just about make out the shape of Maverick. The rest of the valley was in darkness apart from scattered pinpricks of light from distant buildings and the welcoming glow in the Black Bear's windows.

The parking lot was far busier than last time she was here, and Nell could hear music and laughter coming from inside the bar. Her belly was alive with nerves, yet she felt weirdly liberated, as if for once in her life she was doing the fun thing rather than the right thing, and she strode up to the door of the bar with her head held high. Her hair was tied in a high ponytail and she was wearing skinny jeans and heeled boots: when she'd checked her reflection in the mirror she had felt she was just a Stetson and a "yeehaw" short of the full cowgirl. It was a look that suited her mood tonight.

The room was packed with drinkers and diners, but she spotted Brody instantly. He was in the exact same place he'd been sitting last time, his elbows propped on the bar, a bottle of beer in hand, talking to the bartender, who this evening was a pretty young woman in a clingy tank top with long wavy hair. Nell recognized the expression on the girl's face, the sparkly eyes and pouting lips: the Brody Knott effect in all its glory. As Nell watched, Brody glanced in her direction and broke into a grin, the hot bartender seemingly forgotten, and Nell stood a little taller and walked toward him with the confidence of knowing she was being watched and admired.

"Hey," said Brody, standing to greet her. He put his hands on her shoulders and slowly leaned in; for a split second she thought he was about to kiss her, but instead he put his mouth to her ears, his lips brushing her skin, and murmured, "You look gorgeous."

Nell had to smother a giggle; she was still a little unnerved by this new seductive Brody.

"Thank you," she said, "you look"—she stepped back, making a show of looking him up and down—"okay, I guess."

Brody laughed, raking a hand through his tousled golden hair, although his eyes had a hungry look that put Nell in mind of a lion sizing up a lame zebra. It made her wonder how the night might end. "What can I get you to drink?"

Nell was already regretting her decision to drive; if she was going to be the person Brody seemed to think she was, then she needed some alcohol. She chewed her lip, her eyes running over the bottles of spirits. Just the one would be okay, she was sure of it, especially as they were going to be eating later.

"A vodka and tonic, thank you."

"Coming right up, ma'am."

As Brody signaled to the bartender, Nell leaned her back against the bar so she could look out at the room, her nerves easing and her face softening into a smile. The bar area was slightly raised, giving her a view of the whole room, so it was an excellent spot for people-watching, and a rowdy crowd sitting at a large table near the back caught her eye. Judging by the ski jackets draped over their chairs and the clutter of helmets, gloves and goggles on the table, they had come here straight from the slopes, but as Nell was idly trying to work out whether they were locals or tourists, her attention was snagged by a familiar-looking kid walking past their table. Was that...? With a plummeting feeling, Nell registered that, yes, it was most definitely Joe Quaid. The little boy was alone, perhaps returning from a visit to the bathroom; Nell held her breath as she watched him make his way through the room, weaving around other diners until he arrived at his own table, where, to her horror, was Jackson.

Her heart hammering away as if she'd just run a sprint, Nell ducked her head and shrunk against the bar as if she could blend into the woodwork. Had he seen her? She risked a glance over her shoulder, but Jackson was entirely focused on Joe, who was tackling an enormous milkshake.

"Here you go," said Brody, handing Nell her drink. Thankfully he didn't seem to notice that she was currently in fight-or-flight mode. "Let's grab a table."

And then Brody set off in the exact direction of Joe and Jackson, leaving Nell with no alternative to follow, trying to hide behind him as they went. Her gaze skittered around the room, trying to work out where they might be headed, and she let out a huge breath as she spotted their likely destination: an empty table for two, helpfully positioned behind a large pillar. Sure enough, as they approached she could see a sign propped against a glass that said RESERVED FOR BRODY KNOTT in large letters. The sign was laminated; clearly, it got a lot of use.

"The Black Bear's owner, Tanner, is a buddy of mine," explained Brody, as he pulled out a chair for Nell, thankfully the one that meant she'd be sitting with her back to the Quaids.

Still, she could sense Jackson's presence behind her like a furnace, radiating heat, and she was jittery at the idea there might be tap on her shoulder at any moment. She took a gulp of vodka, desperate for the mellowing effects of the alcohol to kick in.

"Hi, Brody." A waitress appeared at their table, hugging the menus to her chest, her fingers twirling her hair.

"How you doing, Donna?" Brody flashed a grin. "Busy in here tonight."

"Sure is." She continued to stare and smile, as if waiting in line for a rock star's autograph; Nell, meanwhile, was clearly just a roadie in this scenario.

After a long moment, Brody cleared his throat. "Um, could we take a look at the menus?"

"Sure thing." Donna rattled off the night's specials, topped off their water glasses and then, with a fluttery wave in Brody's direction, left them to it.

At that moment Brody's cellphone, which was sitting on the table, vibrated with a message, and while he checked the screen Nell took the opportunity to glance behind her. It looked like Jackson was paying the check; with any luck, they would be gone in a few moments. She felt her shoulders relax down from where they'd been jammed up around her ears.

"Sorry about that," said Brody, replacing his phone on the table, face-down. "So what would you like to eat? The chef, Mauricio, is Mexican, he does a fantastic carne alambre. And perhaps we could share some of the—"

"Nell!"

At the sound of the child's voice, Nell stiffened and her eyes closed. Forcing herself to turn around, she saw Joe running toward her, pumped up with sugar and excitement, while following behind was Jackson. Their eyes locked briefly, and even though she was still licking her wounds over what had happened at his house yesterday, it was like an arrow straight to her heart.

"Nell!" Joe bounced up to her, oblivious to any adult awkwardness. "We've just had burgers and shakes and Dad let me stay out a whole hour past my bedtime!"

"Wow, lucky you!" She beamed at him, then forced herself to look again at Jackson. "Hi, how are you?" she asked, as brightly as she could manage.

"I'm good, thanks," he muttered. He had his hands shoved in his pockets and his gaze was flicking toward the door, clearly finding this just as uncomfortable as she was.

Leaning back in his chair, Brody raised his bottle at Jackson. "Hey, man, how you doing?"

"Brody." His mouth twitched in an aborted attempt at a smile. Perhaps Nell was imagining it, but she was sure she caught a sadness in his eyes, and the sight of it brought an echoing twist of emotion inside her. Had Cindy even told him that she'd been to the house yesterday?

"Well, I better get Joe home to bed. Have a good night." Jackson glanced at her, hesitating for a moment. "Nell, I . . ." he trailed off.

"Yes?" she asked, her pulse quickening. She was desperate for him to ask what had happened to her visit yesterday, perhaps suggest they meet up tomorrow, just to give her the chance to explain. Because, if she was being honest with herself, the person Nell really wanted sitting opposite her tonight was Jackson Quaid.

As he opened his mouth to speak she held her breath, but after a moment he just looked away again.

Brody cleared his throat. "Good to see you, Jackson." There was an edge to his voice.

Jackson nodded briefly, aware he was being dismissed. "Enjoy the rest of your stay," he said to Nell, and then quickly steered Joe toward the exit.

Brody watched him go. "Jeez, for a Californian that guy sure is uptight. I have no idea how he ever got together with Cindy."

Nell was still staring at the doorway where she had her last glimpse of Jackson, a dull ache in her chest. Perhaps she should go after him and tell him how she felt? But no, the moment had passed. She turned her attention back to Brody.

"Do you think Jackson will ever get back with her?" She couldn't help asking, even though it hardly mattered anymore.

"With Cindy?" Brody shrugged. "Who knows? She was never right for him. Too wild. Jackson's a real stand-up member of society, but Cindy—man, that girl's always been a free spirit." He chuckled, taking a swig of his beer. "Anyway, enough about Jackson Quaid. I want to hear about you, Penelope. Tell me about your home in London. Tell me about your family. Tell me *everything*."

Nell looked into Brody's face in all its square-jawed, cushion-lipped glory. He was beaming at her, his eyes sparkling, as if she was the most fascinating woman in existence.

"Okay," she said, relaxing into a smile. "But first of all, how about another drink?"

Chapter Twenty-Six

As they talked, the vodka began to work its magic and Nell let herself be swept away by Brody's charm avalanche. He laughed at her jokes, showered her with compliments and seemed to find her endlessly fascinating in a way that no man had since the early days of her relationship with her ex, Adrian—and even that had been a pale version of Brody's turbocharged charisma. He made her feel good about herself in a way that she really needed after Jackson's indifference.

They had just ordered food when Brody's phone buzzed again. He tutted and glanced at the screen, but immediately turned his focus back to Nell, leaning toward her and brushing a strand of hair off her face, his fingers lingering ever so slightly on her cheek. It was such an intimate gesture that it set off a shiver of anticipation inside her.

Brody smiled at her reaction, then propped his forearms on the table. "Nell, the other day, when we were visiting the new lodge development, you mentioned the fact that Darlene was selling the store."

"Oh," said Nell, surprised by the sudden change of subject. "I did, yes."

"You seemed kind of worried about it."

Nell rubbed her neck, unsure whether she should discuss her concerns with Brody. "I just get the impression that Liza DiSouza isn't being entirely straight with Darlene."

"In what way?"

"Well, I can't really be sure"—Nell didn't want to confess to Brody just how much she knew, as she'd have to admit to snooping—"but I'm not sure she's offering her a fair price. Plus, I don't think she intends to keep Fiske's as a store, which I know is really important to Darlene. I just want to make sure Liza DiSouza is being honest with her."

"I get your concerns. There are always going to be some tough decisions when a big company like DiSouza Developments invests in a small town like Tansy Falls. You've got to find that balance between building a better future without trampling all over the past."

"Exactly," said Nell. "And I'm not convinced Ms. DiSouza gets that."

Brody sighed, raking a hand through his hair. "Look, you're protective of Darlene because Megan loved her. I get that. But this isn't your town, Nell. You don't know the history of the place. You've not even been here for two weeks!" He leaned forward, his eyes fixed on hers. "Take it from someone who's lived in Tansy Falls his whole life: if DiSouza Developments doesn't buy Fiske's, nobody else will. Darlene can't afford to be sentimental about it."

Brody's phone buzzed yet again and he rolled his eyes. "Sorry about this. I'd turn it off, but I'm on call tonight. Mountain rescue business."

"Don't worry, it's fine," muttered Nell as he checked the message, her mind still on their conversation about Fiske's. "Um, Brody, what if I had some . . . *specific* information about the sale of the store, that I knew was being kept from Darlene. Don't you think I should tell her?"

Brody frowned. "What kind of information?"

"I can't really say." Nell shifted in her seat. "But it's pretty damning."

"Has Darlene asked for your advice?"

"No," she admitted.

"Has she told you she wants your help with this at all?"

Nell stared at the table. "Nope. Never."

"Darlene Fiske is a tough cookie, one of the toughest I've ever met. She's run that store by herself for decades. She prides herself on that fact, and she won't thank you for getting involved. Let her deal with it the way she wants to."

Nell sighed. "Yeah, that's pretty much what she said to me."

"Well then, you should stay out of it. The bottom line is that if Darlene doesn't sell the store to DiSouza Developments, it'll go with her to her grave, and then her heirs—probably that niece of hers who lives in LA and has no interest in Tansy Falls or Darlene's legacy—will simply sell it to the highest bidder, and who knows what Fiske's will end up as then. At least this way Darlene will be able to enjoy her retirement, rather than being tied to the store and worrying about it for the rest of her days." He leaned across the table toward her. "Darlene wants out, Nell. She's too old to cope with it now, and Liza DiSouza is giving her that chance."

"You're right." She sighed. "I just want what's best for Darlene."

"I know, I can see that. It's just one of the things that makes you so adorable." It was a corny line, and Brody was milking it, but Nell couldn't help smiling. "Trust me," he went on, his eyes widening in emphasis, "this is a fantastic opportunity for Darlene."

There was a sudden crash from across the other side of the room where a band was setting up on the stage. As they both looked around, the drummer noticed Brody and waved; Brody raised his hand in reply. "Nell, I've just gotta have a quick word with Brad over there, okay? I'll be right back."

She watched as Brody crossed the room, thinking over what he'd said about Darlene and the store. It had hit home when he had pointed out that she was a stranger in Tansy Falls. He was right: this wasn't her business and she should stay out of it. The knotty feeling in Nell's stomach that had been bothering her since she read the valuation report finally began to ease, and she relaxed back in her chair, enjoying the pleasurable heaviness spreading through her limbs. Glancing about the room, she noticed a table of girls giggling and pointing at the stage, where Brody was greeting the drummer with a hug. He stood a few inches taller than the rest of the guys onstage, his hair shining like polished gold under the stage lights; even from here, Brody radiated charm. *He's with me*, she thought, happily swigging down the rest of her drink. Perhaps she could have just one more...

Just then, a buzzing sound on the table grabbed her attention. Brody's phone was vibrating again: another mountain rescue emergency, no doubt. What was it this time? A cat stuck up the ski lift? Nell let out a snort of laughter; clearly, she was already a little bit drunk. She glanced at Brody's phone again, nosiness flaring inside her, and had a sudden urge to take a peek at the screen. *Curiosity killed the cat*, she scolded herself—unless the fall from the ski lift got the poor thing first! Stifling more tipsy giggles, Nell looked over to where Brody was still chatting to the drummer: he had his back to her, absorbed in their conversation. A quick look wouldn't hurt, surely. Reaching out a finger, she spun the phone toward her, then pressed a button to make the screen illuminate. Instantly, a message flashed up:

OK babe, but I do need to know if she's seen the F's valuation report. I promise to make it worth your while if you can find out! L xoxo

It took Nell a few moments to process what she had just read, but as the screen went dark again her mouth dropped open. It didn't take much detective work to deduce that the "F" stood for Fiske's, the "L" stood for Liza—and, judging by the tone of the message, that her and Brody's relationship was at least as much pleasure as business. The lovely tipsy floatiness that Nell had been feeling just seconds ago vanished as she reached the obvious conclusion: the reason Brody had asked her out tonight was to pump her for information about the sale of Fiske's.

Or perhaps she had misunderstood? Nell jabbed at the screen again to reread the message, desperately hoping she was mistaken, but there seemed to be no room for doubt; the meaning was as clear as the water in the pool at the foot of Smugglers Leap. Brody wasn't actually on call for mountain rescue tonight, he was on call for Liza DiSouza. And, if that was the case, it would mean that all of this—the compliments, his attentiveness and flirting—had just been an act.

Nell gripped hold of the table, her head spinning. She hadn't even liked Brody! Not in *that* way, anyway. And the worst part of it was that this fake date had ruined any chance she might have had with Jackson, as now he probably assumed they were together. Not that there had actually been anything to ruin, of course. It seemed the only relationships she had these days were pretend ones.

Brody was now coming back across the room toward her, smiling and glad-handing people as he passed, but while his rock-star swagger had once been charming, it now seemed more like arrogance. She suddenly remembered seeing Liza leaving the Black Bear when she'd arrived for lunch last week and wondering at the time who she'd been meeting; well, now it all made perfect sense. A surge of anger shot through Nell and she snatched up her coat and bag, her hands shaking.

Brody sat back down. "Hey, beautiful, sorry about that."

Nell pushed back her chair and stood up. "I'm sorry, I have to go."

Brody's brows slid together, his eyes flicking to his phone. "What's wrong?" Perhaps he'd guessed what she'd done. Well, it didn't matter now.

"I'm not feeling too good." She was scrabbling in her bag for money, desperate to get away from him, to breathe the cool mountain air.

"Do you want me to drive you back to the inn?"

"No!" she almost yelled. "No, I'll be fine to drive." Fishing out a fistful of dollar bills, she shoved them on the table.

"You don't need to—"

"Goodbye, Brody."

She stalked to the exit, hauled the door open and in a final, futile burst of anger, slammed it so hard that the doorframe shook. As soon as she was outside she stopped, tipped her head back, eyes closed, and took in a great cleansing breath. The temperature had dropped since she'd been inside, but the sting of cold on her skin was good, it cleared her head and helped her focus.

Reinvigorated, she strode toward Sue Ellen, who she'd left at the far end of the parking lot next to the road. She didn't think twice about whether she'd be safe to drive after two vodkas: maybe it was the shock of Brody's behavior, but she felt stone-cold sober. Besides, right now Nell wanted nothing more than to be cocooned in Sue Ellen's fake-wood interior. Just sinking into the squishiness of her vinyl seats would be as comforting as a hug from a friend.

Although the parking lot was in darkness, a full moon was high in the sky, painting the ranks of cars uniformly silver. Even so, in the moonlight it was impossible to miss the lurid glow of a bright yellow Jeep. She slowed to a halt, staring at Brody's car, the spark of an idea catching light in her mind. The moonlight bounced off the chrome trim, which was gleaming as brightly as if it had been polished by hand, which, knowing Brody, it probably had been. Nell glanced around, but she was all alone out here. Sue Ellen's keys were already in her hand, and she ran her thumb along the jagged edge, eyeing the Jeep's immaculate paintwork... *No*. As tempting as it was, she was no criminal. But then she spotted a row of industrial-sized garbage cans nearby and before she could stop herself she ran over and lifted the lid of the nearest one, covering her face with her hand against the sudden stink, and grabbed a bag from inside. Adrenaline rushing through her, she ripped the top and shook it out, all over Brody's Jeep. Stinking scraps of food and a large slick of unidentifiable goo spilled out across the hood, oozing into the grill and dripping down onto the wheels. She stood back to admire her handiwork, her heart thumping, and then, fueled by the heat flushing through her body, she went to get another bag and chucked it over the roof, sending eggshells and coffee grounds splattering all over the windshield, clotted wads of wet paper sticking where they fell. With any luck, it would take a lot of scrubbing to get them off.

Wiping her hands on a tissue, Nell stalked back toward the car, her cheeks hot and eyes shining. She may not have danced on any tables tonight, but that had been just as exhilarating, and as she climbed into Sue Ellen and started the engine she got the distinct impression that the car was rumbling its approval.

Chapter Twenty-Seven

So today is your final day in Tansy Falls—and a special moment for me, as I get to return to Mount Maverick. I do hope you've managed to find a nice spot to scatter me, but if not then please take the gondola up and just sprinkle me off the edge. I'll be perfectly happy wherever I land—although do make sure you're not standing downwind or you'll end up with a mouthful of ashes, and while I'm quite happy to spend the next few years in your lungs I imagine the view down there won't be quite as impressive. (Sorry—is that even funny? Honestly, my sense of humor has turned beyond black since The Cancer.) Anyway, darling Nellie, I really hope you've had a wonderful time in Tansy Falls. Hopefully I've been watching you from above and if that's the case I'll try my best to give you a sign today. Watch out for me haunting yooooou!

When Nell got back to her room the following morning after breakfast, she discovered three missed calls on her phone from Mallory. Nell hit the callback button at once. Mallory had probably been calling to make arrangements to meet up before Nell left for the airport tomorrow morning, but Nell could also do with spilling the beans about her evening with Brody. Mallory was bound to help her see the funny side, but her call went straight to voicemail and she hung up without leaving a message. At this time of the morning Mallory would be busy with the cows, so Nell's bean-spilling would have to wait.

After going to bed last night Nell had lain awake for hours, thoughts and emotions pinballing around inside her, making sleep impossible. Brody had texted her shortly after she'd left the Black Bear, asking if she was okay, but she'd ignored the message. Her fury toward him had already faded to a dull niggle: drenching his Jeep in garbage juice had taken care of the worst of her anger. Besides, it wasn't as if she'd ever really fallen for him: the attention had been nice, but if Nell was being honest with herself—and there's nothing like some midnight soul-searching for a dose of brutal honesty—she'd never been convinced she was the irresistible femme fatale that Brody had seemed to believe her to be, which was just as well, as it looked like it had all been a put-on.

Jackson, though, was another matter entirely. Somewhere around 2 a.m., Nell sat up in bed and switched on the light, just to try to drive out the thoughts of him that kept springing like water leaking through the hull of a ship. She would plug one leak, only for another to pop up elsewhere. If only Jackson had answered the door when she'd visited the house; if only he hadn't seen her on a date with Brody; if only she'd had the guts to take a wild gamble and ask him out for a drink. So many "if only"s, it was like a ticker-tape parade of missed opportunities, with each carnival float showcasing yet another time when Nell spectacularly failed to tell Jackson she liked him. Wrapping her arms around her knees and resting her chin, she stared at the wallpaper on the opposite wall, regret lingering like a cold hard stone in the pit of her belly. Well, it was too late now. Tomorrow she was going back to London, and her silly crush on Jackson Quaid—because that's all it had ever been—would fade as quickly as the freckles the mountain sunshine had painted on her face.

She checked the time again: nearly 3 a.m. With a huff, Nell turned off the light and lay back down, switching sides until she found a cold bit of the pillow. At least one good thing had come out of her evening: she was now determined to let Darlene know that she was being swindled by DiSouza Developments. If Liza DiSouza was going to play dirty, then she could too, and as the night loosened its grip on the world outside Nell finally came up with a plan.

The morning sky was every imaginable shade of gray as Nell left the Covered Bridge Inn and crossed Main Street, stepping over the banks of grimy snow that bordered the sidewalks. The prospect of saying goodbye to Tansy Falls in just twenty-four hours' time left her with a hollowed-out ache in her guts; this place had opened her eyes in so many ways she couldn't imagine going back to her life in London and picking things up where she'd left off. Before coming here, she had never thought much about what she wanted out of life: she was an accountant who lived in an unlovely bit of London in a not-quite-right apartment and was terrible at relationships. That was who Penelope Swift was and would be for the rest of her days. Yet over the past two weeks, Nell had glimpsed the possibility of an alternate future for her in Tansy Falls. Just as Polly Swift had struck out into the unknown a century before, Nell had realized that you don't have to stay stuck in the rut you've wound up in: it was possible to find a better way to spend your one precious life, if only you had the guts to take the first step.

As much as she loved the idea of shaking up her life, though, Nell knew it wouldn't happen. She just wasn't brave enough to uproot herself from everything she knew and move across to the other side of the world. And while her life in London might not have been exciting, at least it was orderly and predictable; there was no way she would have let her heart be stolen by Jackson Quaid, or have had her head turned by Brody Knott's fake charms, if she'd been back on home turf.

As she passed by Fiske's, Nell stared up its weatherworn facade, as familiar to her now as the front of her own apartment building. Her natural instinct was to turn off the sidewalk, climb the wooden steps (the third of which, she now knew, squeaked when you stepped on it) and head into the store's welcoming embrace, but instead Nell set her jaw and quickened her pace. She couldn't face Darlene before putting her morning's plan into action; the guilt was bound to show on her face. She would see her tonight at dinner, once the deed had been done and it was too late to back out.

Nell felt her phone vibrating in her pocket. She took it out and checked the screen: it was a local number. Perhaps it was Brody, calling her to accuse her of vandalizing his car? Just let him try, she thought, jabbing at the answer button. She was almost disappointed when she heard a woman's voice at the other end of the line.

"Oh, hi, is this Nell?"

"Yes, speaking."

"Nell, this is Carlee from the Wild Moose Animal Shelter. I'm calling about Maggie and your adoption inquiry. Do you have a minute?"

Nell's heart skipped. "Absolutely," she replied.

"So, I spoke to my director about whether it would be possible for you to adopt Maggie and take her back to England, and while we both agree that you'd be able to offer a perfect home for her, I'm afraid we've decided that at Maggie's age the journey would just be too much. I'm so sorry, Nell. I know how the two of you had bonded."

Nell sank onto a bench next to the sidewalk. "Don't worry," she told Carlee. "I completely understand."

"Thank you, and for trying to help Maggie. And please don't worry, I'm sure we'll find her a good home."

Nell sat on the bench for a moment, her elbows resting on her knees, staring vacantly ahead as she remembered the adoring look in Maggie's misty eyes. She pressed her lips together, her head slumping. Even though it had been out of her hands, she couldn't help feeling like she'd let the little dog down. Well, she told herself, there was nothing more she could do for Maggie now. She *could*, however, still help Darlene. Setting her jaw, Nell got up and set off toward her destination with a renewed sense of purpose.

Nell had walked past Tansy Falls' town hall many times over the last two weeks, admiring the neoclassical brick facade with its grand columns and the ornate gold plaque, but she'd never once considered going inside. Why would she? It wasn't on Megan's itinerary, plus she didn't need to apply for a parking permit or register a marriage. She would have no sooner thought of passing through its porticoed entrance than she would the White House; which, funnily enough, it resembled, albeit on a far tinier scale.

But this morning, instead of passing by, Nell walked up the wide stone steps with as much confidence as she could muster. She hesitated in the entrance, taking in the marble floors and lofty ceilings, then headed straight for the front desk.

"Can I help you?" asked the receptionist.

"I'd like the planning department, please," said Nell, although her voice went up at the end as if this were a question. She wasn't even sure they had a planning department here—or, for that matter, whether it was what she was looking for. Nell's cunning plan was based entirely on guesswork. So she was pleasantly surprised when the receptionist answered at once. "It's on the third floor," she said. "The elevator is to your left."

Beyond the grand entrance hall, the town hall had an aura of functional shabbiness usual to such places, the once-elegant rooms partitioned into boxy offices with the smell of carpet tiles and desk lunches lingering in the air. The planning department was at the end of a long corridor and as she approached her heart sank to see the line of people spilling out of the waiting room. Probably all disgruntled clients of DiSouza Developments, thought Nell bitterly, taking a numbered ticket and readying herself for a long wait. She hadn't calculated on the speed and skill of the man at the counter, though, whose robotic efficiency made Nell wonder if he *were* actually a robot, and within ten minutes her number was flashing up on the screen above his desk.

The man was still finishing off the paperwork from the previous client as she approached.

"Hello, I have a weird question that I hope you'll be able to help me with," said Nell, cheerily.

The clerk slammed an ink stamp onto the page in front of him with the force and focus of a kung fu master smashing a cinder block. "Yes?"

Nell hesitated, attempting to get her rambling thoughts in order. "Okay, so I'm not sure about the processes involved, but say a person—or a company—was buying a business here in Tansy Falls, and had applied for permission to change it into, um, another sort of business. How would I go about finding out what sort of business they were actually planning on changing the original business into?"

Nell winced, hoping he at least got the gist of it.

"Name of the business in question?"

"Oh. Fiske's General Store."

"One moment."

He tapped at the keyboard, staring at his screen. Watching him, Nell felt the whisper of a niggle in her guts. What if Darlene didn't actually want to know what DiSouza Developments had planned for Fiske's? What if she'd made her peace with the uncertainty for the sake of a quick sale and an easy life? She chewed her cheek and glanced at the door, debating whether to get out while her conscience was still clear... No, if Megan had been here, she would have wanted her to help Darlene, Nell had no doubt.

The man pushed back his wheelie chair, grabbed a record card from a shelf behind him and rolled back to the desk, executing the entire maneuver in one fluid motion.

"Fill out this form with your personal details and we will contact you with the information you've requested within five business days." He pressed a button to call the next customer.

Five days? But that would be too late! Nell glanced behind her to see a woman already approaching the desk. She leaned closer to the clerk, her eyes pleading. "I'm sorry, but it's really quite urgent. I don't suppose it would be possible to get the information today?"

The man's eyes snapped up to meet hers. "Five business days," he repeated. "Next!"

Yet as Nell walked away from the counter, her feet feeling as leaden as her spirits, it occurred to her that there was still a way to make this work. It might be a bit underhanded, but wasn't her whole plan decidedly sneaky? She'd come this far, she might as well go the full Judas. Mind made up, she rummaged in her bag for a pen and in the space on the form requesting her personal details she filled out Darlene's name and phone number. Even though Nell would be back in England, Darlene would still discover what Liza DiSouza intended to do with her store. This way might be even better, in fact, as Darlene would never know who'd gone behind her back and requested the information.

"Completed forms in this tray," snapped the clerk, as she approached the desk.

Nell stared at the form in her hand for a long moment and then placed it on the pile.

Chapter Twenty-Eight

When Nell pulled into the parking lot at the foot of Mount Maverick that afternoon, the first thing she did was to scan the area for yellow Jeeps. When she was sure the coast was clear, her hands loosened their death grip on Sue Ellen's steering wheel. Hopefully Brody was stuck at home trying to scrub eggshell off his windshield. Then at that moment, as if summoned by the thought of him, her phone buzzed with a message.

Dude—I'm worried about you let me know you're ok. B.

Nell punched out a reply.

I'm fine though maybe next time tell L DiSouza to do her own dirty work.

She pressed send, then shoved her phone back in her pocket. It may have been petty, but it made her feel a little better.

The wooden casket containing Megan's ashes was sitting next to her on the passenger seat. Nell eyed it warily, trying to imagine carrying the bulky urn while she clambered down the slope to the plateau. It seemed highly likely she'd either drop it or fall off the mountain.

She picked up the casket, put it on her lap and, for the first time, unscrewed the lid, unsure what she would find. Inside there was a plastic bag, of the sort you might put loose peaches in at the supermarket, filled with a fine, gray powder. Nell held it up, wrinkling her nose. Was that it? She had been expecting something a little less, well—dull. A pink velvet pouch full of rainbow glitter, perhaps. That would have been far more Megan.

Staring at the ashes, Nell could feel a crumpling in her chest and a lump forming in her throat, so she tucked the bag inside her backpack.

"Come on then, honey," she said, with a sigh. "Let's go and get you scattered."

It must be right at the tail end of the ski season now, Nell thought, as she made her way through the near-empty sports center. In the boutique, a bored-looking assistant leaned on the counter, staring at her phone, while only one ticket window was open to buy lift passes and there was no line. As she passed by the Maverick Café it occurred to Nell that Megan, never one to pass up on a moment of pleasure, would have definitely wanted to stop for a cinnamon-cream hot chocolate, so that's what she did, requesting extra whipped cream in her friend's honor. She took the drink outside and sat on the terrace, enjoying the warming chocolate and the hypnotic swish of skiers looping down the slope—and hoping that somewhere, somehow, Megan was enjoying it too.

She was just getting up to leave, when her phone vibrated with another message.

What?? I asked you out because I like hanging with you. Liza's a friend and when I told her we were meeting up she asked me to find out some info but that's it. Just business, babe!

Then just as she was trying to compose an appropriately cutting reply, another message flashed up.

How about you take me to dinner tonight to make up for trashing my car?

And he ended it with a wink emoji.

Nell burst out laughing, she couldn't help herself. Brody Knott had some nerve, she'd give him that. Smiling, she deleted the message.

There was no queue for the gondola today and so Nell clambered straight into a cabin by herself. She hugged her backpack to her, reminding herself that she wasn't actually alone: she was with Megan, just the two of them, like so many of the very best times in her life. Nell scrabbled for these happy memories now, determined to make today a celebration of Megan's life, but her mind was refusing to play ball. Instead, it whisked her back to the last time she had seen Megan alive: in the hospice, the day before she died. Nell had sat at her bedside for over an hour, telling her all the things she wanted to say, while clinging to her hand as if her own strength could somehow stop Megan from dying. Megan's eyes had remained closed, though, and in the end Nell gave up trying to stay strong and had broken down, bent double by the force of the sobs she'd assumed Megan wouldn't be able to hear. But after a moment she'd felt the gentlest squeeze on her hand and as Nell looked up, searching Megan's face for a spark of life, she had seen the glimmer of a smile on her friend's lips, a final goodbye.

As the gondola hummed toward the summit, Nell's eyes filled with tears again. Megan had been such a vital part of her life, she knew that for the rest of her life she would feel like a jigsaw with a crucial piece missing. Nell was getting accustomed to grief now, the way it suddenly snuck up and whacked you around the face, but today, instead of giving in, she decided to fight back. She sat up straight, rubbing at her eyes before the tears had a chance to take hold, and forced herself to take some calming breaths, because if Megan could still smile in the face of despair then surely Nell could too. She would never feel complete again, and that grief would always be lurking, but perhaps, given time, she wouldn't feel the shock of that missing piece quite so acutely.

At the top, Nell stepped out of the gondola station and out into whiteness. She looked around, bewildered. The plateau was completely covered in cloud: it was impossible to see much beyond the ground at her feet. Straining her eyes against the fog, Nell felt the first flickers of panic. Without landmarks to orient herself, how was she going to locate the spot Brody had found to scatter Megan's ashes? It didn't help that last time she was here she was too overwhelmed by the mountain to focus on their route.

After swiveling her head fruitlessly around for a few moments, Nell struck out in what she hoped was the right direction. It was eerily quiet up here today, the cloud muffling any sounds apart from her breath and the sound of her footsteps. Occasionally a dark shape loomed out of the fog, but it was easy to believe she was the only person on the plateau.

Nell had been walking for a minute or so when she was startled by an excited whoop nearby, though it faded as quickly as if the whooper had just fallen off a cliff. Hoping it might help her get her bearings, she headed in the direction of the sound; after a few more steps, a signpost emerged from the fog and Nell broke into a relieved smile as she discovered that she was at the top of Goose Gulley, the terrifying ski run Brody had shown her. Somewhere far below she heard the wild cackle of laughter and she shook her head, wondering how anyone was crazy enough to tackle that treacherous slope while effectively blind.

Feeling more confident, Nell set off again, more quickly now that she was certain she could find the way. Sure enough, she soon passed the sign for the blue run she remembered from last time, and moments later Nell saw the orange netting appear from out of the fog, marking the spot where she and Brody had slid down to the outcrop below.

Without pausing, she clambered over the netting, sidled up to the edge and peered over, staring down into yet more white. Last time she'd done this descent it had been nerve-wracking, but today would be considerably worse: she would be launching herself off the side of a mountain with only a few hazy memories to guide her. The irony of plunging to her death while scattering Megan's ashes wasn't lost on her, and she snorted with laughter. It was either that or terrified screams.

Despite the brave face, though, Nell's jellylike legs were already betraying her and she stepped back from the edge. Perhaps she should just scatter the ashes up here? If she chucked them with enough force, chances are some of them would reach the outcrop anyway. Nell fiddled with her ear, thinking over this idea. But no, she couldn't come this far and chicken out. They'd found the perfect spot to lay her to rest—they'd even christened it Megan's Point—so she had to see it through. Besides, she was quite sure that if Polly Swift had been here, she would have knotted her neckerchief in a jaunty fashion and bounded straight over the edge, whistling as she went.

Making sure her backpack was secure, Nell began to sidle downhill, angling her body so she was perpendicular to the slope as she imagined a proper mountain climber would do. The momentary lift this mental image gave her was instantly snuffed out when it occurred to her how poorly equipped she was for mountain climbing. She didn't even have an energy bar with her, let alone an emergency flare, crampons or an ice ax. All she had in her backpack was what she'd take if she was popping out to the shops for some milk, plus Megan's ashes. At least she had her phone, assuming she had any coverage up here, of course. She hadn't even thought to check.

Then, without warning, Nell's foot hit a patch of ice. She let out a cry as she slipped and lost her footing, and then she was tumbling down, her arms flailing, until she slid into a pile of snow and came to a halt. Nell lay on her back, waiting for her shaking limbs and thundering heart to calm, and fighting the urge to scrabble straight back up the way she'd just come down. She'd only lost control for a couple of seconds, but the shock had knocked the breath out of her as thoroughly as if she'd been winded. She was an idiot not to let anyone know she was coming up here. If she didn't make it back, nobody would have a clue where she'd gone. They wouldn't find her until the snow thawed—and up here, that probably wouldn't be until summer. The thought was horrific enough to force Nell to get up and finish the job.

There was the hazy shape of a tree a little way below and Nell shuffled toward it, grateful to have something solid to grab onto. As far as she could remember, if she hadn't veered wildly off course, the outcrop must be just below her, although it was impossible to know for sure as the cloud was even thicker here, pressing against her face like a wet washcloth. She hung on to the tree for a moment and then, with a confidence she didn't feel, Nell forced herself to let go of the branch. She surfed a tumble of loose snow and for a split second it felt like she was falling, adrenaline zipping through her body like electricity, until she landed on something solid. Gasping for breath, she scrambled to her feet and looked around. Next to her there was a single spruce tree, crying out for gifts underneath and a star on the top, while behind her was the gray expanse of a rocky wall. She closed her eyes, letting her head drop back in relief. She had made it; no bones broken.

Nell unhitched her backpack and retrieved Megan's ashes, holding the bag up in front of her.

"So what do you think of your new home, Meg? I guess it's not the best day to appreciate the view." She imagined the magnificent spread of scenery that lay beneath the cloud. "Bet you're sick of being cooped up in that bag. Let's get you out of there."

With fumbling fingers, Nell undid the plastic tie, but then hesitated, unsure what to do next. Should she take a handful of ashes and toss them up into the air, or should she sprinkle them on the ground like birdseed? Perhaps you were meant to just... shake out the bag as if emptying crumbs into the trash? Nell was determined to do this properly, but she was clueless about ash-scattering etiquette.

Remembering Megan's advice about making sure she stood downwind, Nell licked a finger and held it up to ascertain the wind's direction, as she had seen people do on TV. She must have been doing it wrong, though, as her finger felt cold all over. Perhaps she should try the other hand...

Will you just get on with it!

Nell heard Megan's voice as clearly as if she had been standing next to her.

"Right away, honey," said Nell with a smile. Dipping her hand in the bag, she brought out a handful of ashes, scattering some on the snow and then raising up her hand and letting them pour through her fingers, watching as the fine dust was whipped away by the breeze. Without any warning, a sob choked out from deep inside her.

"I miss you so much, Meg," cried Nell, her voice cracking. "Thank you for everything. For being the best friend I could ever have had, for making me a better person and for bringing me here, to Tansy Falls." She sniffed, shaking her head. "I don't want to leave this place, Meg. I don't want to leave *you*."

So this was it: her final goodbye to her friend and the end of the itinerary. Nell couldn't believe it had been only two weeks since she arrived in Tansy Falls—it felt at least ten times longer than that. She thought back to when she first started this trip and how she couldn't wait to get it over with; now she wished it would never end. Not only was she losing her last thread of contact with Megan, she was having to say goodbye to a town that felt more like home than anywhere she'd ever lived, and a place where she'd found hope and happiness again.

And then it suddenly occurred to Nell that maybe *this* was the surprise that Megan had referred to in her letter, when she had written that sticking with the itinerary "would all be worth it in the end." Nell had assumed she'd been talking about a surprise outing or a person she'd meet, but how much cleverer (and how typically Megan) that her wonderful, perceptive friend had foreseen that the magic of Tansy Falls would start to heal Nell's wounded heart.

And as she stared out into the silent whiteness, Nell gave in to the tears that had been threatening all day and let herself cry, wildly and without restraint: for Megan's suffering and death, for Nell's other losses—her baby and her broken relationship—but also for relief, and the understanding that there was always light at the end of the tunnel, no matter how dark it might seem.

Then all of a sudden a tiny red bird darted out of the fog and landed in the spruce, right next to where she was standing, and sat on the branch looking at her with its head on one side. Nell froze, her face soaked with tears, barely daring to breathe in case she scared it away. The bird stayed in the tree for a little while, moving in jerky hops about the branches, before taking flight again. It was instantly swallowed up by the whiteness, leaving Nell wondering if she'd imagined the whole thing.

When Nell arrived back at the Covered Bridge, as shaky and triumphant as if she'd just conquered Everest, she found Mallory in the lobby on a couch by the fire.

"Hey!" Nell bundled her into a hug. "Have you been waiting for me?"

"I was leaving you a note." Mallory waved a folded-up piece of paper as proof. "Busy day?"

"I've just been up Maverick to scatter Megan's ashes. It was... emotional."

Mallory sucked in a breath. "Right. Wow, that must have been tough." She squeezed Nell's shoulder. "Where did you take her?"

"Just below the summit. It's a lovely spot, Brody Knott helped me find it."

"Brody Knott, eh?" Mallory was now scrutinizing Nell with the suspicious look of a teacher being told a tale about a homework-eating dog. "Word on the street is that the two of you went out for dinner last night."

Nell stiffened. "How did you know?"

"News travels fast in Tansy Falls." Mallory paused. "Nell, do you have time to come to Mistyflip with me for a coffee? There's something we should talk about."

The café was almost empty, and Nell and Mallory sat at the large table in the window looking out at the Tansy Falls Historical Society Museum and toasted Megan's memory with coffee and blueberry crème donuts. Nell hadn't appreciated quite how hungry she was until she'd gobbled down one donut and then had gone straight up to the counter and ordered another two. Adrenaline clearly gave you quite an appetite.

"So what is it you wanted to talk to me about?" asked Nell, once she had finished describing her hair-raising descent down Maverick and Mallory had gaped repeatedly and told her she was lucky to be alive.

"Well, to start with I wondered what was going on between you and Brody—although just tell me if it's none of my business. Small-town snooping tends to rub off."

"No, it's fine. Brody came to visit the Smugglers Leap falls with me yesterday, and while we were there he asked me out for dinner, and I just thought—why not?"

Mallory didn't need to say anything, as her eyebrows said it all for her.

Nell held up her hands. "I know, both you and Darlene warned me about him, but I figured it would be a bit of harmless fun."

"And was it?"

"I guess so, right up until the moment I found out that he was basically spying on me for Liza DiSouza."

Nell was expecting this to be a bombshell, but Mallory just rolled her eyes.

"Well, duh, the whole town knows Brody's sleeping with Liza DiSouza."

Nell stared at her, openmouthed. "Why didn't you tell me?"

"Because first of all it's obvious, as those two are literally perfect for each other, and secondly I had no idea you were even considering going on a *date* with him." Mallory shook her head incredulously, although her expression quickly softened. "You're not upset about it, are you?"

"Oh no, not at all! I just feel a bit stupid, that's all. And covering his Jeep in garbage made me feel much better."

Mallory burst out laughing. "Girl, Meg would be proud of you." She squeezed Nell's hand. "But what did you mean when you said Brody was spying on you? Why is Liza DiSouza interested in you?"

Nell shifted in her seat, sighing. "It's a long story."

Mallory checked her watch. "Deb can cope with the triplets for a bit longer. So come on—spill."

It was a relief to finally get it all off her chest. Nell confessed everything to Mallory: her concerns over the sale of Fiske's, how she'd sneaked a look at the DiSouza Developments valuation report and her trip to the town hall that morning.

"Well, I hope Darlene appreciates everything you've done," said Mallory, after Nell had finished. "Although you do know she'll be furious when she finds out."

"Yeah, I do. But I had to do something." Then a thought suddenly occurred to Nell. "Mal, how did you know I'd gone to dinner with Brody last night?"

"Jackson told Lucas he'd seen the two of you at the Black Bear."

Nell blinked, thrown as ever by the mention of his name.

"The thing is," Mallory went on, fiddling with her wedding ring, "I get the impression that Jackson is quite into you."

Nell took a sharp intake of breath and held it as Mallory went on.

"He's not said as much outright, but he's been talking to Lucas about you and asking questions, which isn't like Jackson at all. He's usually pretty private."

"Okay..." Nell was making a huge effort to sound calm.

"I would have said mentioned it before, but there wasn't really anything to tell—well, nothing concrete, anyway. And I wasn't sure you'd be interested in him." Mallory looked at her. "So are you? Interested, that is?"

A grin spread across Nell's face. "Yes, I am. I really like him, Mal." She bit her lip, struggling to contain her excitement. "Ever since I first saw him, I've felt this kind of—weird attraction to him."

"Not that weird, really," said Mallory. "He is pretty gorgeous."

"No, I know. Isn't he?" Nell felt as light as if she were floating. "He actually invited me around to his house the other day, but when I turned up Cindy answered the door. I'm not sure whether he even knows that I stopped by."

Mallory nodded. "He does—Cindy told him. Apparently she gave him the third degree about who the 'cute redhead' was." She chuckled at the thought. "Jackson was going to try to rearrange your visit, but then he saw you with Brody last night, and..." She trailed off, but the implication was clear. "That's why he phoned my husband. To ask what he should do."

"What did Lucas tell him?"

"Well, he went around to the old Philpott place last night, they had a few beers, and basically Lucas told Jackson to stop being so darn cautious. Anyway, he's inviting you over to his place tonight."

Nell's stomach gave a flip. "Jackson is?"

"No dummy, Lucas." Mallory rolled her eyes. "Of *course* Jackson! Not that I'm supposed to know about it." She fished in her pocket and pulled out the note she'd waved at Nell earlier. "Jackson wrote this for you, and I *may* have accidentally read it." She grimaced. "Sorry."

Nell took the note, but didn't open it. "So Jackson's got you and Lucas running his personal errands for him, has he? Couldn't he have brought this over himself?"

"Calm down, missy. Lucas offered to drop it off because he was going to be driving past the inn's door, but then we had a cow crisis this morning—there's *always* a cow crisis—so I offered to do it for him." She glanced at the note in Nell's hand. "Aren't you going to read it?"

She hesitated, then smiled and unfolded the note.

Nell, I'm really sorry about the other day. I'd love to have the chance to explain, and give you that tour I promised. Dinner tonight at 7?

He'd written his phone number at the bottom of the message.

She looked up to find Mallory staring at her in anticipation. "Well?"

Nell chewed her cheek. "I'm meant to be having a farewell dinner with Darlene tonight, and she's been so good to me..."

"Oh, Darlene will understand—in fact, she'll be thrilled. In case you hadn't noticed she's been trying to get you and Jackson together ever since you arrived. As, of course, has Tansy Falls' matchmaker-in-chief, Dewitt Hoffman. So will you go?"

Nell thought for a moment. Surely if there was ever a time to get out of her comfort zone, it was now. "If Darlene doesn't mind... absolutely," she said, breaking into a grin.

"Excellent." Mallory held up her hand for a high-five. "I'm expecting a full debrief tomorrow morning, okay?"

Nell clapped her hand, her eyes sparkling with excitement. "You're on."

Chapter Twenty-Nine

The sun was dipping below the horizon as Nell drove down the driveway toward the old Philpott house. The thick cloud of earlier had fragmented into threadbare wisps, glowing pink and gold in the twilight, and there was a softness to the air that whispered of spring.

The windows of the gray house shone with a warm light that cast shadows on the sparse patches of snow in the lee of its walls. Nell's feet crunched on the loose dirt of the drive as she walked toward the house, the steady rhythm of her steps working to calm her racing heart. She was wearing jeans and a sweater and only a touch of mascara and blush; tonight, she had come as herself, the no-frills version. She was leaving Tansy Falls tomorrow, so she'd decided she might as well lay all her cards on the table for Jackson: *this is who I am, take me or leave me.* As Nell walked up the steps to the porch, she held fervently onto the hope that it would be the former.

She tapped at the door, shattering the stillness and spooking something in the undergrowth that quickly rustled to safety. Moments later there was the patter of fast-approaching feet and the door flew open to reveal a beaming Joe. He was wearing Star Wars pajamas that were a little too short and his hair was sticking up as if it had just been toweled dry.

"Nell! My dad said you might read me a bedtime story. Will you? Please?"

"I would love to," she said, smiling.

"Hi, Nell." She raised her head to see Jackson walking up behind his son, wiping his hands on a dishtowel. Perhaps it was because he was on home turf (and because, for once, she hadn't blundered in unannounced), but in the few strides it took him to reach the front door she sensed a difference in him, a sort of rugged physical confidence, as if he'd just been out hunting bison or corralling horses. His hair, which usually seemed content to do its own thing, had been swept off his face, the better to frame the bold "T" of his brows and nose, and he was wearing a battered denim shirt that was pale and frayed at the cuffs. Nell could imagine feeling the softness of the material between her fingers, and the thought made her catch her breath.

"Welcome to the old Philpott house," he said, with that charmingly crooked grin.

"Well, I have been here a few times before, you know," said Nell, "during the course of my lengthy stalking career."

"That was you? The crazy mud woman?" He made a show of checking her out under heavy lids, and she felt his eyes running over her body as acutely as if he had been touching her. "Well, I gotta say, you scrub up pretty good."

Flustered, Nell held out the bottle of whiskey, the same one from her earlier visit here. It was a good job she didn't like the stuff, otherwise she'd have probably cracked it open after her doomed encounter with Cindy. "This is for you, to thank you in advance for letting me have a go on your tire swing."

"Thank you, that's very kind. Come on in."

As practical as Nell's boots were, they were tough to get off, and as she stood on one leg, tugging at the heel, she wobbled and would have toppled over if Jackson hadn't reached out and caught her elbow. Their eyes locked, and Nell felt a lurch in her stomach as if she were plunging down the highest dip of a rollercoaster.

"Can I show Nell my room now, Dad?" Joe was hopping around them, oblivious to the electricity crackling between the adults.

Jackson let go of her arm. "Joe's been quite excited about your visit, as you can probably tell."

"Come on, Nell, let's go!"

Up in his bedroom, Joe showed Nell all his Lego creations and introduced her to each of his stuffed animals by name. As godmother to Megan's eldest girl, and surrogate auntie to all three of her daughters, Nell knew the games that kids enjoyed, and Joe was an enthusiastic playmate. She felt perfectly at home in this cozy room with this sweet boy and tried not to dwell on the fact that this could be the only time they would hang out together.

They were arranging Joe's vehicles into a traffic jam that had already looped twice around the room when Jackson's head appeared around the door.

"I thought Nell came up here to read you a bedtime story," he said.

"Dad, she's gonna do that in a minute, but we've got to finish this first. It's *important*."

"Uh-huh." He looked at Nell. "You okay there?" Then he mouthed: "Need rescuing?"

She shook her head, smiling. "We're having a great time. Besides, I think we're nearly done." She glanced inside the toy bucket. "Looks like we're down to just a couple more cars, a tugboat and a dinosaur on wheels."

Joe fixed his dad with a triumphant smirk and went back to his arranging the toys.

"Well, how about a drink to help you with the final push?" Jackson held out a tumbler, the ice cubes clinking. "I took a guess and made you a Negroni. Hope that's good?"

Nell wasn't sure if it was, as she'd never tried a Negroni before, but it felt like a night for new experiences. "Thank you," she said, glancing at the traffic jam. "Hopefully I won't get caught for drunk driving."

Fifteen minutes later, after a quick story and a long good night—Joe being as relentless as a criminal attorney in his efforts to fix a date for when they would next meet—Nell headed downstairs. She took it slowly. It was going to be just the two of them now, without Joe's chatter to ease things along, and the prospect of being alone with Jackson was giving her stage fright.

Following the murmur of music, Nell went through an archway and found herself in an open-plan kitchen and living room. Bowls of nuts and olives sat on the island and the embers of a fire glowed in the grate, but there was no sign of Jackson.

Nell hesitated in the doorway, surprised by the room in front of her. Adrian, her ex-boyfriend, had been scrupulously minimalist, to the extent that he even considered framed family photos "clutter," and she had assumed this was just a man thing. Not this particular man, though, it seemed. Jackson's home was dotted with intriguing items, each perfectly suited to its space: a Persian rug in jewel colors that looked gorgeous on the dark wooden floor, a painting of a forest hanging over the mantelpiece, a squat stone sculpture—its abstract curves conjuring the image of a mother

and baby—and at least a dozen framed family photos. And in the
center of the room was a vast wooden table, its top made out of a
slice of an entire trunk, with enough room to seat a football team
plus its opposition. The wood was elaborately figured with swirls
and feathering, the colors running from honey to darkest chocolate,
while the edge followed the natural curves of the tree. Nell walked
over to look at it more closely; the top was as lustrous as polished
stone and soft to the touch.

She heard the front door close and turned to see Jackson in the
doorway carrying an armful of logs.

"This table is stunning," said Nell. "What sort of wood is it?"

"California black walnut." Jackson crossed over to the fireplace and
arranged the logs in the grate. "It's a slab from one of the first trees I
worked with when I was training to be a forester. The trunk had been
cut open and I just knew I had to preserve the pattern."

Jackson came to join her. They were standing inches apart, close
enough for Nell to smell a clean citrusy scent on him.

"Did you know," said Jackson, after a moment, "that the color of
wood is actually derived from the infiltrates that a tree draws from the
soil where it grows? That's why even within a species its color can vary
dramatically." He traced his fingers over the table; in the soft light,
his skin looked as burnished and golden as the wood. "This tree was
from the Sierra Nevadas in California, where I grew up, but the color
would be very different in a walnut grown on, say, the limestone bluffs
of Iowa." He stared at the table for a moment, then turned to Nell,
wincing. "Sorry. I can be a bit of a tree geek."

"Not at all. Never apologize for passion." That last word hung
heavily between them and Nell's cheeks reddened. Why did he always
make her feel as if she was turned inside-out, as if all her feelings were

on display? "I mean, I can see why you're so, um, enthusiastic," she stammered.

Thankfully, Jackson changed the subject. "Nell, I need to say sorry to you for the other day when you came over and Cindy answered the door."

"It's okay."

"No, I should explain. Cindy has this not-so-great habit of turning up unannounced to see Joe, which was what happened the other day. I was working in the office at the other end of the house and didn't hear you knocking. Cindy should have come and gotten me, but..." He grimaced, running a hand through his hair. "I hope it wasn't too awkward."

"Honestly, it's fine." A question about the wedding ring on Cindy's finger hovered on Nell's lips, but she thought better of it. "Besides, I'm here now, and this time I'll be getting fed, so—win-win, really."

Jackson shot her a relieved smile. "I better go up and say good night to Joe. Make yourself at home, I won't be a minute."

After he'd gone, Nell sat on a stool at the island picking at the nuts, even though she was too full of nerves to have any room for food. Judging by his kitchen, Jackson liked to cook: Nell counted four different types of olive oil, their bottles so ornate they could have housed perfume, and there was an array of cooking utensils hanging from a grid above the stove, some of which she couldn't even guess at their purpose. Nell munched an olive and turned her thoughts to the evening ahead, her insides fizzing up like a shaken can of soda at the possibility of what might happen. She couldn't remember feeling this strong an attraction toward a man since—well, not ever, really. She'd had the usual teenage crushes, a handful of not-quite-right romances in her twenties and then, of course, there was Adrian, who had seemed so smitten when they met that he'd basically flattered Nell into a relationship. Looking back over the rubble of her love life now, it occurred to her that she'd never actually *chosen* any of these past boyfriends: she'd let herself be picked, as if she were a ballplayer being called up to bat. Her own desires and feelings hadn't really come into it; just the idea of being found attractive by someone had been enough for her. In fact, wasn't that exactly what had happened when she'd agreed to have dinner with Brody?

Nell downed the last of her Negroni, unsure whether the fire burning inside her belly was from the alcohol or this epiphany. Then she remembered some advice Megan had given her after Adrian had dumped her. "Next time, honey, you need to be a more active participant in your love life," she had said, stroking her hair. "Find someone who you feel is right for you, rather than someone who thinks you're right for them." It hadn't made much sense to her at the time, but now Nell knew exactly what Megan had meant.

"You've got quite a fan there," said Jackson, appearing in the doorway. "Joe just asked if we could visit you in London next week."

"He's a really sweet kid," she said, resisting the urge to ask what Jackson had replied.

"He is, though I'm evidently biased." Jackson headed to the fridge. "I hope you like paella. My mom is Spanish, so I was weaned on the stuff."

"I love it," said Nell, squirreling away this nugget of information like a precious jewel; she wanted to know everything about him. She watched as he rolled up his sleeves and started to chop an onion. "Can I help at all?"

"No way, you're on entertainment duty. How about you tell me about your friend Megan and this itinerary I've been hearing so much about?"

It was easy from that point on. Nell's self-consciousness evaporated as she retold the story of how she and Megan had met and their friendship over the years, then moved on to the itinerary—which she realized, with a little thrill of pride, that she'd actually managed to finish (apart from the skiing part)—and her visit to Tansy Falls. Meanwhile, Jackson was making swift work of the pile of vegetables in front of him, slicing at such speed Nell feared for his fingertips.

"Are you secretly a professional chef?" she asked, watching him expertly dismember a squid.

"I'm not, but my mom is, and I picked up some skills from her over the years when I was growing up." He put a hula-hoop-sized paella pan on the stove and looped a bottle of oil over it. "I love cooking, but I don't often get the chance to do it for an appreciative audience. Joe has a typical six-year-old's appetite, so it's a pleasure for me to be able to cook for someone whose idea of a gourmet dinner isn't hot dogs and Doritos."

"Well, as much as I too enjoy a Cool Ranch chip, I can tell you that I'm thrilled to be cooked for."

As the paella bubbled away on the stove, Jackson told Nell about his idyllic childhood in California. To a girl who grew up in a commuter town where the closest thing to the wilderness was a grassy desolate lot behind the grocery store, it sounded straight out of a storybook: running wild in the mountains with just his dog for company, family dinners in the backyard—four generations all together—lit by stars and fireflies, road trips to LA in an old Ford pickup with his buddies. And Jackson had such a poetic turn of phrase he made even everyday things like walking to school sound like a verse from a Bruce Springsteen song.

The paella was about the best thing she'd ever tasted, but Nell had little appetite. Their conversation flowed as easily as the fast-running river Jackson described fishing in as a kid. She thought back to the day she'd first seen Jackson (had that really only been two weeks ago?) and the inexplicable connection she'd felt to him even then. It had been absolutely real, she realized now. She reckoned they could have talked all night and not run out of things to say.

They had just finished dessert, a deliciously creamy lemon thing that tasted like it had been prepared by a French pastry chef, when Jackson pushed back his chair.

"All set?" he asked, standing up.

Nell took in the expectant look on his face and felt a chill down the back of her neck. Was he asking her to leave? She had assumed he'd been enjoying himself as much as she had, but it certainly wouldn't be the first time she'd misread the signs.

"Um, sure," she said, reaching for down to pick up her bag, her stomach plummeting with disappointment.

Jackson frowned. "I don't think you'll need to bring that. I mean, you don't want to risk your stuff falling out into the creek. That swing's pretty wild."

"Oh! I just thought..." Nell grinned. "Never mind."

"I'll give you a tour of the backyard as well," said Jackson, as they put on their coats and boots. "We need to do this right, for Megan's sake."

"Do we need to take a flashlight?"

He opened the door onto what seemed to be absolute blackness. "No, it's a clear night, the stars will be enough." He smiled at her and Nell caught a glimpse of her own excitement mirrored in his face. "You sure you want to do this?" he asked, teasingly.

"Are you kidding?" She gawked at him. "I've been waiting to do this for the past two weeks."

Chapter Thirty

Their first steps away from the house were in total darkness, but Nell's eyes adapted fast, and by the time they came out from under the trees and were heading down the hill to the creek she felt silly for having asked about a flashlight. With the multitude of stars and an almost-full moon it would have been bright enough to read a book.

Nell had always thought of the night as something that deadened the world, blotting out color and dulling detail, but this particular night was as transformative as sunshine or a rainbow after a thunderstorm, changing the landscape around the old Philpott house into an entirely new and enchanted place. In the moonlight the snow that lingered in the folds of the earth shone with a strange blue light, overlaid with a cross-hatching of shadows from the branches above, and from every direction came the soft sounds of night: otherworldly hoots and cries, rustling in the dead leaves on the forest floor and a low sighing that sounded to Nell like the ancient trees readying themselves for bed.

The tire swing was fixed to a sturdy branch of a large tree—a northern red oak, according to Jackson—and dangled about ten feet above the widest part of the creek, creating a natural plunge pool. Tonight, the water was still and inky black, but in the summer, it must have been a perfect spot for a swim.

Jackson brushed the dusting of ice crystals off the tire and held the rope out to her. "Here you go. It's all yours."

Their eyes met and they grinned at each other, as if they were sharing an amazing secret, and then Nell clambered on, swallowing down the excited laughter that was ready to burst out of her.

"Ready?" asked Jackson.

She nodded, her eyes sparkling.

"Hold on tight." Then he pulled back the tire and let go.

Nell let out a cry, unable to keep it in. She hadn't been on a swing for years, but as she went soaring upward she felt a swooping in her body that whisked her straight back to being eight years old. As she urged the swing higher, her whole being was consumed by sensation: the wind whipping back her hair, the weightlessness of flying, the giddy list in her stomach as she plunged back to earth. Again and again she flew up into the sky, the stars blurring together as if she were shooting into a far-off galaxy at warp speed.

Gradually the swing began to slow, the rope creaking where it was looped over the branch, but like a child Nell shouted: "Higher! Higher!"

Jackson laughed, catching her when she flew back and giving her an almighty push.

Nell whooped as she swung up again, leaning as far back as she dared with her legs stuck out in front of her. How amazing this must be in the summer, when you could let go of the rope at the very highest point, that moment when you feel like you're hanging frozen in midair, and tumble down into the cooling water below.

"Worth the wait?" called out Jackson.

"I never want to get off!"

Jackson laughed. "Okay, kid, but you've got five more minutes, then I've got something else I want to show you."

*

Once she was back on solid ground Nell's legs felt as wobbly as a sailor's after a long voyage, but her insides were sparking with adrenaline.

"That was amazing, thank you!" She beamed at Jackson, pushing her hair off her face. "Where to now, boss?"

"Just up here. It's not far."

"Will Joe be okay?" It felt like they were a long way from the house.

"Absolutely." Jackson patted his pocket. "I've got an intercom on my phone. If he stirs, I'll know about it."

As they followed along the banks of the creek, the ground steadily rose upward. The creek was much narrower here—Nell reckoned she could have leapt from one side to the other—and the water was flowing more rapidly, chattering down over a tumble of rocks. She looked up toward the crest of the hill and caught another glimpse of the sky, wondering again at the number of stars. How could there be so many more here than there were in England? Where were they hiding back home?

As they approached the top, Nell noticed a tree trunk lying next to the bank and when they got nearer Nell realized it had been carved into a bench, just big enough for two.

"Did you make this?" she asked Jackson, admiring the workmanship.

He nodded. "Take a seat. It's quite a view."

Nell did as he suggested and there, right in front of her, was Maverick. It was looming over the treetops, its dark shape revealed only by the absence of stars. Looking up at the very top, where she had been only the day before, Nell felt an almost spiritual sense of awe. It wasn't just that the mountain was imposing, although even in darkness she could feel its presence, but Maverick held a far deeper significance for her now. In her mind it would be forever linked with Megan, each of them a part of the other, both keeping watch over Tansy Falls.

Jackson sat down next to her, and as she stared at the mountain it was as if the beauty of the view, the memory of Megan and the anticipation of what might happen with Jackson all came together, and Nell was hit by such a wave of euphoria that she was lifted out of herself, just for a second, and she knew that this would be such a special moment in her life that she wished she could bottle it to enjoy it again whenever she wanted.

After a little while, Jackson cleared his throat. "I wanted to ask you something," he said. Nell's focus was now entirely on the man sitting by her side; she noticed she was holding her breath, waiting for whatever would happen next.

"Last night, when I saw you with Brody... I mean, just say if it's none of my business—"

"No, no, it's okay." Nell was relieved to have the chance to clear the air. "Brody helped me find somewhere to scatter Megan's ashes on Maverick, but that's as far as our relationship goes."

"Good. That's... a relief." He flashed her a quick smile. "You know, Joe asked me if the two of you were dating after we saw you last night. He can be worryingly mature for a six-year-old kid."

"Oh, I have *zero* interest in dating Brody Knott," said Nell, a little more vehemently than she'd intended.

Somewhere up in the trees, an owl hooted, its call echoing around the darkness. Jackson tucked his hands in his pockets, his knuckles brushing her thighs as he did so.

"You can be a hard woman to read, Nell Swift," he said quietly.

She turned to look at him, astonished; she had thought it was the opposite. "Really?"

"Yup. These last two weeks, whenever we've met it's felt a lot like you've been trying to get away from me."

"*What?*"

He laughed at her expression. "Honestly! When we went to the covered bridge—man, this is going to sound crazy—I really felt we had a sort of... *moment*. But it was like you couldn't get away fast enough. I was pretty disappointed."

"But I felt that too! I thought it was just me, though."

"Didn't it occur to you that I might be interested when I chased you to the sugar shack and went through the whole of that damn tour just so I could invite you to the house?"

"Truly? No, it didn't. Besides, I wasn't sure about the situation between you and Cindy." She took a breath. "I noticed she was wearing a wedding ring..."

"Well, that's because she's married."

Nell shot him a quizzical look.

"To Brook Brookman," said Jackson, as if it were obvious. "The other guy."

"His name's Brook Brookman?"

"Yeah—and believe me, it suits him." His brows lifted, and Nell giggled. "Cindy and I are cool now, but, though I can't regret it because I've got Joe, we should never have gotten married. We just weren't compatible. She never really got the tree thing, for starters." He glanced at her, amusement crinkling his eyes. "She used to tell people that there were three of us in our marriage: me, her and an eastern white pine."

Nell smiled at him, a rush of tenderness softening her heart. *I get the tree thing*, she wanted to tell him—but she hesitated, the moment passed, and they lapsed into silence. Nell kicked herself inwardly, infuriated at herself for holding back, and in that moment she came

to a decision. Just this once she wasn't going to shy away from the
intensity of her feelings or passively wait around to see what would
happen. Now was the time for action. *I choose Jackson.*

Nell angled her body to face him and it seemed like the air around
them was vibrating with possibility. "So tell me," she asked. "Am I
hard to read right this minute?"

Jackson's face was inches from hers, silvery pale against the darkness, and the thought that this gorgeous man might like her as much
as she did him turned her insides to liquid.

"No," he replied, slowly shaking his head.

They looked at each other for a long moment, their gaze signing
an unspoken agreement, and then Jackson reached up to touch her
face, his fingers brushing her lips with a tenderness that made her gasp.
And then slowly his mouth moved toward hers, and at the moment
their lips touched Nell closed her eyes and tumbled into the chasm
of desire that had opened up inside her.

There wasn't a hint of hesitation or awkwardness in their kiss:
their bodies were perfectly in tune, like dancers who'd rehearsed for
months for this one incredible performance, moving together as one.
Time melted away and with it Nell's consciousness, her entire being
consumed by the sensations that were shooting through her body
like explosions of light, each more dazzling than the last. She had no
idea how long they kissed for, but when they reluctantly pulled apart
their faces were a mirror of wonder and delight. Unable to find any
words, they both collapsed into giggles. Jackson put his arm around
her shoulders, pulling her against his side, and they gazed out at the
mountain, too overwhelmed to keep looking into each other's eyes.

"I wish this had happened two weeks ago," said Nell after a little
while.

"Me too. I have wanted to do that since the moment I saw you covered in mud on my driveway." He dropped a kiss on top of her head. "So, what now?"

"Now I go back to London."

Jackson pushed a strand of hair off her cheek, looking at her with such tenderness it made her stomach flip all over again. "I was worried you were going to say that," he said eventually, with a heavy exhale.

They kissed again, more urgently this time, Jackson sweeping Nell up into his arms and onto his lap, clutching her to him as if he had just pulled her out of a stormy sea. Yet even as her body was irresistibly drawn to him, her mind was already pulling away, because as incredible as this moment was, it was just that: one moment, one date. This perfect kiss wasn't too little, but it was certainly too late. No matter how strong their initial attraction, it wasn't enough of a foundation for a long-distance romance. And so even though tonight should really be the start of something, deep down Nell knew that it was already over.

Chapter Thirty-One

The alarm on Nell's phone bleeped with the throbbing persistence of a migraine. She hadn't set it since coming to Tansy Falls, and its harsh alert whisked her straight back to a dull Monday morning in her bedroom in London. It wasn't a nice feeling at all.

Reluctantly, Nell turned over to lie on her back, staring at the ceiling. The memory of last night loomed in her mind. *Jackson.* At the thought of him she was swept up in a heady rush of emotion, echoes of pleasure pulsing through her body. It had been the most incredible kiss of her life—but it was never going to happen again. Nell groaned, covering her face with a pillow to block out reality. When they had said goodbye in the early hours of this morning (just three hours ago, in fact) they had clung to each other with the desperation of the drowning, neither of them wanting to let go, but now that they were apart it might as well have all been a dream. Nell felt as if she'd been given the most amazing present only to have it snatched away again.

She checked the clock: 7:08 a.m. In less than three hours she would be leaving Tansy Falls, the itinerary and her adventure over, but before then she needed to pack her suitcase, meet Mallory for breakfast and drop by the store to say goodbye to Darlene. As much as she longed to stay in bed for the rest of the day, hiding under the covers until the plane for New York left without her, she knew she had to get up.

She couldn't run away forever; her home, her job—her whole life—it was all back in London.

Usually careful about such tasks, Nell threw everything into her suitcase without even bothering to fold her clothes, then showered and dressed as quickly as possible to maximize the time she had left in town. Jackson had wanted to come over before she left, but Nell had asked him not to. It was going to be hard enough to leave this place without the added wrench of forcing herself to walk away from the one man she had ever really fallen for.

"I'll call you every day," Jackson had promised her, as they had said goodbye on his porch with his arms around her, the gray light of dawn already smudging the horizon. "Maybe Joe and I could come over for a visit."

But Nell knew it was never going to happen. Weeks and months would tick by, their feelings for each other, which seemed so intense now, would gradually fade, and in time they would move on with their lives with just the memory of that one incredible night to occasionally raise a smile. It would be far better, Nell told herself firmly, as she zipped up her bag, if she just put the whole thing behind her and moved on with her life. She forced down the lump that had appeared in her throat, took one final look around the pretty little room and headed for the door, her heart as heavy as the suitcase she was dragging behind her.

Down in the foyer, Nell found Connie talking to Piper at the front desk, while Boomer stood at Piper's feet waiting patiently for his morning walk. The warming scent of baking wafted from the kitchen, and Nell guessed that Piper had already been hard at work since the early hours.

"Nell!" Piper's face lit up and she held out her arms. "I hoped I might catch you before you left. How has your trip been?"

"Amazing. I've had such a wonderful time. Thank you for everything you've done—and you too, Connie, you've both been so welcoming. The Covered Bridge has been like a second home." Looking into their smiling faces, she felt a heaviness in her chest. "I really don't want to go," she added, hoping that if she kept talking she wouldn't start crying. "I'm going to miss Tansy Falls so much."

"You'll be back to see us again, I hope?" asked Connie.

"That would be lovely," said Nell. "I hope so too."

A group of people had come down to the foyer while they had been talking and were now hovering by the reception desk.

"I'd better deal with these guests," said Connie. "Safe travels, Nell. We'll see you again, I'm sure of it."

As Connie turned away, Piper steered Nell toward the fireplace where it was quieter, Boomer trotting behind.

"Nell, I've been wondering if you managed to put your mind at rest over the sale of Darlene's store? I could tell it was worrying you when we spoke the other day."

Judging by her furrowed brow, Nell wasn't the only one who was worried about Liza DiSouza's plans for Tansy Falls.

"I've done what I can," said Nell, "but it's Darlene's decision now."

At that, she thought back to her visit to the town hall and wondered how soon the planning department would get in touch with Darlene. Perhaps, by some miracle, Liza DiSouza was intending to keep the store as a store after all, and Nell had been worrying unnecessarily? Well, it was out of her hands now.

"Try not to worry. I'll keep an eye out for Darlene," said Piper, as if reading her mind. "I know she's perfectly able to look after herself, but none of us wants to see the character of Tansy Falls destroyed. I promise I'll do what I can to help."

"Thank you," said Nell, giving Piper a hug. "I'll miss you guys." There was a gruff woof at their feet, and Nell looked down to find Boomer staring up at her, tongue lolling. "I'll miss you too, Boomer," she laughed, burying her face in his fur.

As Piper and Boomer headed out the door for their walk, Nell spotted Mallory coming in the other way. She was carrying two coffee cups and a Mistyflip paper bag, out of which came the aroma of warm baked goods.

"Hey, sorry I'm late!" She sounded a little out of breath.

"Hi! I thought we were having breakfast here?" asked Nell, eyeing the takeout.

"No time. We need to get going."

"Where to?"

"Aha, it's a surprise!" Mallory waggled her eyebrows cryptically, then flicked her head toward the door. "Come on."

Nell hesitated, her mind already envisioning a desperate last-minute dash for her flight. "I've got to drop by the store to see Darlene. I'm not sure I'll have time..."

"It won't take long," called Mallory over her shoulder, already heading for the door. "The truck's just outside. You can tell me about dinner with Jackson on the way."

Mallory was driving Dewitt's truck, a charming old red Dodge from the sixties that with its cheery headlamps and curved hood looked like something out of a Pixar movie. What it had in character, though, it lacked in suspension, and as they rumbled out of town in the direction of the Hoffman farm Nell's teeth rattled over every tiny bump and dip.

"Come on then, where are we going?" she asked, as Mallory took several attempts to crank the truck into a higher gear while clutching her coffee between her knees. "Are we going to say goodbye to Deb and Dewitt?"

Instead of answering, Mallory dipped her hand into her jacket pocket and pulled out an envelope, which she dropped on Nell's lap. She picked it up—and she let out a gasp as she took in the familiar curly handwriting on the front. It was addressed to her, and it was from Megan.

"What is this?" she asked, her eyes wide.

"The last item on Megan's itinerary."

"But—why? How?"

Mallory smiled, taking in Nell's gobsmacked expression. "You remember I told you that Megan and I spoke back in January and she told me about your visit and the itinerary?"

"Yeah…"

"Well, she said she was going to send me something for me to give you on your last day in Tansy Falls. Your final challenge." Mallory checked the rearview mirror and swung off the main road. "She wanted to keep whatever it is a secret until the very last moment."

Nell stared at the envelope. "So *this* is the surprise she was talking about in her original letter to me? What was it she wrote—something about the end being the beginning." She looked up at Mallory. "This is it?"

"It is. But Megan swore me to secrecy, so obviously I couldn't say anything to you before." She raised her eyebrows. "Exciting, huh?"

Nell nodded, dazed. "Do you know what's in here?"

"Nope. She just told me where I should drive you and that's it."

Nell looked down at the envelope again, which she was gripping in her hands as if it were an unexploded bomb. "Shall I open it?" she asked, her voice a whisper.

"No, not yet. Not until we get there. Which should be just about...now." And with that Mallory braked, the truck juddered to a halt and Nell, who had been so entranced by the envelope she'd had no idea where they were going, looked up and discovered that they had pulled up alongside a meadow that was overgrown with grass and scrub.

Mallory was already opening the door and jumping out. "This way," she called, dragging Nell out of her reverie and back to the mystery at hand.

They clambered over a ditch marking the side of the road and Mallory forged a way through the thigh-high undergrowth toward a ruined barn that stood near the woodland bordering the far end of the meadow. Its stone foundations looked sturdy enough and the roof was still intact, but the wooden walls were slumped perilously to one side. It put Nell in mind of a game of Jenga, with the next move certain to bring the whole thing tumbling down.

"Right, this is as far as I've been told to take you," said Mallory, planting her hands on her hips.

"So what now?" asked Nell, looking around.

"Now you open the darn letter!"

Mallory was jigging on the spot in her excitement, but Nell was almost scared to find out what was inside. It felt like Megan was talking to her from beyond the grave—and she had a stomach full of butterflies at the prospect of what she might have to say.

"Come *on*," urged Mallory, "the suspense is killing me!"

Shooting her a quick smile, Nell opened the envelope and, with trembling hands, pulled out the letter inside.

Chapter Thirty-Two

Surprise!! It's me again! Damn, I so wish I could see your face right now...

Anyway, congratulations, my darling! I'm sure you've done a fantastic job over the last two weeks, and I'm so proud of you for taking on this challenge. I imagine the journey hasn't always been easy, but hopefully, looking back, it was worth it. I trust you've had some fun and met some awesome people along the way. And now (drumroll, please) I have one final, special task for you. Are you ready? Because this one is going to take all your courage.

Okay, first things first. I want you to put down this letter and take a really good look around at what you can see. Go on, do it now, I'll wait...

Frowning, Nell did as Megan had asked, making a slow 360 turn while taking in her surroundings: the hills, woodland, the farms dotted about the valley and the gray ribbon of the road weaving up to Maverick in the distance. This landscape was perfectly familiar to her now, its blend of beauty and grit speaking to her soul in a way no place had ever done before. She noticed Mallory was watching her,

her brows bunched in confusion; Nell just shrugged and made a face as if to say, *beats me*, then got back to reading the letter.

All done? Did you have a really good look? Excellent. I really hope you liked what you saw, because this glorious little patch of Tansy Falls real estate—all two and a half acres of it—now belongs to you.

Nell gasped, a hand rushing to cover her mouth.

"What is it?" squealed Mallory. "What does it say?"

"I'm...I'm not really sure, I haven't finished reading it." Nell looked up. "But I *think* Megan's giving me this land."

Mallory grabbed hold of Nell's arm, her eyes bulging. "Go on, quick, read the rest!"

You have questions, right? Of course you do. So I'll try to answer them for you.

Way back in the mists of time (the '70s) my Aunt Nancy and Uncle Bill were newlyweds happily living in New York City. Then one summer they were invited to a friend's wedding in Tansy Falls. Back in those days the town was even sleepier than it is now, but the two of them fell in love with the place and that very weekend, Aunt Nancy—who is quite a character— spotted a FOR SALE sign on this very plot of land and insisted that Uncle Bill buy it, the idea being that they would build a house here. (I get the impression that land was pretty cheap in those days, so maybe this isn't as crazy as it sounds.) After a few more visits, though, Uncle Bill and Aunt Nancy learned that one of the prettiest houses in town had come up for sale—yup, you've guessed it, the old Philpott place—and in the end they moved there instead, though they still kept hold of this land. Over the years Aunt Nancy had various mad ideas about what to do with it, from breeding reindeer to building a sweat lodge in which to hold Native American healing ceremonies (I told you she was a character) but none of these plans came to fruition, and it remained untouched. So when Ben and I got married they gave it to us as a wedding present, with the idea being that we might build a vacation home on it for our family. I was totally up for it, but the girls came along soon after and parenthood got in the way, so I didn't even get a chance to bring Ben out here for a visit—and then, of course, cancer turned up and ruined the party.

When I found out I wouldn't be getting better, Ben and I had a talk about what to do with the land, and we both agreed that we would like you to have it, as a thank-you for being the best friend a gal (and her husband) could have hoped for. Ben doesn't have any links to Tansy Falls; you, however, now do. While I know it's a long shot, I'm hoping that maybe, just maybe, Tansy Falls has charmed you the way it did Aunt Nancy, Uncle Bill and me, and that the idea of putting down roots here is something you might just consider. Speaking frankly—us dead people can do that, you know—the city has never been right for you, honey. You're the kind of person who needs space and trees and fresh air, and Tansy Falls can offer you that in spades.

Which brings me back to the subject of the itinerary, and my reasons for putting this adventure together for you. I suppose I could have just said when I was dying, "I'm leaving you some land in a little town in America and I think you should go and live there, okay?" But you'd have told me that I was crazy, and rightly so. I needed you to see Tansy Falls, to experience the place for yourself and hopefully fall in love with it the way I had. I know it will take a leap of faith for you to move your life here, but if my death has showed you anything, I hope that it's the importance of being bold, grabbing opportunities and taking risks. You've had a tough few years, honey, and life has thrown you some curveballs, so if anyone deserves a fresh start in a beautiful place surrounded by special people it's YOU, my dear, sweet Nell. (And I'm using the word "deserve" deliberately here, because I think you need reminding that you have every right to build yourself a wonderful life, and do whatever it takes to find happiness.)

Of course, you may well have hated it in Tansy Falls, in which case at least you've had a vacation! By all means sell the land and spend the proceeds on a lifetime supply of fabulous shoes; you have my blessing, whatever you decide. But I'd really like to have you in the neighborhood, and, if I know you at all, Penelope Swift, I have a feeling that you might like that too.

Until we meet again, my darling,
Meg

Nell lowered the letter, her heart galloping, and at that moment the sun appeared from behind the clouds, bathing the valley in a golden light. Ridiculous though it was, Nell was struck by a powerful certainty that this was Megan smiling down at her, and as she squinted into the brightness, dazzled in every sense of the word, she felt a tear rolling down her cheek.

"Thank you, Meg," she murmured, shaking her head in awe. "Thank you for giving me another chance."

Wiping her face, Nell now looked around again, marveling at her surroundings through fresh eyes. The ramshackle barn, that gnarled, old tree that looked like a stooped wizard, the expanse of waving grass, wildflowers and budding boughs: all this belonged to her! It was as if Megan had waved a magic wand and granted her dearest wish. Elation surging through her, Nell had to stop herself from whooping and spinning with delight. And although Megan was undoubtedly right, and that it was going to take all her courage to build a new life in Tansy Falls, the very least Nell could do to honor her memory was to live life the way her friend had always done: without fear, and to the fullest.

Breathless with excitement, Nell looked around to find Mallory, who had wandered off a little way to give her some privacy.

Walking over to her now, Nell beamed at her. "Well, it looks like you and I are going to be neighbors," she said, as Mallory's face lit up at the news. "I don't suppose you're looking for another farmhand, are you...?"

*

"Man, this is so exciting!" squealed Mallory, as she spun the steering wheel and turned the truck onto the road back into town.

"I still can't quite believe it," said Nell. "I feel like you're going to tell me this is all an elaborate joke."

"Nope—this really is happening, honey!" Mallory banged a triumphant palm on the steering wheel. "Dang, that girl was clever! I guess the next thing is to sell your apartment in London. Is that what you're thinking, Nell?"

"That's the thing. I'm trying *not* to think right now. I'm just enjoying the dream of moving here, because when I do start thinking about it practically, about the reality of what would be involved—the red tape and emails and having to pack up thirty-seven years of life and move it across the world... Well, it feels like a heck of a challenge."

"But why?" Mallory glanced at her as if it was blindingly simple. "I'm no expert, but I'd have thought with the proceeds of a London apartment you'd be able to build a pretty fancy house here and still have plenty of change left over. You'd be more than welcome to stay with us at the farm while the work was completed—we've got plenty of spare rooms. And you'll have no problem finding a job here." She was almost bouncing in her seat with excitement now. "The world is your cow, honey—you just gotta do the milking!"

Nell laughed at her. "But that's just it, Mal. I've never actually milked a cow before."

They were now pulling up outside Fiske's General Store. Mallory left Dewitt's truck herringboned across two spaces then bounded up the front steps, with Nell following on behind. It wasn't yet 9 a.m. and the CLOSED sign was still showing at the door.

Mallory banged on the window. "Darlene? It's us. Nell and Mallory." She shielded her eyes, peering through the square of dark glass. "Hellooo? Anybody home?"

Moments later, they heard the thud of a bolt being drawn back and the door opened with its familiar jangle to reveal the tiny sprightly figure of Darlene, her white hair hanging loose and witchy about her shoulders and a loop of chunky green beads at her throat. Instead of her usual smile, though, she had a dour look that became even more severe when she turned to Nell.

"Well now, I've just had a call from the planning department at the town hall," she said, folding her arms. "Sounds like you've been doing some detective work, Miss Swift."

They'd called Darlene already? Nell opened her mouth to make an excuse, thought better of it, and swiftly shut it again.

Darlene nodded curtly, satisfied that she'd located the culprit. "You'd better come in. Mallory dear, will you give us a few minutes? I need to have a little talk with Nell."

"Sure, I'll go and put some gas in Dewitt's truck." As she turned to go, she flashed a grim look at Nell and mouthed, "Good luck."

I'm going to need it, thought Nell, following behind Darlene like a condemned woman.

Chapter Thirty-Three

As they walked toward the back of the store, Nell tried to scramble together her defense. Not that she had much in the way of supporting evidence for her case. Darlene had told her to stay out of her business numerous times and she had ignored her. It didn't matter how good Nell's intentions were, Darlene had every right to be furious.

Laid out on the counter were the best cups (the non-chipped ones), a pot of coffee and a plate of cookies that were scenting the air with vanilla and cinnamon. All the makings of a cozy party, if it wasn't for the subzero atmosphere.

Nell perched on one of the stools, her spirits sinking at the thought of the conversation ahead. She'd only been awake for a couple of hours, but she'd already had the giddy highs and plummeting lows of an emotional roller coaster.

Darlene took the stool opposite and poured the coffee without saying a word; judging by the set of her mouth she was clearly waiting for her to provide an explanation. Nell had no idea what she could say to make it better, but an apology seemed a good place to start.

"I'm so sorry, Darlene, truly I am. I had your best interests at heart, I promise."

The older woman just raised an eyebrow.

"I know you told me to stay out of it," Nell plowed on, "and you have every right to be angry—but honestly, I was just trying to protect your store."

Darlene stirred milk into her coffee and tapped her spoon briskly on the mug, but still didn't say a word.

Nell dropped her head, feeling wretched. "How did you find out that it was me who went to the planning department?" she muttered at the floor.

"Dan Bixby told me."

"Who?"

"I believe you met him when you paid a visit to the town hall?"

Nell thought back the robotic clerk in the planning department. "You know him?"

"Of course I know him, he's Lorna Bixby's eldest," scoffed Darlene, as if this would mean something to Nell. "Anyway, Dan phoned to tell me that he'd had a very pretty redhead in his office yesterday pretending to be me."

"But I wasn't pretending to be you, honest, Darlene! I just thought they wouldn't have the information about DiSouza Developments plans for Fiske's until after I'd gone, so I thought I'd leave your contact details and..."

Even to her own ears, though, it sounded like a lame excuse.

"Didn't it occur to you that if I'd wanted to know, I'd have asked for those plans myself?"

Nell looked down at her hands and nodded.

"And yet you went ahead and asked for them anyway."

"But I was so worried that Liza DiSouza wasn't being honest with you! I know how important it is to you that Fiske's stays as the general store, and after the valuation report..."

She only just managed to stop herself before blurting out something even more incriminating.

"Ah yes, the valuation report." Darlene took a ladylike sip of coffee. "What did you make of that, by the way?"

Nell's insides turned cold. "I'm sorry?"

Darlene chuckled at the look on her face. "Oh, this isn't my first rodeo, honey. You seemed so desperate to get your hands on that report that I knew you might take a look when I left you minding the store that day."

Nell hunched her shoulders, miserably. Why hadn't she kept her nose out of it? Instead, she'd managed to alienate one of the people she liked the very best in Tansy Falls. She stared miserably at the floor, wishing it would swallow her up.

"However," Darlene went on, "your obvious concern for me and the store did actually have an impact." At this hint of a reprieve, Nell glanced up. "After Ted Libby gave me his thoughts on the valuation report, I showed it to another attorney. *Just* for a second opinion, mind. And while I completely stand by dear Ted's abilities, the other attorney did flag some potential, uh, areas of concern." Darlene brushed an invisible speck of dirt off her leg. "You know, I could have lived with Liza DiSouza undervaluing the store if it guaranteed a quick sale, but when I found out that she was planning on turning Fiske's into a sushi restaurant"—she threw her eyes skyward—"well, let's just say I'll be reconsidering my plans."

"A *sushi* restaurant?"

"Oh yes. Turns out Ms. DiSouza has plans for a cocktail bar and sixty-seat restaurant with a teppanyaki counter, whatever the cow-kick that is."

"But that's terrible! It would destroy the character of Tansy Falls."

"It certainly would," agreed Darlene.

Neither spoke for a little while, the only sound the ticking of the antique clock over the cash register.

"You know, I've run this place on my own my entire life," said Darlene after a pause, gazing around the store. "That's an awful lot of years making my own decisions, being my own boss and not having to listen to anyone else's opinions. But while I may well be proud, I'm not stupid. When you were so concerned about the contract—well, it was quite plain that I should take a closer look." Finally, her face relaxed into a smile. "And I'm very grateful to you for making this stubborn old goat do just that, because if you hadn't, then my great-grandaddy's store would have been turned into some jumped-up diner flogging raw tuna to out-of-towners."

And with that, Darlene held out her arms to her, and Nell gratefully sank in for a hug.

"Thank you, sweetie," Darlene murmured into her hair. "Megan would be very proud of you."

After a moment they sat up again, and Darlene took Nell's hand and gave it a squeeze.

"I'd like to give you something," she said, "as a token of my appreciation."

"You really don't have to. I'm just happy that some good came out of my meddling."

"Well, I'm going to. I was planning on giving you a gift anyway, a little memento of your visit to Tansy Falls." Darlene's squinted thoughtfully at the shelves. "A pair of llama socks, perhaps? Ooh, some birch-scented bath oil? That's always very popular... Maple cookies? Maple candy? Maple beer? Come on, sweetie, what would you like?"

Nell considered this for a moment. "Well, I suppose there is something..."

"Yes?"

"What I'd *really* like is to know what the problem is between you and Deb Hoffman."

Darlene dropped Nell's hand as if it was scalding hot. "Child, you are just about the nosiest person I have ever met," she said, although her expression softened again just as quickly. "I'm afraid I just can't tell you that, honey. How about a nice Mount Maverick jigsaw instead? Over two thousand pieces!"

"Please, Darlene, I promise I won't tell anyone."

Darlene took a deep breath and then let it out very slowly. "I'm sorry, Nell, but I can't tell you and the reason why I can't is that I don't remember."

"Remember what?"

"What the issue is between me and Deb Hoffman." She flapped her hand as if trying to swat a fly. "Oh, I know there was a big falling-out decades ago, but I can't for the life of me remember what it was over. Not a clue."

Nell blinked. "But you must be able to remember!"

"You just wait until you get to my age, it won't seem so hard to believe then, I guarantee you that."

"We could find out. I could get Mallory to ask Deb?"

"No point. Deb doesn't remember either."

"How do you know?"

"Dewitt told me. He's been trying to get me and Deb to talk for years. That's why he came around the other day, to have another go at it. It's absolutely pointless, but he refuses to quit, bless his soul."

"So if neither of you remember, what's stopping you from clearing the air with her?"

Darlene stared at Nell like she'd just suggested selling Sue Ellen for parts. "Why, the principle, of course! Until she apologizes, I'm not talking to her."

"But what if she's not the one who's in the wrong?"

"Of *course* she's the one in the wrong!" Darlene drew herself up so she was sitting ramrod straight. "That woman is arrogant and pig-headed, always has been. Whatever it was, it was bound to be Deb Hoffman's fault—no question."

Nell would have persisted, even though she was well aware this was probably a head/brick-wall situation, but they were interrupted by a knock at the front door.

"Ah, that must be Mallory," said Darlene, visibly relieved to have an excuse to drop the subject. "Don't you dare tell her what we've been talking about," she added, shooting Nell a flinty look.

Nell grinned. "Don't worry, I won't. And Darlene, thank you again for forgiving me."

"Megan would have been exactly the same. I'm just grateful to you for caring so much about my little store."

"And about you."

"Thank you, sweetie." There was another, louder knock. "Now go and let Mallory in before she breaks down the damn door."

But when Nell opened the door, it wasn't Mallory. It was Liza DiSouza.

On seeing Nell, Liza's beauty pageant poise wavered for only a millisecond. No doubt she would have had a report from Brody about the other night, but from the look on her face you'd think Nell was her favorite person in the world.

"Well, hello there! It's so wonderful to see you again. How are you?"

Nell's lips curled into a smile; two could play at this game. "I'm good, thank you, Liza. I actually just came round to say goodbye to Darlene, as I'm heading back to London this morning."

"Oh, that's a real shame." Liza stuck out her bottom lip, oozing fake sincerity. "Have you enjoyed your vacation in our little patch of paradise?"

Nell flinched at her use of "our" (what did this woman care for Tansy Falls, apart from milking it for profit?) but she nodded. "Oh, very much so. I've met some wonderful people here."

"Yes, I heard you've been keeping busy during your stay," said Liza, silkily. "Getting very *involved* in the local community." She pushed past Nell. "Just stopped by for some of your delicious coffee, Darlene," she trilled, waving her pink cup.

"Come on in, honey!" called Darlene, clambering off her stool to greet her. "I was hoping you might stop by."

Liza threw Nell a tight-lipped smile—a smile that clearly said, *I've won*—and pushed past her in a cloud of perfume that was either Chanel or trying very hard to be. She air-kissed Darlene and then draped herself over the counter with the confidence of somebody who owned the place; which, Nell supposed, Liza assumed she pretty much did. Meanwhile, Nell hovered by the display of llama socks, busying herself with some light refolding while waiting for the fireworks to begin.

"I don't suppose you've got that almond milk I mentioned to you the other day?" Liza asked, as Darlene poured her coffee.

"Nope," she replied. "Just actual milk."

Even from her vantage point by the socks, Nell glimpsed a flash of irritation beneath Liza's spidery lashes. "Never mind, I'll just take it black. But you really should consider stocking some dairy alternatives, Darlene. People are thinking much more carefully about their choices these days."

"It's funny you should say that," said Darlene. "Because I've been having a careful think about *my* choices too."

"Mmm?" Liza took tipped her head to the side, her perfectly groomed brows raised in polite interest.

"Yup. And I've decided not to sell the store to you after all."

Liza froze. "Excuse me?"

"The deal's off, *Miz* DiSouza."

The perma-smile on the New Yorker's face faded. "Is that so?" She put down her cup and glanced at Nell with a look that could have been arrested for attempted murder.

"Well, whatever the issue is, Darlene, I'm sure we can sort it out."

"The issue is that you gave me your word you'd keep Fiske's as a store, yet now I learn that you're intending on turning it into a sushi restaurant." Darlene planted her hands on her hips. "Can we sort *that* out?"

If Liza was thrown by the news that her plans had leaked, she didn't show it.

"Darlene, I'm afraid whoever's advised you on this matter"—here, she fired another steely look at Nell—"has no idea what they're talking about. You'll not find anyone willing to buy Fiske's and keep it running as a store. It's neither profitable nor sustainable. The value is in the land, not the business." Her voice was icily calm, but Nell could see the tension in her jaw. "Perhaps I should have been more up-front with you about our intentions, and for that I apologize, but honestly, I'm doing you a favor. If you won't sell Fiske's to DiSouza Developments, then I'm afraid you're going to be stuck working here for the rest of your days. I mean, just look at this place!" She surveyed the room, not even trying to conceal her contempt. "Who's going to want to take on *this*?"

At that moment, Nell felt a prickle down the back of her neck, like a breeze or the lightest touch of someone's fingers, and an idea popped into her mind. On the face of it, Nell could see it was a ridiculous idea—totally irrational—yet she couldn't ignore it, because at the same time it felt perfectly right. It was similar to the way she had felt when she'd first laid eyes on Jackson: like the universe was taking charge, and, if she trusted it, things would unfold in exactly the way they were supposed to.

Without a second thought, Nell cleared her throat.

"I will," she said. "Darlene, I'd like to buy the store."

Chapter Thirty-Four

Liza and Darlene swiveled to look at her, both goggle-eyed.

"Nell?" Darlene's fingers were fluttering at her cheek.

Liza, meanwhile, had recovered from the shock and was now looking so furious that Nell could almost see the smoke coming out of her nostrils.

"Are you really sure?" asked Darlene, her eyes searching Nell's face for reassurance.

Nell opened her mouth to tell her that, yes, she was deadly serious, but instead the momentousness of what she had just offered to do slammed into her like a forty-ton truck. Had she actually lost her mind? Having seen the DiSouza Developments report she was pretty sure she would be able to afford the store (as well as the proceeds from her apartment and a generous inheritance from her late granny, she'd been saving diligently since she first started work for a rainy day that hadn't yet come) but she'd just taken on the not-so-insignificant project of moving her whole life to Tansy Falls and building a house here—and now, on top of that, she was offering to buy a business as well! It was a nice idea and all, but she didn't know the first thing about working in retail. Where did you get the stuff to sell in the store? How did you know what prices to charge? Did you just...pick a number? Nell didn't have a clue. She didn't have a home here (unless she pitched a tent in the ruined barn on her land) and as much as she knew Tansy Falls was where she wanted to be, she was still an outsider. Would the locals accept a flatlander taking over such a beloved town institution?

Nell felt as if she was being buried under an avalanche of doubts and questions and reached a shaky hand for the tabletop to keep herself steady. She would just have to tell Darlene that she had been too hasty and, as much as she'd like to buy the store, she wouldn't be able to after all. It had been a moment of madness. Darlene would understand, she was sure of it.

As if sensing her doubts, a sneer spread across Liza's face. "Well, what a surprise, it looks like someone's having second thoughts." She flicked a handful of pink acrylics at Nell. "Go away, honey. You leave this to the grown-ups to figure out…"

Slumping with defeat, Nell risked a glance at Darlene: the old woman shot her a quick smile, shaking her head as if to say "it doesn't matter," but the light had gone out of her eyes. Nell stared at the ground, her cheeks burning and stomach clenching with nausea. *If this is how staying in your comfort zone makes you feel,* she thought, *then perhaps it is wiser to get out of it.* And with this thought, the photo of Polly Swift on the Wilderness Trail appeared in her mind, the young woman's face shining with the same determined spirit that she'd seen in the photo of the teenage Megan that Brody had shown her; and Nell realized, as a fluttering started up deep inside her belly, that this was *her* Wilderness Trail moment. She was standing at the start of the trail, gazing up at the ancient trees and the path ahead, and she could either shoulder her backpack and set off into the unknown, or she could go home, marry a man she didn't love and spend the rest of her life wondering, *What if?*

Her pulse pounding, she strode over to Darlene, Megan's advice about being bold and taking risks spurring her onward. *I've got this,*

Meg, she thought, any doubts now vanishing from her mind. Nell knew the road ahead would be rocky, but she was ready for the challenge—for all of them.

"Darlene, I would love to buy Fiske's," she said, her voice steady. "If you're willing to sell it to me, of course. I don't have a lot of money, but I'll certainly be able to match what DiSouza Developments has offered, and I can promise you that I'll run it as a store and do my best to keep Fiske's as the heart of Tansy Falls."

Darlene's face crinkled with delight. "Honey," she said, sticking out her hand, "you've got yourself a deal."

Behind them there was an enormous sneeze. "Ugh, that damn animal!" screeched Liza, trying to shoo away Cat, who had jumped up next to her. Oblivious to her flapping, Cat sat down on the counter and delicately licked his paws.

Liza let out a grunt of fury, swinging around to face Darlene. "We had an agreement!" she shrieked.

"We did," said Darlene. "But we don't anymore."

"This is absolutely unbelievable!" Liza grabbed her cup, her face crumpled with anger. "You'll be hearing from my attorney." She spun around to jab a finger at Nell. "And if you think you can make a success of this...this...*junkyard*, then you're an even bigger fool than you seem." Then she spun on her heel and stalked toward the door. "Oh, and by the way, Darlene," she spat over her shoulder, "your coffee is *disgusting*."

"Give my regards to Brody!" called Nell, as Liza threw open the door and slammed it so hard that the bell fell off the hinge.

Nell and Darlene stared after her for a second, then turned to look at each other, their eyes sparkling like naughty kids who'd just been told off by their teacher.

"Are you absolutely sure about this?" asked Darlene, clasping her hands.

Nell looked around her, taking in the book corner, the overcrowded shelves, vintage shop signs, the stacks of boxes and random antiques. The thought that this place would soon be hers sent tremors of excitement up her spine.

"As sure as I've ever been."

Darlene clutched her hands to her chest. "Oh, I'm so pleased! And don't worry too much about the money, sweetie, it's really not that important. I'm quite sure we can come to an arrangement. I just want this place to go to someone who cares for it as much as I do. Oh, and of course you must have the apartment above the store too. I've got a little house up in the woods that I'll be very happy to move into full-time. I've already planned on growing potatoes and keeping chickens, possibly a goat or two..."

"I haven't had a chance tell you yet, Darlene!" Nell slapped a palm to her forehead. "Megan's left me some land just outside town. Looks like she wanted me to settle in Tansy Falls all along."

Darlene gasped. "Well, I'll be," she murmured, her eyes wide. "Megan had this all planned out! Oh, that brilliant, wonderful girl..."

On the counter nearby, Cat started up a rumbling purr, clearly fishing for attention, and Nell reached out to scratch the patch of white fur beneath his chin.

"I hope you like dogs, Cat," she told him, "because I think there are going to be two of them living here quite soon."

Nell could just imagine two little baskets snuggled up behind the counter: one for Moomin, of course, and another for Maggie, if the animal shelter would still allow her to adopt the sweet old terrier.

Just then there was a pounding at the front door, which sent Cat skittering off the counter in alarm.

Darlene pursed her lips. "That will definitely be Mallory," she said, threading her arm through Nell's and heading toward the entrance. "That girl knocks like a darn Hoffman."

When they opened the door, they found Mallory cowering and shielding her face.

"Is it safe to come in?" she asked, mock-terrified. "I've just passed that woman from Maverick Lodge storming out of here like you ran at her with your scythe, Darlene."

Darlene gave her a light slap. "Foolish child," she muttered, but her eyes were crinkling with amusement.

Mallory grinned, and then nodded behind her. "Nell, there's someone here to see you."

She looked to where Mallory had gestured, and the world tipped on its axis as she saw Jackson striding up the steps toward her. If he was embarrassed by the audience of women gathered on the porch, he didn't show it: his dark eyes were focused unwaveringly on Nell. She took a step toward him until they were standing together, her hands aching to touch him and a delicious itch flaring inside her at the memory of last night.

"I know you told me not to come and say goodbye," he said, "but I had to speak to you before you left."

"Jackson, I..."

He touched her arm. "Please, just let me say something first."

Mallory and Darlene melted away into the store, leaving the two of them alone on the porch, although as they went Nell heard Darlene mutter to Mallory: "Didn't I tell you those two were perfect for each other? Like peas and carrots, the pair of them..."

The early morning clouds had now disappeared and in the warmth of the sun the plinking of melted snow from the store's roof mingled with the rumble of traffic on Main Street, but all this faded away as Nell gazed into Jackson's eyes.

He took a breath, as if gathering his nerve. "Nell, I know we've only just met, and that we live thousands of miles apart, but I—I like you. I really like you." He broke into a crooked smile, and Nell's heart lurched. "What I'm trying to say is that even though I know we're going to be apart, I'd really like us to be together. And hopefully, in time, to be together physically—in the same place—and not just emotionally." His brows bunched together and he ran a hand through his hair. "Does that even make sense?"

Nell laughed, feeling like she'd been drinking expensive champagne. "Perfect sense."

"So what do you reckon?" He reached for her hand, his fingers entwining hers. "Shall we try?"

Nell paused for a moment. "Things have changed since last night, Jackson."

"Oh?" His hand tensed on hers.

She nodded. "The thing is, I've just found out that Megan has left me some land in Tansy Falls, and I've also offered to buy this place from Darlene." She turned to gesture at Fiske's gold-lettered sign, then looked back at Jackson and made a face. "Crazy, right? So if you really meant what you just said, then..." She trailed off, shrugging. "Looks like we can be together pretty soon after all."

Jackson stared at her as if she'd just slapped him. Nell scanned his face, taking in his raised brows and parted lips, and a bubble of nervousness rose and popped inside her. But after what felt like minutes, his face finally relaxed into a look of sheer happiness.

"Well, that is"—he took a breath while Nell held hers—"the most wonderful news."

And if his smile and the certainty in his voice weren't enough to convince her, Jackson then dipped his head toward her for a kiss. As their lips pressed together Nell spun up toward the stars again and Jackson wrapped his arms around her and lifted her up off the floor, clutching her to him so that she was literally floating off the ground, and Nell would have happily stayed like that forever if she hadn't heard the scrape of a door and the sound of someone clearing their throat behind them.

"Sorry to disturb you, lovebirds," came Mallory's voice, as if from very far away, "but don't you have a flight to catch, Nell?"

With a huge effort Nell broke away from their embrace, but her eyes were still fixed on Jackson, who was gazing down at her as if he couldn't believe his luck.

"Do you want to come and see the land Megan's left me?" she asked him. "We could drive there now."

Jackson grinned, stroking her cheek. "I would love to. But what about that flight?"

Nell gazed up at him, fireworks of happiness bursting inside her. *You were right, Meg*, she thought, *Tansy Falls really* has *captured my heart.*

"I guess it will just have to leave without me," she said with a smile.

Reading Group Guide

Dear Reader,

Tansy Falls doesn't actually exist, although it feels very real to me now, but it is inspired by a little town in northern Vermont where my dad and stepmom live, just near the slopes of the mountain on which Mount Maverick is based. It's the sort of place where strangers greet you with a smile and a "good morning," moose wander through your backyard, Christmas is always snowy, and crime is virtually nonexistent—apart from the occasional rogue black bear breaking into someone's kitchen and stealing avocados from the fridge (true story).

The idea for Nell and Megan's tale came out of my own experience of losing loved ones to cancer—something, sadly, far too many of us can relate to—after my mother and brother-in-law died within a short time of each other. Personally, I've always found nature to be one of the greatest healers, and I could well imagine someone like Nell—who, like me, lives in a city—finding peace and happiness amidst the mountains and maple trees of beautiful Vermont. This book is also something of a wish-fulfilment for me personally, as I have often driven past the meadow with its tumbledown barn that Megan gifted to Nell and wished that I could build a little house there too!

I do hope that you'll join me for my next visit to the Vermont hills in *A Secret at Tansy Falls*, but in the meantime, if you have any questions or comments, please get in touch with me via Facebook, Twitter, or Instagram, as I love hearing from readers.

All best wishes,
Cate

Q&A with Cate Woods

What message(s) would you like readers to take away from The Inn at Tansy Falls?

Central to Nell's story is the saying "A life lived in fear is a life half lived." I remember when I first heard this as a child, because it struck such a chord with me. I was an anxious kid, and up until that point had instinctively shied away from experiences that made me fearful, but this phrase transformed my way of looking at the world. I understood that it was okay to be scared, but—to borrow another inspiring phrase—you should feel the fear and do it anyway. It's since become something of a personal mantra, and there have been numerous times throughout my life when it has encouraged me not to take the safe option just because it might be the least challenging. For instance, soon after having my first child I was back at my job writing for a magazine when I was offered the chance to ghostwrite an autobiography for a celebrity. The prospect of leaving a stable job with all its benefits for self-employment and an uncertain future seemed terrifying, but I decided to take the leap and it has opened up a whole new, fulfilling career for me writing books.

Is there a particular supporting character in the town of Tansy Falls that resonates most with you? Are there any characters based on loved ones?

I have a huge soft spot for Darlene. I just hope I'm that cool when I'm in my eighties, plus I admire her ability to speak plainly! Also, I'm afraid to say that I find Brody Knott extremely appealing. What can I say? I'm a sucker for boyish charm and a cute smile. Meanwhile, Megan is an homage to all the strong, stylish, fearless women in my life, particularly my oldest and best friend Freya.

Was Nell's discovery of Miss Polly Swift of Tansy Falls based on any tales of historical events, ancestors, or idols in your own life?

Polly Swift is actually an amalgam of three women who were trailblazers in Vermont's hiking history. Hilda Kurth, Kathleen Norris, and Catherine Robbins made headlines across the country a hundred years ago when they became the first women to hike the length of the Long Trail, which stretches 273 miles from Massachusetts to Canada and was the inspiration for the Wilderness Trail in the book. During my research I came across a sepia photo of these young women—who were known as "the Three Musketeers"—and was captivated by this grinning trio in their headscarves, pants, and sturdy lace-up boots, at a time when most women were still trussed up in formal gowns. The general vibe amongst the (male) journalists who wrote about their adventure seems to be utter astonishment that females could achieve such a feat *on their own*. According to one newspaper report, the women battled rain, hail, and a rabid hedgehog (that they killed with an ax), and yet still managed to complete the trail in twenty-seven days, keeping their spirits up by playing "the peppiest songs they could think of" on a ukulele. The clearly dumbfounded journalist adds: "They have had no scares and have carried no firearms and have scorned male escorts." Words for us all to live by, I think!

Boomer and Simba added heartwarming details to this story. Do you have any pets that are dear to your heart?

Oh yes! I come from a dog-obsessed family. We joke that my dad loves his dogs more than his kids. Perhaps because there were always several of them around when I was growing up, I never used to be that bothered about pets—until, that is, I got a dog of my own a few years ago. She is a coton de Tuléar called Beanie and I *finally* get what all the fuss is about. She is a wonderful companion, and just petting her instantly lifts my spirits. So yeah, thanks to Beanie I am a certified dog bore now. Wanna see a photo...? (Oh, and a shout out to our three pet goldfish, Elton, John, and Rocketman, too.)

In a time where many heroines and main characters in romance and women's fiction are in their twenties and early thirties, why was it important to you to have Nell be in her late thirties?

Part of the reason is that I'm in my forties now, and I feel that it's important to acknowledge that you love just as passionately and as stupidly and deeply as you grow up as you do in your twenties. I find writing about older women more interesting because they've had more time to find their groove and work out who they're meant to be—or perhaps it's just because they're more battle-scarred! Also, I do think the late thirties is a particularly tricky and therefore interesting time for women. I mean, we always have some societal expectation piled upon us, but that tipping point when you're approaching forty feels particularly intense.

Discussion Questions

1. Megan appears only very briefly in flashbacks, but how well do you feel you know her by the end of the book? How effectively do her letters to Nell convey a sense of her character?

2. When Nell first lays eyes on Jackson, she describes having a strong feeling that he will somehow be significant in her life. Is this love at first sight, or is it something else? Is this a feeling you've ever experienced?

3. One of the themes of the book is about how life happens when you get out of your comfort zone. What would you say is your own personal comfort zone? Have you ever forced yourself to step outside it?

4. Do you think Nell was correct to assume that Megan sent her to the Tansy Falls museum to see the Polly Swift exhibit, or was it just a lucky coincidence?

5. The countryside of Tansy Falls has a powerful effect on Nell, helping to heal her heartache. What effect does being in nature have on you?

6. If you were vacationing in Tansy Falls, would you rather stay at the Covered Bridge Inn or at Maverick Lodge? Do you agree with Piper that Maverick Lodge could potentially ruin the character of Tansy Falls?

7. What do you think Nell's future would have looked like if she hadn't decided to come to Tansy Falls? Do you think she would have found a way to live more authentically without Megan's help?

8. If there was a movie of this book, who do you imagine playing the main characters?

9. What do you think is the greatest love story in the book? Is it the one between Nell and Jackson, Nell and Megan, or Nell and Tansy Falls?

Acknowledgments

First of all, a huge thank-you to my father, Andrew, for all the research and advice. Despite being born a flatlander, he is a mountain man through and through.

Thank you to the whole Bookouture team and particularly my fairy book-mother, Kathryn Taussig, without whose editorial brilliance, support and guidance this book would still be a series of Post-it notes. I would also like to thank my fantastic agent, Rowan Lawton, for making it possible for me to be a published writer.

Finally, thank you to my husband, Oliver, for everything. Honestly, I feel sorry for anyone who's not married to you.